GODS OF JUSTICE ™

Edited by
Kevin Hosey and
K. Stoddard Hayes

Illustrations by Mark Offutt
and Joel Gomez

Dallas, Texas

Published by:
Cliffhanger Books, Dallas, Texas
www.cliffhangerbooks.com

First Cliffhanger Books trade paperback edition (July 2011)

Cover and interior design by Kevin Hosey

Published in the United States of America

Heroic Tales

To everyone who dreams of righting wrongs
and fighting for justice. More power to you.

Kevin Hosey

For all the real heroes who devote their lives
to helping the helpless, protecting the
innocent, and resisting bullies and tyrants.

K. Stoddard Hayes

The Mass Grave of John Johnsons

Micah Urban

IT WAS A long night, just the dead and me.

The body bags were the cheaper, blue, non-vinyl kind with handles. There were forty-four in all. Someone had written numbers on each of them with a permanent marker, probably the order in which they had been brought out of the mass grave discovered on Kampe's farm—in the remains of the lake that had disappeared into the local system of caves one night last week.

Now they filled my cooler, occupied all the gurneys I could find in the little clinic called Green Garden. They even lined the hall between my office and the morgue. In an effort to keep the temperature down on my side of the building, I turned off the heat and propped the outside door open to let in the frigid January air.

It was past midnight. I wasn't a young man any more. I was tired and hungry. Late nights like this reminded me that I was now closer to fifty than forty.

After eating a cheese Danish, I went back to the morgue and opened the bag marked with a sloppy 27, the most easily accessible corpse. The only definite conclusion I could come to after a precursory examination was that the body had once belonged to a male. The next three corpses had little else to contribute to the matter. All were males of a similar height and build; all lacked distinctive identification marks.

Discouraged, I retreated to my office, warmed by a space heater.

After making myself a fresh pot of strong coffee, I sat down at my computer. I typed up some notes and read my email. I debated canceling all of my appointments for the remainder of the week, but thought better of it. There was no way I was going to be handling this particular case all on my own.

I called the State Police forensics lab in Rockford for help. The trooper in charge of the lab told me right off that my case was too big for them, and recommended I contact the FBI. The Chicago field office told me to contact the Minneapolis field office who referred me back to Chicago. Cutting out the middle man, I called D.C. There, after fifteen minutes on hold, I talked to a man with a deep voice. He did not introduce himself, but he was very curious as to who I was and why I was calling. I answered all his questions and asked if there was any assistance the FBI could offer.

"Mister Murray," Deep Voice said. "I want you to know that we've been expecting your call."

I sat up straight in my chair. "You have?"

"We have standing orders to be on the lookout for your call."

"Really?"

"Do you have something to write with, Mister Murray?"

"Yeah." I reached for the nearest scrap of paper and managed to just barely keep up with the phone number he rattled off. "Is this a special branch of the Bureau or something?"

Deep Voice chuckled. "Yeah. Or something."

The number the FBI gave me turned out to be the direct line to the Federal Office of Super-Heroes.

What had I stumbled onto?

I had a very helpful customer representative take all my information and in less than five minutes, I was approved for support. They would be sending a special forensics team from Omaha to Green Garden just as soon as possible. My main contact went by the name of WhoDied.

WhoDied was famous in my trade. Some might say infamous. He was said to be able to identify human remains no matter how badly decayed or how little remained of the corpse, and he would do it on site. Some said he was psychic; others said he was a hoax.

Hoax or not, he arrived with superhuman speed.

One moment I had put my head down on my desk, and the next, I glanced up to find a trio of strangers standing in my doorway. They all wore costumes and masks.

I rose and ran a hand along the front of my shirt to try and iron out the wrinkles.

WhoDied stood there, the office door opened wide, letting out the heat. He wore a cowl that showed only his mouth and chin; the eyes were hidden behind dark lenses. Under a hooded cape, he wore tights of a macabre decoration—black above the chest and white below. "R.I.P." was emblazoned across his stomach above a large question mark. Thick black gloves went up nearly to his elbows. The entire getup hung limp on him, denoting a frame of skeletal substance. He kept his back rigid, his shoulders squared and his head up.

Before I could get a good look at the other two masked strangers, the hero closed the gap between us, coming to a stop on the far side of my desk. "Doctor Abram Murray?"

I nodded.

"WhoDied."

I stumbled over what to call him. Should I call him Who? Was that too informal? Should I call him Mr. Died? Too formal? I ended up nodding my acknowledgement and held out my hand. I kept it simple. "How are you?"

WhoDied stepped back. "No touching. That could contaminate me."

I withdrew my hand; I brushed my palm off on my jeans, and having nothing else to do with my fingers, I stuck them into my front pocket.

"You left your door open," said a feminine voice.

I looked past WhoDied to one of the other two, a girl I wagered was barely old enough to drive. She was half a foot shorter than WhoDied. Her cowl, like WhoDied's, exposed the lips and chin, but it also opened above the brow, exposing black hair pulled tight into two shoulder-length braids. Her eyes were hidden behind violet lenses. Above her full-length black tights she wore a Mandarin dress depicting a map of the world. Gray gloved hands held the straps of a large, neon blue bag.

WhoDied introduced her as Locality.

His other aide, whom he called Four-D, was a boy—maybe fourteen—who wore simple black tights with motorcycle boots and a belt with an hourglass buckle. He didn't wear a mask, but had a black bandana pulled high across the bridge of his nose. Acne stretched across his forehead and up past his hairline, well into his crew cut.

I explained about the many bodies I was trying to preserve, my lack of space for storing them, and my improvisation. Locality nodded her head, but WhoDied made no acknowledgement. He just stood there, motionless. Perhaps he was staring off into space. Perhaps he was taking in every detail of me and my office—garishly lit by fluorescent bulbs which made my 1960's toothpaste green walls appear all the more minty.

WhoDied looked at me and asked, "What have you learned so far?"

I reached for the yellow legal pad on which I had jotted all my notes. "There are forty-four bodies." I explained about the Kampe's vanished lake where the bodies were found and the badly decomposed state of the few corpses I had looked at.

"And where are the bodies now?" he asked, as if he hadn't seen them stacked all over on his way in.

My mouth opened—I was ready to tell him that most of them were right outside in the hall, but it was such an obvious answer that I felt stupid saying it. I said nothing and shut my mouth. Behind WhoDied, Locality offered me a shrug, from which I gathered the momentum needed to ask, "Which do you want to see first?"

"Do you have a favorite?" he asked.

I glanced back to Locality, who smirked.

Realizing the hero wasn't being serious, I stood up and led the FOSH forensics team down the aisle of body bags to the morgue, where I introduced them to Body Number 27.

WhoDied moved fast. Before I could even think of stopping him, he had climbed up on top of the gurney and straddled the body; then he spread apart the lips of the bag and proceeded with an up-close inspection of the corpse.

I didn't know what to say or do. Rooted where I stood, I merely stared in grotesque fascination, wondering exactly what his powers were.

"Just wait," whispered Locality from behind me. "It gets better."

WhoDied opened a pocket on the cuff of his right glove. It was a deep pocket, for he pulled out a surgical scalpel. He held it up to the white light and turned the blade first this way then that. Then he leaned down and reached inside the exposed, decomposed body cavity with the blade. His hands disappeared from sight and went to work. A moment later, he sat up, scalpel in one fist, human tissue in the other. He held the scrap of meat up to the light, examining its color.

"The liver," WhoDied said, "is surprisingly rich in memories."

I took a step closer, expecting he would hold the snippet out for me to examine as well. Instead, he plopped it into his mouth.

I blinked. I turned to Locality. "Did he just...."

She nodded.

I looked back to the hero. He seemed to be savoring the morsel as if it were gourmet cuisine. I was transfixed by the repulsiveness of the deed. "Why?"

"That's just the way he works." Her voice was flat, unwavering in the light of the spectacle. "The way he's always worked."

WhoDied actually licked his chops, as if enjoying the aftertaste. Then he swallowed.

I felt my jaw drop—it was the only reaction I could muster. He looked directly at me. My mouth closed so hard my teeth clacked.

Dismounting the corpse, WhoDied squared his shoulders and raised his chin. He looked directly at me without shame and announced, "His name was John. John Johnson."

I tried several times to say something intelligible, but could only manage a shocked, "Really?"

WhoDied nodded.

In a hushed tone, I asked Locality, "How accurate is he?"

She dipped her chin. "One hundred percent."

Turning back to WhoDied, I smiled. "So. John Johnson."

WhoDied rested a hand on the gurney and—for just a moment—looked very old and tired. Then he regained his composure. "And he was a superhero."

My ears perked up. "A superhero? Do you know which one."

A frown creased his lips as he nodded. "We were friends once. Long ago. The world knew him as Rex Solaris."

The first time I had seen Rex Solaris on TV, I was a boy. He had been helping the survivors of an earthquake in Nicaragua. I sat in front of the television for hours that day, hypnotized by this modern day Olympian saving life after life. He even rescued a whole schoolroom of children my age. It was to one of these school children that he gave his famous belt buckle—a golden sun engraved with an 'R.'

I remember wishing I had been trapped in that schoolhouse, that Rex Solaris would've saved me and given me that buckle. A lot of children did.

Rex Solaris was the Mick Jagger of Superheroes. He made doing good look sexy.

Unlike his government counterparts, who wore cheesy costumes with stiff names, Rex Solaris was a style all unto himself. Before him, a superhero never would've worn black, let alone a black, rhinestone studded jumpsuit. A FOSH agent never would have had unkempt brown hair, sideburns to his chin and a thick bushy mustache.

But in 1972, Rex Solaris did. And he didn't just look good, he was endowed with super strength, super speed, super senses, and he could fly.

What woman could resist him?

My mother, Polly Murray, came into the room for a bit and watched the news with me. She was cool and calm. Between puffs of her cigarette she told me that Rex Solaris was my father. When my jaw dropped, she said she wasn't joking.

I went outside to play after that. I tested my abilities to see if I had superpowers of my own, but I didn't. I had to work very hard just to be average. It crossed my mind that my mother was crazy. By the time I was in high school, I had lost interest in what she was saying, so she stopped telling me.

"Rex Solaris." I looked down at the body anew.

I wondered if WhoDied would be able to tell me if the hero really was my father by sampling my flesh, but this was a passing whim left over from childhood. I didn't really care anymore and there was a lot of work left to do.

"Take me to the next body," WhoDied ordered, as if he couldn't see the pool of body bags that spilled out the door of the morgue and extended all the way down the hall.

I chalked it up to professional theatrics and led him over to the next gurney, presenting Body Number 16 as if I had just conjured it out of thin air.

WhoDied extracted a mint from a tin he kept tucked in his left glove. Only after he had munched the pill to pulp did he unzip the body bag and continue with his ghoulish performance.

"Liver's missing," he commented. Then, after a moment, he produced another sample of meat. He held it up to the light and after a moment discarded it. Then he reached back inside. "Stay away from the pancreas."

I raised an eyebrow in Locality's direction.

"Gives him indigestion," she explained.

"Ah."

Looking back at the FOSH hero, I was just in time to witness him tasting a bit of Body 16. His head dipped and his tongue ran the meat all over his cheeks and teeth.

Without warning, WhoDied spat the sample out onto the floor.

"Anything wrong?" I asked, eyeing the spot on the tile where his spit mixed with decayed human flesh.

"Horribly." He turned to me, his lips stretched into a disgusted scowl.

WhoDied reached for his left glove and once more brought out the tin of curiously strong mints. Popping the lid, he emptied the canister into his palm, opened his mouth wide and poured in the whole handful. He munched for a minute and then swished the mixture back and forth, thoroughly cleansing his palate.

I took a cautious step back, waiting for him to spit out what was left of the mints. Instead he swallowed them in several small gulps. When he was done, he took a deep breath, inhaling the frigid air through his teeth.

Then WhoDied reached back into the corpse's body cavity with his scalpel and retrieved a fresh sample from even farther in. He tasted this directly, forgoing the visual inspection he had performed with the other specimens. He sucked on the flesh as if it were a gobstopper.

I cast a sideways glance at the sidekicks.

"I don't know," Locality said as she watched her mentor. "I've never seen him act like this before."

The silent boy, Four-D, shrugged.

We watched as WhoDied moved on to the next body. Here he extracted a bit of the tongue. He placed this between his teeth only long enough to be sure of something and then he spat it out; he turned for a fourth set of remains.

I quickly stepped between him and Body Bag 12. I grabbed him by the shoulders and forced him to stand still. "What in God's name are you doing?"

WhoDied stared at me and I stared back.

"What I am doing," he said, "is stumbling unto the most fascinating murder mystery I have ever come across."

After he finished his fourth test, WhoDied returned to Body 27. He stood at the head of the gurney and placed a hand lightly atop the corpse's chest. Turning to the three of us, he announced, "This is John Johnson." He then sidestepped to Body 16 and patted the head. "*This* is John Johnson." At the third corpse, he jovially slapped his palm against the decayed shoulder. "*This* is John Johnson." He gestured behind himself at his most recent attempt to help me, Body 34. "And *that* is John Johnson."

WhoDied, in my silence, walked up and looked at me in earnest. "I wager that every one of these victims is John Johnson."

"So," I said in my most scholarly voice, "somebody out there is killing people named John Johnson?"

"No." The barest trace of excitement could be heard in his raspy words. "Someone has killed John Johnson forty-four times."

"The *same* John Johnson?"

"Yes."

"Rex Solaris?"

"*Yes!*" He was positively giddy.

I looked around at the eight gurneys that were crammed into the morgue. My gaze wandered over to the refrigerator units where seven more bodies were stored and I thought of the bodies lining both sides of the hall outside the door. Finally, I stared deep into WhoDied's empty black lenses.

12

"That's impossible."

WhoDied held up a slender finger. "Don't confuse impossible with improbable."

I was pretty sure I meant impossible, but I didn't argue. Instead, I went to Body 27. I spent the next few minutes studying the decayed features for any recognizable markings. There was a distinct, knotted mess of hair around the chin and a faint line along the left shoulder that might've been a scar. I moved on to Body 16 and spent all of thirty seconds locating the same features.

Casting an uncertain glance back at WhoDied and his sidekicks, I squeezed between the gurney and the counter, making my way to a corpse WhoDied had yet to touch. The blue bag was marked with a large number five. I unzipped the bag and took a look at the body, which also had a tangled beard and shoulder scar.

I rested a hand on the gurney and turned my attention back to WhoDied. "All these bodies are the same man?"

He nodded.

Despite the cold, a bead of sweat trickled down into my right eye. "Are you sure?"

WhoDied pointed in turn to 27, 16, 12 and 34. "About the ones I've sampled? Yes. But I should sample the rest of the victims to make sure."

I watched the trio work.

WhoDied would examine each body first. After sampling the meat of the dead, he would say a few words before stepping aside to let Locality through. She no longer wore her gray gloves, and her performance consisted of nothing more than running her hands along the contours of the corpse. She would then rattle off a string of numbers as she cleaned her skin with the hand sanitizer she kept in her bright blue satchel.

Four-D carried a yellow legal pad and would jot down everything said. Before moving on to the next body, Four-D would pull his bandana down and lower his head until his nose was practically touching the body. He would then inhale deeply, scribble his own notes and pull the bandana back up into place.

WhoDied explained the process. Locality had the ability to determine where a person died by touching the flesh of the corpse. The numbers she rattled off were longitude and latitude, but she could also provide the specific details of the scene right up to which direction the body had been facing when taking the last breath. Four-D, by smelling the body, somehow knew the exact time of death—not how long the body had been decaying, but the exact moment life actually left the body, down to the second.

I could've gone back to my office. I could've caught another catnap. But I was fascinated by the show.

"Everything is becoming much clearer," WhoDied said.

We were all sitting in my office. I **was** in my chair, WhoDied sat across from me, and Locality and Four-D stood close enough to my space heater to keep me in the cold.

"Clearer?" I leaned on my desk. "How so?"

WhoDied glanced over the notes Four-D had made and then handed the yellow legal pad to me. "Look through the list. You should come to the same conclusion."

The page was broken into four columns: identity of the victim—which was John Johnson from top to bottom—a set of coordinates, additional information about the location, date and time of death.

The coordinates meant nothing to me. I perused Locality's additional information and recognized the places listed. Corbinsville, Griffith, Bradley. They were all towns within ten miles of the mass grave of John Johnson.

I turned my focus on the last column. The exact date was never repeated. Even the times of death were scattered throughout the day, and though the large majority of deaths had occurred during the night, more than a dozen had occurred in middle of the day. The only discernable pattern was that all of the listed dates were in the future.

Looking up only with my eyes, I peered over the notepad at WhoDied. "Are you saying that these murders haven't happened yet?"

WhoDied pointed to Four-D. "No. He is."

I looked to the boy. Back straight and head high—much like his mentor—he possessed a steely resolve in his gaze as if he was daring me to challenge him.

"He's never been wrong," Locality offered.

I shifted my gaze to WhoDied sitting on the edge of his chair. "Are you saying that our murderer is a time traveler?"

"Yes." WhoDied almost smiled. "Isn't it marvelous?"

"So...." I stared at the dates a moment longer and then dropped the legal pad on my desk. Leaning back in my chair, I crossed my arms over the gentle bulge of my belly. "Let's say we *are* dealing with a time traveler. How do you kill the same person over and over again, you know? I mean, once you've killed John Johnson in 2012, then there's no John Johnsons left to kill in 2013 or 2014 and so on down the line."

Another smile tried to emerge from the corners of WhoDied's lips. He pointed to the sky. "Unless you start killing John Johnson at the end of his life then work your way backwards." When I didn't reply, he leaned forward and said in a hushed tone, "Blew your mind, didn't I?"

He had.

"Who...?" I sat up straight. "Who could do this?"

WhoDied sat back in his chair. I wasn't expecting an answer, but he gave me one anyway. "I don't know. My brother, WhoDidIt, passed away last year. He would have been the one to ask."

Locality and Four-D nodded their heads in agreement.

I pushed my chair back from my desk, stood up and stretched. "So who do we call now?"

WhoDied looked at his folded hands resting on his lap. "No one."

Resting my hands on the edge of my desk, I looked down at him. He did not look up at me. "Isn't there someone who can help figure out who is killing John Johnson?"

"There are a few people I could ask," WhoDied admitted, "and I'm sure they would be able to piece it together eventually, but we don't have time for that. And the grim reality is that it doesn't really matter. The killer is a time-traveler and for all we know at this time he may only be a ten-year old boy."

"May not even be born," Locality conjectured.

"Too true," WhoDied agreed. "If only we had more time."

"More time?"

WhoDied sprang to his feet and planted his finger on my desk in the middle of the notes. I followed his direction and stared at the date for Body 15: January 23, 2012—two days away, in the parking lot of a roadside diner near Griffith where I had eaten a few times.

I looked up at WhoDied. "So what do we do?"

"I'm thinking it will probably be best if we let John Johnson know what is happening."

"You know where he lives?"

WhoDied was silent as he reclaimed his chair. "No. Not exactly."

He told me what he did know.

Rex Solaris and WhoDied had worked together in FOSH, back in the early '60s. Then Rex Solaris had been lured away from the bureaucracy of FOSH to the newly created corporate entity called "The Union of Superheroes." As the first famous member of the Union, Rex Solaris was lavished with wealth and perks to make any celebrity jealous.

Rex Solaris was a notorious lady's man. His numerous encounters with his pretty, young groupies were well documented in the tabloids. But what only the government knew was that a number of these trysts resulted in children. The government kept tabs on all children born to known Persons of Extraordinary Power.

In the early 90's—at the end of the Cold War—the security surrounding this top secret information was breached and the files were leaked. The parents of the children were notified so that they could take the appropriate action and secure their children from threats.

The file on Rex Solaris's offspring was hefty.

A rumor persisted on the internet that when his contract with the Union expired, he settled in the Midwest, near a high concentration of his offspring, watching over his children from afar.

WhoDied looked at a map of the local area I had given him. "Based on the locations that the John Johnsons were killed, I'd say we're in the right area. But even if we could find him, there's no guarantee that he'd let us in to speak to him."

"But surely he'd talk to *you*?" I said.

WhoDied shook his head. "There's no guarantee. What would really be helpful is if we could find one of his children. That would be a certain ticket in to talk to him."

Before I could stop myself, I was saying, "Well, I might be able to help with that."

"Oh? Who do you know?"

"Me."

I told them about my mother's claims regarding my pedigree.

"And you believed her?" Locality asked.

"No. Well, yes. Sort of." I turned to WhoDied. "I wanted to, when I was little. But as I grew older, I assumed she was delusional."

WhoDied stared at the jade lion statuette on my desk. Just when I was beginning to wonder if he had fallen asleep, he said, "This could work." He sat up straight. "Provided we can find Johnson in time."

It was my turn to sit in a contemplative funk. I went over the name of anyone I knew who might be able to locate John Johnson. There was only one name which persistently popped up—someone who knew the area better than the other lifelong residents.

WhoDied must have been reading my body language, because he

asked, "You know someone?"

"Maybe." But I was pretty sure that I did.

Sheriff Walter Swit knew everyone within twenty miles. He didn't know anyone by the name of John Johnson; however, there was a Jon Jensen living out by the abandoned quarry who fit the description of our forty-four corpses. The man was a hermit who had moved to the area in the mid-nineties. The sheriff even offered to drive me out there—perhaps he felt guilty about burdening me with the bodies. Regardless, I had a ride so I settled for directions.

The FOSH transport was an ambulance that was matte black from top to bottom. The windows were as darkly tinted as the lenses covering WhoDied's eyes. All the lights were covered with smoke tinted plastic. Inside, behind the driver and passenger seats were two captain seats and a bank of state-of-the-art equipment.

Locality drove. I was given the passenger seat.

By nine o'clock in the morning, we were parked on the side of a wooded road across from a dirt drive that led deeper into the forest. A simple metal swing gate cordoned off the private path from passing traffic—not that there was much of that. A large "No Trespassing" sign was chained to the metal crossbars.

As I peered through the bare branches for any sign of civilization, WhoDied announced from his seat in the back, "We'll wait here."

I turned and looked back at him. "You want me to go alone?"

"We might not be welcome."

"*I* might not be welcome."

"You're his son, aren't you?"

"I don't know." I didn't. Not really. I had my mother's accusations. "What if I'm not? What if he vaporizes me with his heat vision?"

Locality laughed.

"He doesn't have heat vision," WhoDied said.

Half a mile into the trees I found a clearing that was home to a log cabin, a two story piece of art that easily could have taken half a million dollars even in a bad real-estate market.

The steps did not creak or groan as I slowly made my way up to the deck. There was a well-worn rocking chair and table. Drapes were drawn shut in all the windows.

I knocked on the door and waited.

17

After several minutes without a response, I peered in the window through a sliver of an opening in the curtains. It was dark inside. I couldn't even distinguish the furniture from the walls.

When I went back to the door, it was open. Standing there was a man who resembled a lumberjack only slightly more than he resembled the bodies at my morgue.

"Hi," I said.

"Hello." There was calmness to his demeanor more fitting of a monk than a rock star celebrity.

"My name is Abram," I said. "Abram Murray."

He stretched his neck, cracking his joints. He smiled politely at me. "I know who you are, Abram. How did you find me?"

John invited me into his home.

Beyond the initial recognition at the door, he made no further mention of whether or not there was any special tie between us. I opened my mouth to ask him if he was my father, but I lost my nerve. What if the answer was no? What if it was yes? I said nothing.

He took me to his kitchen. There, over a meal of reindeer stew, I explained the situation. John listened while he finished his bowl. When he was done, he stood up, went to the stove and dished up a second helping. Turning around, he asked, "What does this all have to do with me?"

I stirred the remains of my stew. "The bodies are you. All of them."

He raised an inquisitive eyebrow, then came back and sat down. He tapped his fingers rapidly on the table. He picked his spoon up and held it over the bowl. "How sure are you that these bodies are me?"

"WhoDied said they were."

John set the spoon down. "Marcus is here?"

"*Marcus?*"

John smiled. "That's WhoDied's real name."

"Ah." I nodded. "He's here. Why? Do you have reason to doubt him?"

"No." He shook his head. "I trust him with my life."

"Well, that's good." I placed my hands on the table, folded. "Because according to him, you're going to die on Monday."

John stared down into his own eyes.

"When did this one die?" he asked.

I double-checked the note pad for Body 12. Before I could tell him, WhoDied announced from behind me, "August 9, 2031."

John focused on the faint scar which traced the curvature of the left shoulder. "I was fighting Doctor Red back in '82. He had a knife made out of...I don't know what. Something alien maybe?"

"I understand the lab tests were inconclusive," WhoDied answered.

John didn't look back. "It's the only time I've ever been cut by a blade. It never did heal right."

He stretched, cracked his neck, and looked back at us. The Zen-like calmness he had first displayed had given way to an aura of disturbed seriousness. "Show me the one who dies Monday."

We went out into the hall. I led the heroes towards the open exit, where Body 15 resided two spots from the end. His only comment upon seeing the corpse was: "I just bought this shirt. I haven't even worn it yet."

WhoDied stepped up besides John and rested a hand on his old friend's shoulder. "You don't have to die in it."

After John Johnson left, I turned to WhoDied. "What now?"

WhoDied was looking out the door at the daylight flooding in. "We're going to go back to the hotel. I have some calls to make. Would you be able to stay here a little bit longer? I have a colleague who should be arriving shortly."

Looking at my watch, I tried calculating how long I'd been up—thirty-two hours. I yawned. "What time is he supposed to be here?"

"He was supposed to be here this morning."

I stayed.

A deep, dreamless sleep was shattered with one fell swoop of something heavy and blunt across my left shoulder. I jumped out of my chair before I was fully awake.

Standing on the far side of the desk was a caricature of a man. What hair he had was unkempt and a sickly yellowish white. His skin was a leathery tan, yet so tight against his form that his dark veins bulged, disappearing from sight only where his circulatory system was hidden by liver spots.

He was dressed in a tuxedo and tapped his cane impatiently against the floor.

"You Abraham Murray?" he asked. His voice was high-pitched.

"Abram Murray," I corrected. "Are you Mod?"

"No one calls me Mod anymore." He hefted his cane into the air and let it fall across my desk. "What's with all the bodies? Marcus didn't say anything to me about having to take a look at so many bodies."

"No. There's only one body that we need you to take a look at."

Mod stabbed the floor with his cane. "Then show me that. I don't have all night."

I led him to Body 15. From where we stood, I could look out the open door and see the brake lights of an idling car.

"You left the door open," Mod announced as I squatted down and unzipped the body bag which held Monday's corpse.

I ignored the remark. "This is the body we wanted you to examine."

For a moment of silence, Mod stared down at the body. Then he sniffled. After wiping his nose with a handkerchief, he turned to me. "You tell Marcus that his powers were drained—taken completely away. Then he was stabbed in the heart with a steak knife."

And then the mysterious Mod was out the door, into his car, and gone into the night. I wasted no time in calling the number WhoDied had provided me and told him the diagnosis.

The news was exactly what he wanted to hear.

Lady J's was a twenty-four hour diner nestled between a gas station and a closed-down truck stop. Garnished with red neon lights and windows that wrapped around the front two-thirds of the building, it had a beacon of a sign that rose over a hundred feet into the air and bore a rendering of Rosie the Riveter as a carhop.

I sat with WhoDied, Locality and Four-D in the FOSH van, idling at one of the pumps at the gas station. I had the passenger's seat and a pair of government binoculars.

WhoDied was in the driver's side captain chair watching a streaming feed of what was happening inside Lady J's on a bank of flat screen monitors. In the passenger side captain chair was Locality, who had her eye on another set of screens which displayed various views of the surrounding parking lot. Beside me, in the driver's seat, Four-D ate a donut, taking occasional sips from his hot chocolate.

I put the binoculars down and looked at my watch. Less than fifteen minutes to go. The killer could be arriving at any second. I raised the lenses to my eyes again and looked inside.

Aside from John, there were five other patrons. Two college-age boys in a far corner booth, an older couple several tables away, and a lone man at a counter seat who looked like a trucker. Behind the counter there was a cook and a waitress, who from time to time actually went out to wait.

They were all FOSH agents.

20

John kept to himself, reading the morning paper and eating his steak and eggs.

My mind wandered. I found myself wanting to believe the stories my mother told me when I was little.

"I've got movement," Locality announced, her voice excited, but professional.

I was already moving the binoculars back to the entrance when WhoDied responded, "Where?"

"East side."

A blurry figure crossed my vision. Before I could focus, however, the new arrival was approaching the diner door—his back turned to me.

"Where did he come from?" I asked.

There was a silence I mistook for being ignored. I looked back to see her shrug.

"One moment he wasn't there, the next he was walking across the parking lot."

"Do you want to watch?" WhoDied asked, keeping his eyes on the monitors in front of his face. "Abram?"

I handed the binoculars to Four-D and crawled into the back of the FOSH van; the sidekick followed me. We jockeyed for comfortable positions between WhoDied and Locality, but gave up and turned our attention to the action about to start inside.

The killer wasn't at all what I imagined.

He was tall and lanky; he had close-cropped hair that was either blonde or white—it was hard to tell from the video feed. One of the camera angles had a good shot of his face. He couldn't have been more than twenty-five. Before the black eye and swollen lip he was now sporting, he could've had a distinguished career as a model. He was dressed in thin, white body armor that was visibly damaged; a silver circle emblazoned on his chest was spider-webbed with cracks.

He weaved and staggered and bumped into stationary objects on his way to John's table.

"He's either drunk or seriously hurt," Locality commented.

Could this really be the man who murdered Rex Solaris so many times? WhoDied reached over and turned up the volume.

The killer landed roughly in the chair opposite John, who put his fork down and swallowed his last bite of steak. "You new around here?"

The killer shook his head. "Not really, no." Then he nodded. "But in a way, yes."

John stretched his back and cracked his neck. "You seem a bit confused. What happened? You look like you've been knocked upside the head pretty good there."

"My name is Sorbere, Mr. Johnson. Though you don't remember it, we've met before."

"Oh?"

Sorbere tipped is head down without lowering his eyes. "The reason *you* don't remember it, is because for you, it hasn't happened yet."

He rested his arms on the table, his white-gloved fingers landing well within John's personal space. "You see, I've traveled here from the year 2060 to find you."

"That has to be an interesting power—to travel through time."

"That's not my power, Mr. Johnson. That's modern technology."

"What a wonderful world you must come from."

"On the contrary, Mr. Johnson, it's a very dark world where true superheroes are an endangered species. Oh, we have plenty of pretenders. Plenty of villains—far worse than any you've ever encountered. But there's never been anyone who can compare to you."

"Flattering." John forced a smile. "And you're here, why? Because you need me?"

"Yes. I need you."

"And you came back almost fifty years just to find me?"

A lopsided grin broke out on the killer's face and then faded away. "Sadly, in my time you've already passed."

"I'm sorry to hear that. But I'm afraid you've come all this way for nothing. I'm retired now."

"I know. That's what you said when I first met you, in my time."

"You said I had passed in your time."

Sobere shrugged. "The world thought you had been dead for years, but rumors persisted that you were holed up in the backwoods, somewhere, living the life of a hermit while the world went to hell." A thin smile spread across his face. "So I looked for you. And I found you. But you wouldn't help me. So to teach you a lesson, I absorbed your powers— that's what I do, Mr. Johnson, I absorb the powers of others."

"So you've come all this way to absorb my powers?"

Sorbere did not say anything, but a cold look in his eye seemed to confirm everything.

Despite the immediate danger to him, John did not draw back. "So if you've absorbed my powers once already, why do you need to absorb them again? Unless it wears off. It does, doesn't it?"

"The first time it lasted a year." Sorbere took off first one of his white gloves and then the other. "But each time I take your powers, it seems to wear off faster."

"*Each* time?"

The killer slowly moved his bared hands in John Johnson's direction. "The last time, it only lasted two days."

John didn't flinch. "What do you need my powers for?"

"It's not your powers that I crave. Not anymore."

Sorbere laid his bare hands on John's wrists. "You have no idea what it feels like knowing that you—and only you—can take the power *and* the life of the greatest superhero the world has ever known."

He closed his eyes and concentrated; after a minute, though, he opened them wide. He looked to John Johnson and then around at the rest of the people in the diner, all of whom had stopped what they were doing and were looking in his direction.

"What's going on?" Sorbere asked. The man from the future leveled accusing eyes at John. "My powers are gone." He stood up, knocking his chair over backwards and turned to the undercover FOSH agents. "Which one of you shut my powers off?" he screamed.

No one answered.

The villain made a move for the door, but by the time he could turn around, John blocked the way.

Sorbere dodged left and went for the waitress, who was standing nearby. She was in her fifties and petite. Sorbere did not notice the weapon in her hand as he wrapped his forearm about her neck. He was also oblivious to the other FOSH agents, who were now all visibly armed and pointing their own weapons in his direction.

"Nobody move," the killer began. But before he could finish his threat, his hostage had slipped out of his grip, sidestepped out of his reach and shot him square in the chin with her stun gun.

Muscles throughout Sorbere's body convulsed. He landed hard on the ground, his extremities twitching now and again.

Even before his vitals were taken, he was being restrained.

It was 5:46 AM and John was still alive.

As government agents finished cleaning up the restaurant—taking down their equipment and turning the restaurant back over to its normal staff and clientele—WhoDied, Four-D and Locality saw me safely back to the clinic. They parked next to the side entrance, which had been open now for three long days.

I turned around in my seat and looked back to WhoDied. "What do I do with the bodies?"

"You don't have to worry about those," WhoDied told me. "FOSH wanted the corpses moved somewhere more secure so they picked them up while we were at the diner."

"Well." I nodded. "Okay, then."

"You look bummed," Locality said. "Were you expecting them to fade into nothingness?"

I smiled at the thought. "Maybe."

WhoDied leaned forward and put his hands together, fingertip-to-fingertip. "The world doesn't work that way, Mister Murray. We didn't pre-vent anything, we just . . . changed course slightly."

I looked around the van—at all the equipment, at the superheroes. I glanced out the window and through the open door to the dark hallway, now empty; then I turned back to WhoDied. "Is there anything else you need from me before I head out?"

"No." He stuck out his hand. "Thank you for your help."

I studied his offered palm. He was clearly no longer concerned about contamination, so I reached over and shook his hand. "Thank you."

Four-D gave me a curt nod.

"Take care," I told him. Turning to Locality, I said, "You too."

She smiled. "Always."

I stepped out of the FOSH van into the cold and watched them drive off into the sunrise. Then I turned and went inside, shutting the door be-hind me.

I was not alone.

John was waiting for me in my office. He was sitting behind my desk, studying the same jade lion which WhoDied had earlier found fascinating. As I came in, John looked up at me. "Do you know what this is?"

"It's a lion," I replied, shedding my red parka; I tossed it over the back of one of the other chairs.

"It's not just any lion." He smiled. "This is Ishi, the favorite lion of the Emperor of Japan."

"Oh?" I came to a stop before my desk and looked down at the mighty

24

Rex Solaris. "How do you know that?"

John set the lion down in its original resting place. "He told me so when he gave it to me."

I examined the statuette anew. My mother had given it to me when I went off to college.

"Go ahead, Abram." John got to his feet. "Ask me."

I turned to him. "Ask you what?"

"Ask me the question you've wanted to ask me since we first met."

It took me several tries, but finally I managed to find the words. "Are you my father?"

He nodded. "Yes."

Feeling a little light headed, I stumbled back and fell into the chair reserved for my guests. I nearly missed and ended up on the floor, but somehow I kept my perch. Stars exploded in my vision, then faded away.

"I'm very proud of you," he told me. "You saved my life."

I shook my head. I had done little more than make a phone call.

"You did," he affirmed. He rested his hands on my desk. "But we're not done yet."

He picked up a familiar legal pad. "Sorbere is still coming for me. As far as he's concerned, he's already killed me forty-three times."

"So he has to be stopped again and again?"

John dropped the legal pad; he nodded. "FOSH is assembling a team to prevent the future murders. Naturally, I'll help in any way I can."

"So will you be heading off to Washington?"

"No. The team will be based locally." He looked around at my office and then back to me. "They asked if I had any recommendations for the team. I hope I didn't overstep my bounds, but I recommended you. You don't have to do it if you don't want to."

I looked up at John Johnson, Rex Solaris—my father, who wanted my help. I smiled. "I wouldn't miss it for the world."

Daughter of Nyx

Kelly Wisdom

I FOLLOWED MIA into the Bureau chapel, filing in behind the rest of our neighbors to take our seats on the hard wooden pews. Once everyone was settled, the officiant standing at the front of the room raised his arms, a fur-lined robe draping his ample body.

"Hey, Veronica," Mia whispered. "He doesn't seem to be missing as many meals as the rest of us, huh?"

"Shh," I said. "You want to have to pay more atonement?"

"Let us rise and recite the Oath," the officiant said. When he spoke, his breath fogged out in tiny white puffs.

The benches creaked as we stood. I forced myself to mouth the words, lest I be chastised by the under-officiants prowling the aisles.

"I promise to obey the Bureau, created for my welfare and protection, in all things. Let this be my oath, or my life be forfeit."

The last line stuck in my throat.

Once we'd all fallen silent again, the officiant looked out over the crowd as if we were a bunch of unruly school kids. "The Bureau would like to address the rumors that a Child of Keres has been spotted here in the University Quarter," he said.

Sinking lower in my seat, I pressed my back against the pew and swallowed uneasily around the growing lump in my throat.

The officiant continued. "These evil creatures arose as abominations of nature after the environmental disasters of the Ancient Age. They spread like vermin over the earth as the continents came together to form the Landmass. Their so-called civilization was nothing but a hotbed of violence and degradation. A human with wings is an aberration, should not even be called human, so it is no wonder that they promoted unnatural ideas of social equality, unnatural liaisons between themselves and humans, as well as unnatural behaviors among their own kind. It is said they even lay with animals, being part beast themselves."

I clenched my teeth and tried to breathe calmly.

"When the Bureau was formed a century ago, its first priority was to eradicate the Keres race. Brave men of the Bureau fought these bloodthirsty creatures and eliminated them from the face of the earth. The battle took many years, but we won. The last Child of Keres was put down nearly twenty years ago. None have been seen since. There are no Children of Keres in this Quarter, in this city, or on this planet. Anyone stating otherwise will be subject to higher levels of atonement."

There was anxious shuffling and coughing from the pews, but no one said a word.

"The Bureau will now accept your atonement," the officiant said.

People began to slide from the pews and walk toward the front of the chapel, where a line of under-officiants stood holding baskets, each adorned with a different color ribbon. Black for curfew-breaking, yellow for sedition, green for not attending chapel, red for deviance. I watched the under-officiants check names off their lists as my neighbors dropped pennies in the baskets. Pennies they had sweated for in mines and factories, or, if they were students like Mia, pennies they had begged, borrowed, or sold their possessions or bodies to get.

Mia walked to the front and tossed a penny in each basket, not bothering to see her name checked off the lists.

"Let's get the hell out of here," she said when she returned.

We pulled our coats tightly around us and walked out into the night.

"So that sermon seemed to kind of upset you," Mia said.

"Did it?" I kept my face still.

"Yeah. How come?" She grinned impishly. "Have you seen one of the wretched beasts?"

"Cut it out," I said. "You want more atonement? You can't afford the ones you owe now."

"I'll just have to rob a Guard or something. Or that officiant tonight. I could cut up that furry cloak and make three coats from it."

In front of Mia's building, we stopped so she could dig her keys out of her bag.

"You know," I said, "I should probably just head home."

"Don't be silly," Mia said. "You've got time before curfew."

"Not much time."

"I thought you wanted to hang out more," she said. "To 'take this thing to the next level,' isn't that what you said?"

"I did, yes, but...."

27

"Don't you want to be with me?" she asked.

"You know I do."

"No, I don't know. You come around one day, then you disappear for weeks. Now, suddenly, you're back again. You've never even stayed over." Her voice kept getting louder.

"Can we take this conversation inside, please?"

"Thought you'd never ask." She jingled her keys in my face.

Once inside, Mia sat on the battered couch and waved me over. She pulled the batteries from her transistor radio and licked them. "These should have enough juice to get us through the evening report."

"Please. I can't listen to that shit."

Mia regarded me with inquisitive green eyes.

"It's depressing," I explained.

"No shit," she replied. "But don't you want to know what's happening out there?"

"What's the point? I mean, what can anybody do about it? Nothing. So, what does hearing about it do for me? Nothing except get me all frustrated and pissed off." *Which is not good for me.*

"You think there's nothing anyone can do?" Mia shifted suddenly, bringing her feet up under her body in a crouch, as if she might spring at me like an animal. "What about all of us students out there demonstrating? You think that's 'nothing'?"

"Wait. Are you still going to the demonstrations?" I demanded.

"Of course. Why don't you go?"

"I'm not a student."

"You don't have to be a student to demonstrate."

"I wish you wouldn't go to those things. It's too dangerous."

"Why aren't you a student, Vee?" she asked, ignoring my warning.

Ah. The question I could not answer.

"I already have a job," I said.

"As a dishwasher in a pub. And do you find that work fulfilling?"

"Don't mock me." My back began to quiver with anger. "I'm not like you. I'm not meant for school like you clearly are. I can't understand even the titles of those science books you read."

"It's not just science, it's twentieth-century quantum physics," she said.

"See," I said. "I don't even know what half those words mean."

"It just infuriates me that most of the Lecturers treat quantum physics like it's alchemy. I'm something of a joke in the department. 'Oh, there goes Mia with her silly books from the Ancient Age.' They think Einstein was a fictional character."

"Who?"

"Albert Einstein. He was a menial worker in some kind of office in a place called Switzerland, which apparently was part of what's now the Fornian Desert. Can you believe that used to be a temperate zone? Anyway, Einstein was...."

Mia recounted Einstein's entire life story to me. But it did not seem amazing in the least. And then she explained his ideas, which sounded like impossibilities. I sat listening, content to hear the lilting tones of her voice even if I couldn't grasp the import of her words, until the fire had died down leaving us both breathing small clouds of mist. Mia reluctantly wound up her tale and left the warmth of the blanket to stoke the fire.

"I got lucky down by the tracks today," Mia said.

"Oh yeah?" I eyed her waifish body as she tossed a few more pieces of coal into the stove.

"Yep. Found a few lumps as big as my fist. Had to fight off some dude taller than you for them." She grinned, an impish glow suffusing her features. "Worth it, though. That'll keep us toasty till you have to go. Unless you decide to stay, that is. Then we'll have to find other ways to stay warm."

Ignoring her suggestion, I looked down at my rough hands, nearly twice the size of Mia's. "I should get your coal for you. You shouldn't have to fight."

"Pshht." Mia slapped my arm dismissively.

Surprising myself, I reached up and caught her hand mid-slap and squeezed the cold, tiny fingers. "I mean it," I said, pulling Mia's fingertips to my lips.

"Vee," Mia whispered.

I paused, staring at her fingers still held to my mouth. Lifting my gaze, I found her green eyes piercing me. She tugged at my hand, and I melted into her. Our mouths came together eagerly.

"I've wanted this for so long," she murmured, holding me tightly at my ribs, the tips of her fingers dangerously close to my back.

I tried not to flinch.

She must have noticed the subtle stiffening of my body. She pulled ever so slightly back.

"You okay?" Mia murmured.

I nodded. "Mm-hmm."

Mia didn't hesitate to lean back in and trace a series of light kisses across my neck, her hands continuing to stroke my torso, which was covered by two shirts and a bulky sweater.

Surely she won't feel anything, I thought.

The warmth that had flooded my body at the first touch of Mia's lips turned to pure ice as her hands reached my waist and inched under the hem of my sweater, grazing bare skin.

I bolted off the couch, furiously tugging my clothes back down.

"I'm sorry, Mia," I blurted. "I can't."

Mia's wide eyes followed me as I paced the small square of rug between the couch and the fire. "Can't what?" she demanded.

"You know."

"I *don't* know, Vee. Tell me."

"I can't...sleep with you. I'm not ready."

Mia stood up and pushed past me into the kitchenette. She pulled coffee powder down from a shelf, filled a kettle with water, and placed it on the hot plate.

I stood in the doorway, observing the quiet anger in her actions. "You don't want me to do anything I'm not ready for, do you?"

"Of course not."

"Then...why are you mad?"

Mia kept her eyes on the chipped countertop. "I'm not mad, Vee," she said. "I'm frustrated. I need to know where this is going."

"I need to take things slow. Can't you wait?"

"Waiting isn't the problem. I get the feeling that you'll never be ready. It's just like your attitude toward school."

"What does school have to do with this?"

"I can't put my finger on it, Vee. There's just something...closed off in you. Some part of you you're just not willing to share. You're happy to work cleaning up after drunks in a dingy pub instead of actually making something of yourself. You're happy to have half a relationship with me instead of really giving yourself to someone. Maybe it's because I'm a girl," she said quietly. "Maybe you should try it with a guy. Maybe you're not as *Aberrant* as you think."

The skin of my back twitched at her use of Aberrant, a term frequently used by the Bureau.

"You don't know what you're talking about, Mia," I said.

"I know that you act disgusted when I touch you."

"I'm not disgusted, I'm...."

"Yes?" She stopped and placed a hand on her tiny hip in an attitude of expectation. The kettle screamed, but we both ignored it. "What are you, Veronica?"

I'm more Aberrant than you can possibly imagine, I thought but couldn't say. "I'm just not ready."

"Bullshit. Why don't you just find some guy who doesn't disgust you? See if you can get one of those Bureau-approved, leading-to-marriage, oh-so-normal relationships. Quit trying so damn hard to be something you're not."

I stood there, trembling with rage, one second away from tearing off my shirt and showing her the truth.

Through gritted teeth, I said, "Screw you, Mia."

She eyed me calmly. "I wish you would."

I stormed out the door and into the night.

The frigid air assaulted me. I threw my trench coat around me as I walked. Anger boiled in my stomach; my back twitched uncontrollably. I had to calm down. Faster and faster I moved my feet over the sidewalk as if I were on a treadmill, trying to move the whole world behind me.

It was near curfew, and the streets were mostly deserted. No one in the University Quarter dared stay out after the nine o'clock bell. A Center City financier might be pardoned for a minor curfew infraction, but a student or a dishwasher...? It was best for the lowly not to tempt the Bureau Guards patrolling the nighttime streets.

The 8:55 warning tone sounded from the university's bell tower. I knew I needed to get back to Mia's—my own flat was too far. However, I kept walking, blowing out furious puffs of breath like a steam-car.

I was so tired of lying to Mia. So tired of hiding. But I had to hide. I had to lie.

My boots scraped against the cobblestones as I came to a halt, my insides a confused jumble of guilt and frustration. The 9:00 curfew bell tolled its solemn pronouncement.

"Shit!" I hissed, and turned around to find myself staring into the grinning face of a Bureau Guard.

"Indeed," he drawled, consulting a silver Bureau-issue timepiece.

In the pale light of the streetlamps, I saw at once that he was only a Delta-Level Guard. He was equipped with an outdated, clunky gaspack instead of one of the heated steam-cars the Alphas and Betas drove on their patrols. Two bulky gas canisters clung to his back; tubes emerged from each canister to arc over his head and point groundward, making him look like he had stick-figure wings.

The thought of a winged Guard caused a snicker to bubble up unexpectedly. It escaped my lips before I could squelch it.

His expression darkened. "And what's so funny, girl?"

"Nothing, sir," I said, pulling my face straight.

"You know you're out after curfew, yes?"

"Yes, sir. I'm very sorry, sir. I was just heading—"

"I don't see any valid excuse for violating curfew, do you?"

I didn't know whether it was best to press my innocence or just agree with him. I went with compliance. "No," I said. "There's no excuse for my actions, sir."

"So you admit your guilt, thereby forfeiting your right to a trial—"

"Wait. No—"

"—and I am thereby free to mete out punishment as I see fit."

I'd heard horror stories of what the Guards could do. My breath started coming in quick, shaking gasps. I looked around for help, but the streets were empty.

I thrust my hands out in front of me in a desperate gesture. "Please, sir, I—"

"Yes?" he said, surprising me. I hadn't expected him to respond.

"Wh-what can I do?" I stammered.

A smirk creased his fleshy face. "I'm so glad you asked," he said silkily, covering the distance between us. "There's nothing I like so much as a friendly, helpful girl, willing to take instruction."

Then his doughy fingers were prodding at my clothes, delving through the layers covering my torso.

"No," I said, swatting at his arms.

"Now don't be unfriendly," he said, touching the bare skin of my stomach. "This doesn't have to be unpleasant."

"I said no!" This time I pushed at his chest.

The weight of his gaspack caused him to stagger a few feet back, but he came at me again. Now he was angry.

"Quiet!" he ordered, clamping one hand over my mouth, while the other fumbled back under my shirt.

But I was angry too. Angrier than I'd ever been. The twitching in my back became a vibration that intensified. And then the secret I'd been hiding all my life finally exploded through my clothes for the Guard to see.

Black-feathered wings unfurled from their hiding place and burst through my clothes. They stretched to their fullest extent, as if in relief from years of being hidden.

"Holy shit," he spluttered, backing away from me. "W-w-wings!"

"Very perceptive," I said, my calm words masking the storm raging inside me.

"Vermin!" the guard blurted. "You're supposed to be extinct. Wiped out by the Bureau. But you're alive!"

"Well done me."

"And now I've got you. I can take you in." His voice trembled. "I'll...I'll be famous."

He came toward me cautiously, arms outstretched, as if he were approaching an animal in the wild. My body responded instinctively. I took two running steps, flapped my wings—and flew.

I felt as if my wings had taken possession of my being and I was simply dragged along in shock. Before I knew it, I was soaring above the rooftops of the Quarter.

"Whoo-hoo!" I yelled, as joy replaced the fear in my chest. I'd had wings my entire life, but I had no memory of flying. Even though the cold air whipped my face and stung my eyes, I'd never felt such pure pleasure. Better still, I'd escaped the Guard. He might tell his colleagues he'd seen a winged human, but no one would believe him without proof.

Alighting on a rooftop near the university, I paused to catch my breath. A high-pitched hiss reached my ears, like air escaping a balloon. I turned in horror to see the Guard using the hand controls to direct his gaspack over the lip of the building, a menacing gleam in his eyes.

"Did you think I'd let you get away, my prize?"

"What are you thinking, flying that thing up here?" I screamed, momentarily stunned into forgetting my predicament. Bureau-issue gaspacks were notoriously undependable.

The Guard landed awkwardly on the roof, taking a few heavy, stumbling steps before stopping. "Just give it up, Aberrant," he panted. "You won't escape me."

I was so sick of that word. I wanted to hit him, to kick him, to scratch out his eyes.

To *kill* him.

Instead, I turned and leapt from the roof, my wings catching air.

The next moment seemed to happen in slow motion.

I heard the crunch of the Guard's boots as he stepped to the ledge. I looked back to see him adjust the gaspack's hand controls and drift into the air. And then the pack malfunctioned, its characteristic hiss becoming a sputter. He was no longer drifting—he was plummeting.

I screamed and dove after him, but he fell too fast.

Nothing could be worse than the noise he made when he hit the ground. At least, that's what I thought until I dropped into the alley beside him and saw the dead eyes protruding from his slightly flattened face.

I turned from the body and vomited. My stomach empty, I faced him again, curling over his broken frame as small, hysterical sobs escaped me.

"I'm sorry," I whimpered futilely. "I didn't want—"

A window scraped open in one of the apartments above me. I backed

34

away from the Guard, ran down the alley, and flew back into the night. I flew wildly, erratically, over buildings I could barely make out through my teary, wind-stung eyes. I needed to get somewhere safe, and quickly. I finally landed in a dark alley near Mia's apartment building. Luckily, the curfew bell had cleared the streets of residents, but the Guards were never far away. I muttered a desperate prayer not to see another one. I couldn't get my wings to retract. Against my will, they beat a nervous staccato that echoed down the alleyway like war drums.

Eventually, I was able to slow my breathing. When I removed my ripped coat and shirts, my wings finally folded back under themselves. I righted my clothing as much as possible.

Mia's was close, so I headed there. I just hoped she would let me in.

She must not have been deeply asleep—she answered my soft knock after only a minute. Her hair was bed-mussed, but her eyes were alert.

"What do you want?" she said.

"I—I really need to t-talk to y-you." My body seemed to suddenly feel the cold. I realized I was shivering uncontrollably.

Despite her obvious anger, Mia noticed my distress. "Have you been outside all this time? Are you crazy? It's after curfew. And you're freezing."

She bustled me in the door and settled me back on the couch. The coals in the stove were just barely glowing. While she stoked the fire, I pulled a blanket around me, desperate to bring warmth to my shuddering limbs. My muscles began to ache.

Mia disappeared into the kitchen. I must have fallen asleep for a few minutes because the next thing I knew she was pushing a cup of steaming broth under my nose.

"You need to drink this."

I let her put the cup to my trembling lips.

"Th-thank you," I said after I'd taken a few sips. The broth warmed me from within, and my shivering slowly began to abate.

We sat in the dark without speaking; the only sounds came as I continued to sip the broth until it was gone.

Finally, Mia asked, "Did someone attack you?"

She must have noticed my clothes.

I wasn't sure how to answer. I said, "Not exactly, no."

"Are you okay?"

No, no, no, no, no, no, no.

"I'll be fine," I said.

She rose. "Well, okay. Then I'm going back to bed. You can have the couch tonight."

She turned to go. In my mind I felt the wind rushing over me as I flew, heard the gaspack run out, saw the Guard fall. I couldn't let the moment pass. I needed to tell her.

"Mia, I've got...I mean, there's something I have to...I need to—"

"Save it." She cut me off. "Tell me in the morning."

"But—"

"Good night."

She was gone. I huffed out a breath of frustration and huddled down to attempt sleep.

It took me a long time to stop replaying the Guard's fall in my mind. Eventually, I must have dozed, for when I opened my eyes again the fire had died down. Even so, I was finally fully warm, hot even, from sleeping so close to the stove. I shucked the blanket off me and stretched my arms.

My wings gave a slight flutter, as if they too wanted a stretch. Would it be like this from now on? Since they had finally experienced the fullness of what they could do, would they be itching to be free all the time?

Oddly, the thought didn't worry me. In fact, I felt quite giddy. My wings twitched again, and a giggle escaped my lips. A giggle. From me.

Then I remembered the Guard's dead eyes, and sobered up.

It was time to tell Mia.

I pulled my coat over my shoulders and headed for her room. My stocking-covered feet shushed over the wooden floor. Mia lay in her narrow bed, breathing deeply, curled up on her side like a child. Dark strands of silky hair fell over her cheek, which looked even paler than usual in the moonlight. She looked so small and fragile. And even though I knew that she was tougher than I'd ever be, I felt an overwhelming need to protect her from harm.

"Mia," I whispered, touching her face lightly with one finger.

"Huh?" She jerked awake. "What's wrong?"

"I have to show you something."

"Can't this wait?"

"What I've got to show you will explain why I hide from everything and everyone, why I'm content being a dishwasher and not going to school." I had to force the rest out over the lump in my throat. "Why I won't let you make love to me."

"You sure know how to get my attention. I'm listening."

I backed up a few steps from the bed. "For now, just look."

Mia sat up further and wrapped her arms around her knees. I slowly

36

removed my overcoat. Then my sweater. Then each of my undershirts, until I was standing before Mia, naked from the waist up.

"Well, I like it so far," Mia said archly.

My wings seemed to have caught my nervousness. They huddled against my back, trembling slightly.

I took a deep breath and turned my back to Mia.

"What have you got on?" she asked.

"Nothing," I said.

And, with another deep breath, I relaxed. My wings unfurled. They gave an involuntary flap—no, strike that. I flapped them. I flapped *my* wings. I had to stop thinking of them as something alien to my body.

Mia gasped. "*Oh*! Oh my *god*. What the—"

I heard her leave the bed, heard her bare feet padding toward me.

"Wings," Mia said.

"Yes."

"You have...*wings*."

"That's right," I said, still facing the wall, my arms crossed over my bare chest. "Big, freakish, crazy, black, bird wings."

"No." Mia's voice was solid now. She put her hands on my waist, below my wings, and turned me around. Her eyes were full of tears. "Beautiful, amazing, glossy, sable bird wings. Can I touch them?"

"Aren't you...I don't know, frightened? Repulsed? Freaked out?"

"No," she said. "But I *am* turned on."

"By...wings?"

"Yes. Now can I please touch them?"

I nodded, and she pulled me into a hug. My cheek rested gently on the top of her head. Her torso pressed against mine as her arms encircled me and her hands reached into the feathery depths of my wings.

"They're so...warm," she said. "And soft."

Mia's fingers explored parts of me that had never, ever been touched. It felt so good it hurt. Suddenly I was crying.

"Do you want me to stop?" she whispered.

I shook my head, feeling the tears slither down my face and onto Mia's hair. Holding her more tightly to me, I let the sobs come as she continued to stroke and fondle every bit of wing she could reach.

When she was done, she took my hand and led me back to the bed, and we scooted under the covers together. The wings were a bit of a problem. My emotions were over-stimulated, and I kept flapping the sheets around. We giggled as we shifted positions, maneuvering my wings out of our way. Then our hands found each other, and the giggling ceased.

When I woke up, my wings were curled up flat against my back, like two sleeping puppies.

"So, those things *can* behave." Mia lay propped on one elbow, staring at me.

"I suppose," I said with a grin. "They've been hidden under sweaters for years, so I can't blame them for being a little hyperactive."

Mia traced a finger lightly down my arm, and I shivered with pleasure.

"What I'm curious about," she said, "is what happened last night to make you decide to finally show me. And why are your clothes torn up?"

A cold feeling of dread filled my stomach, and my grin vanished. After Mia had touched my wings last night, I'd forgotten all the horror that had come right before. Reality hit me like a brick.

"Mia, I...I really screwed up."

She took my big hand in her little one and squeezed fiercely. "Tell me."

"I was so mad when I left. I just kept walking, even after curfew."

"You ran into a Guard."

"Yes," I said. His dead eyes still haunted my mind. "He...you know how they are, he harassed me, you know, and after our fight I was so worked up...and I didn't think, I just got so mad. And my wings tore through my clothes all of a sudden—they've never done that before—and he saw me, so I flew away. I haven't flown since I can remember and I just flew into the air like I'd been doing it all my life. And he had a pack on and he came after me. I guess the pack was low because suddenly that hissing noise stopped and he just dropped."

"He fell out of the sky?"

"Yes."

"How far?"

I shook my head, tears blurring my vision again. "Too far. I flew after him, thought I could, I don't know, catch him or something, anything, but I wasn't fast enough."

"Oh...shit. He died?"

"I heard him hit the ground. I saw his...eyes."

Mia gathered me up in her arms again and rocked me like a child. I couldn't stop the whimpers that escaped me.

"Shhh," she said, smoothing my hair, stroking my twitching wings. "You're okay. There's nothing you could have done."

I leaned into her arms and let her murmurs soothe me.

When I was calm, Mia suggested we get out of the flat.

"Food," she said. "You need food. Let's go down to the pub."

So I re-bundled my body and wings in my ripped clothes and readied myself to face the world.

Down on the street, tiny flakes of ash-colored snow drifted out of the sky to land on our exposed faces and fingers like knives of ice.

"Acid snow," Mia said bitterly. "Another wonderful consequence of the Bureau's environmental policies."

We took a corner booth in Lindon's, a dingy pub where Mia's friends often gathered. The waiter, whose frayed cuffs and dark-ringed eyes gave him away as a student, greeted Mia by name before taking our order and hustling away.

Mia opened her mouth to speak, but at that moment a guy with straggly hair squeezed into the booth beside her.

"Did you hear?" he demanded.

"Hear what?" Mia asked. "Oh, Veronica, this is Sam. Sam, Veronica."

"Hello," I said.

"Hi," Sam said. "But listen. Somebody's killed a Guard."

I went rigid in my seat. Mia took my hand under the table and began stroking my palm with her thumb.

"Oh my god!" Mia exclaimed, sounding exactly like Sam's pronouncement was news to her. "What happened?"

Sam leaned in and Mia and I both responded in kind, our three heads bent low over the ring-marked table.

"No one knows," he said. "They found him in an alley by Baker Street. His gaspack had apparently run out and he fell off a damn building."

I saw the Guard's eyes in my mind and my wings gave a shiver. I pressed my back hard against the booth.

"Turns out," Sam said, "he was chasing someone. Someone...who could *fly*."

"What?" I hissed, unable to stop myself. "How do you know that?"

Mia clenched my hand even tighter.

"Yes," Mia said, "why would you think that? That he was chasing someone who could fly. The idea seems preposterous."

"It would, I agree," Sam said. "Except that someone looked out a window and saw a girl with wings crouched over the dead body. A girl who then flew away."

My hand trembled in Mia's. Her soothing thumb-strokes had ceased. She stared in horror at Sam.

"I know!" Sam's face was beaming. "A winged human! The rumors must be true! Somehow one survived! And she's on *our* side!"

"How do you know that?" I snapped.

Sam gave me a withering look. "Of course she's on our side. How could she not be? Plus, she killed a guard."

"Maybe it was an accident," I said.

Sam shrugged. "Who cares? The point is, it will send the Bureau a message. We are *not* powerless. We can fight back. We already have the numbers. Students and radicals outnumber the Bureau-friendly three to one. But people don't show up to the demonstrations because they're scared. They've seen too many people disappear into the Bureau's custody. But if we had a symbol of strength, a symbol of hope like this winged girl…well, the people might be more willing to stand up and fight."

Sam paused, breathless with excitement. At that moment, the waiter returned with our food. I forced myself to eat so I didn't have to talk. Mia started picking at her meal, her eyes taking on that distant look they had whenever she wrestled with a complex idea.

Once the waiter disappeared, Sam said, "I can't believe we might have a Child of Keres on our side. A freaking Daughter of Keres!"

"Don't use that name!" I snapped.

"Why not?" Sam asked.

"That's what the Bureau called them," I said.

"The Bureau gave them those names and painted them as monsters to justify the genocide," Mia explained. "Most people had never seen a winged human, since they'd been banned from the city. If the masses thought of winged humans as Children of Keres, well, if you know your Greek mythology, the Keres were thought to be bloodthirsty demons with sharp teeth and claws and…"

"Stop talking like an encyclopedia," I cut in irritably.

"Forget it," she said. "Eat up."

Sam leaned back in. "There's going to be another demonstration today. People are energized by this Daughter of Ker—uh, I mean, winged human."

Mia's eyebrows raised, but she continued to eat.

"Penance Square," Sam continued. "Two sharp. Will you be there?"

He clearly wasn't asking me. Mia gave a tiny nod. Sam grinned and slid out of the booth.

"Maybe the Daughter of Keres herself will make an appearance," he said, and was gone as quickly as he'd come.

"I need to get out of here," I said to Mia when we were alone.

"All right," she said, pushing her plate away. "Let's go to your place."

Mia tossed some coins on the table, then took my arm and steered me out into the street. The snow fell heavily and gathered on surfaces in thick gray clumps. Students bustled around us, their threadbare coats pulled high on their necks to keep out the cold.

I don't think I could have found my way without Mia. My mind spiraled in a blind panic. Every second I feared that my wings would come flying out for all the world to see, and people would start pointing and yelling, "Look! The freak!"

The walk home passed in a fearful blur. I found myself suddenly at the front door to my building. Once we were safely inside, I crumpled onto the floor and put my head in my hands.

"What am I going to do?" I whispered. "I'm screwed. Totally and completely screwed."

Mia wasn't listening. I heard her rummaging around in my bedroom.

"You are so messy," she yelled. "How can you find anything in here?"

I got up and walked down the hall.

"What are you doing?" I demanded.

"Looking for clothes."

"Mia. What am I going to do?"

She put her hands on her hips and gave a deep sigh. "I don't know what you're going to do," she began slowly, "but I can tell you what I think you should do."

"Which is...?"

"Join the cause. Reveal yourself. Let the people see that you are not a Child of Keres."

We stared at each other over my piles of discarded clothing. I wanted to scream at her, to tell her she was crazy, to tell her I hated her, to tell her to get the hell out. But she held me in her gaze and wouldn't let me go.

"We called ourselves Children of Nyx," I whispered. "The ever-gentle Mother of Night gave birth to us, and to her we would one day return, my mother said." The word *Nyx*, which had existed only in my mind for so long, sounded strange aloud.

"Then join the fight so you can show everyone the truth about your race," Mia urged.

"Mia," I pleaded. "I can't."

"Yes, you can," she said simply. "Here." She held up my favorite black leather bomber. The silver chains and studs adorning the jacket jingled as she beat the dust from it. "Your unfortunate fashion sense will help here. The chains across the front of this jacket will offer some defense. Where are your scissors?"

I got the scissors from the utility drawer and handed them to her, watching dumbly as she began cutting holes in the jacket.

"While I'm doing this," she said, "go put on the clothes I laid out on your bed. But first bring me a black t-shirt."

I obeyed because I didn't know what else to do. Soon I was arrayed all in form-fitting black clothes, with steel-toed boots laced up to my knees. Mia had altered the t-shirt and jacket with slits for my wings to escape. Finally she handed me a pair of black leather gloves and a black rucksack.

"You can wear this over your back in case your wings end up on the outside of your clothes and you need to hide them. But it shouldn't hinder your flying, I don't think. If you had a weapon, you could keep it in the sack, too." Her eyes brightened with the idea.

"No weapons," I said.

"Okay, fine," she said. "For now. But one day you'll need them if you're going to lead the fight against the Bureau. They have *lots* of weapons."

All at once the force of what she was suggesting hit me. I threw down the rucksack and started pulling off the outfit.

"No. No. No, no, no, no, no!" I screamed. "I don't want to!"

Mia grabbed me by the shoulders and shook me.

"Snap out of it, Vee!" Her voice was harsher than I'd ever heard it. "Do you think I want to go to all these demonstrations, risk getting shot or beaten by some asshole who sleeps every night in electrically heated rooms while I have to fight grown men for coal? Of course I don't. I hate living this way! But I have to." Her voice softened as she brushed her fingers across my cheekbone. "I want a life with you, Vee. And that's never going to happen unless we fight for it."

She took a breath and went on. "I read a book about an ancient uprising once. A people rose up against their tyrannical leaders and defeated them. And one of the rebel leaders said something that has stuck with me since I read it. He said, 'The tree of liberty must be refreshed from time to time with the blood of patriots and tyrants.'"

"Do you want me to get killed?"

"I want you to *fight!*" The words echoed off my walls. "You have a gift and you need to use it. Accept that you're unique. The world *needs* you."

"I'm not unique," I said. "I'm deformed."

That shut her up. Her lips pressed in a thin line; her eyes filled with angry tears. "If that's what you think, you might as well stay home. Stick your head back in the ground where it's comfortable."

"Mia—"

"I've got to go. It's almost two." She shoved her thin arms into the sleeves of her coat. "Will I see you there?"

I kept my eyes on the floor.

When the door slammed shut, I took off my boots and crawled in bed, pulling the graying sheets over my head. But even with my eyes closed, I could see the disappointment and anger in Mia's eyes. Her words ricocheted against the walls of my heart.

Stick your head back in the ground where it's comfortable.

I'd spent my whole life hiding, with good reason. My people had been hunted and exterminated by the Bureau. After my family was taken, I became the sole surviving Child of Nyx. And I wouldn't have lived if the Bureau had known of my identity. If I were to expose myself now, I'd be arrested and killed.

I want you to fight!

It was stuffy under the sheets, so I came up for air. I thought of Mia, out on the streets, pressing to the front of an angry crowd. A brilliant, but comparatively powerless young student willing to take on the Bureau. *She* was the one that should have been given wings.

Goddamnit. I was going to have to give her mine.

I tossed off the covers and retrieved the pieces of the costume Mia had devised. I added one more touch—my father's battered old aviator goggles, which he'd shoved in my hands the day he was taken. He must have worn them to keep the wind out of his eyes when he flew. They were a bit too large for me, so they'd also serve to hide my face. I wanted to protect my identity for as long as I could.

Fortunately, my building was located a mere block from Penance Square. As I left the apartment, the clock on my wall read 2:10. I raced up the stairs to the roof and rushed to the edge. Over the top of the next building I could see the mob of students and other protesters who'd packed themselves into the Square.

What would they all think when I flew down into their midst? Would it even matter?

Mia thought it would.

I stepped out onto the ledge and took a deep breath. Exhaling, I unfurled my wings. They slid easily through the slits in my shirt and jacket.

I looked down, readying myself for flight. When I'd flown the night before, the decision had been instinctive—I had been airborne before I had known what was happening. Now I had to force the fear down and believe that, once the building was no longer under my feet, I'd remember how to fly.

Another breath, and I dropped off the edge. My wings caught the air.

I soared straight for the far end of the square where a line of Bureau Guards, armed with batons, faced off against a seething tide of protesters. The plump, rosy cheeks of the Guards in their fur-lined cloaks formed a stark contrast to the lean, pale faces of the students clad in thin, tattered coats. Swooping down over the Guards' heads, I caught the first glimpse of fingers pointing at the sudden appearance of a girl with wings.

At the center of the line of Guards stood the snow-dusted statue of Elden Stuart, founder of the Bureau. His upturned palm, representing the Bureau's generosity (or so we had been informed as schoolchildren) was covered in bird droppings. I came to a precarious perch on Elden's shoulder, high above the reach of the Guards.

As I looked around for Mia, I noticed the crowd fall eerily silent. Hundreds of faces turned up to me, waiting in anticipation for what I would do next. Did they expect me to speak? My body began to tremble; one foot slipped off Elden. The crowd gasped, then sighed in relief as I regained my footing.

The silence lengthened, until finally I saw a familiar dark head bobbing its way along the front line toward me.

Mia shot me a brilliant smile as she reached the statue and clambered her way up onto the pedestal Elden's feet rested upon. I saw Sam was there on the ground under Mia, having given her a boost. Once she was up, he handed her an enormous speaking cone.

Planting herself in front of Elden Stuart's effigy, Mia turned to address the large crowd.

"Behold!" she yelled into the cone. "A Daughter of Nyx!"

The Bureau Guard closest to us shifted his feet and tightened the grip on his baton.

"One winged human lives! " she continued. "The Bureau has lied to us! She is no bloodthirsty Child of Keres! The Bureau created that name to justify the extinction of her people. She is a gentle soul, yet she is willing to help us make a stand against the tyranny of the Bureau! To help us make a stand for freedom!"

The demonstrators erupted into wild noises of affirmation. Movement out of the corner of my vision tore my gaze from Mia. I saw two Guards move from their positions to carry on a whispered conversation. They seemed to reach some agreement because one nodded sharply and returned to his place while the other pulled a communicator from somewhere in the folds of his cloak.

I wanted to leap down and warn Mia, but the cheers had abated. She took up the speaking cone once more.

"The Daughter of Nyx can inspire us, but it is up to us to take up the cause of truth. The last remaining winged human will fight. But she cannot fight alone. I'm asking you this day to stand up and take the fight beyond this Square. Stand with us! Stand against the Bur—"

The Guards suddenly grabbed her. I was too slow. One Guard pulled her feet out from under her while two more held back Sam and Mia's other student friends. The world seemed to stop. I watched, frozen in fear, as Mia fell. I heard her skull crack against the corner of the pedestal. She hit the ground, and her murderer gave her two more blows to the head with his baton for good measure.

"*NO!*" I screamed.

I dove from my perch onto the Guard who had killed her. He crumpled beneath my weight, and his head hit the cobblestones with a satisfying smack. I heard fighting explode around me. But I was oblivious to everything except taking out my grief and anger on the Guard's body. I have no idea how much time passed before Sam extruded himself from the fight to pull me off him.

I gazed at the blood on my gloves in awe, barely registering Sam's yelling in my ear. "He's dead, Nyx, come on! We need to get out of here!"

Heaving Mia's body over his shoulder in a fireman's carry, he grabbed my arm and dragged me through the crowd to a dark alley off the square.

"I know you want to say goodbye," Sam said. His voice was low and urgent. He kept looking over his shoulder. "But you must do it quickly and return to the battle. More Guards will be here any second."

"Battle?" I said stupidly.

"We've been preparing for this for a long while. You and Mia were the perfect catalysts to start a war that's been brewing for ages. But the Bureau will be sending reinforcements. We need *you* to distract the Guards."

"Mia's dead, you ass!" I screamed in his face. I was verging on hysteria. How could I explain to him that all the oxygen had been sucked out of my world? That the stars had been torn out of my sky?

Sam regarded me in silence.

"How can I distract them?" I finally asked.

"Fly. Get them to chase you. We'll have others backing you up, but we've got a plan to attack the Bureau Tower itself and we need most of our people for that. So a quick goodbye is all you've got time for."

He laid Mia against a brick wall in the alley and stepped back to let me kneel by the body. The fatal injuries had all landed on the back of Mia's head. Other than a trickle of blood along one temple, her face was unmarred. I wiped the blood away with my sleeve and dropped light kisses on each of her closed eyelids. She seemed so much smaller than she had in life.

"Goodbye, Mia," I said, choking on the words. Tears leaked under my goggles, making my cheeks itch.

I could feel Sam's impatience behind me. I smoothed one hand down Mia's dark head for the last time. Sticking my coat cuff under the goggles, I dried my face.

"I never got to tell her I loved her," I said, whether to Sam or to myself or to the frozen sky above, I wasn't sure.

Sam was the only one with an answer. "You'll just have to win this war for her, then."

So I spread my wings and followed Sam back into the fray.

Going My Own Way

Dayton Ward

NOW

Heat seeped through Daniel Balin's insulated coat and pants, sweat ran freely down his chest and back, and his breathing echoed within the confines of his respirator mask. All around him, flames washed over the blackened walls, licking upward in search of new fuel to consume. Dark smoke choked the corridor, billowing outward from the depths of the burning warehouse. Daniel ignored it, knowing that the rest of the company was dealing with the fire itself. His job was to keep pressing forward.

"It's getting pretty thick in here, Danny," said his partner, Andrea Lucas, as she moved down the hallway in front of him. The flashlight mounted on her helmet tried to pierce the smoke, but the beam disappeared into the thick clouds and offered no help as the two firefighters navigated the building's interior. "Maybe you ought to take point."

Daniel moved ahead of her. "No problem." His own flashlight beam was only a nuisance to him in a situation like this, which was why he hadn't bothered to turn it on in the first place.

Despite the best efforts of the building's safety marshals as well as the first firefighters to arrive on the scene, two employees remained missing. They were believed to be in the warehouse's basement level, where the medical supply company's chemicals were stored. According to the manager on duty, the basement also contained a large fireproof vault. If those people were still alive, they might try to hole up there if they were unable to find another way out of the building.

"*Danny,*" came the filtered voice of the fire company's captain, Bill Leisner, through his radio earpiece. "*We've got hoses going on the front of the building. Where are you?*"

Taking a moment to check his bearings against the copy of the map hastily drawn by the company's manager, Daniel keyed his mike. "Almost at the end of the main hallway. Looking for the second stairwell now."

"*Don't take too long,*" Leisner replied. "*The whole place is liable to come down before this is over.*"

"Roger that," Daniel said before gesturing for Andrea to follow him.

"Can you see anything?" she asked, her voice muffled by her mask.

The answer, as usual, was simple enough.

He could see *everything*.

Twenty Years Ago

Dr. Paul Murasaka sat behind his desk, watching as Jack and Mariel Balin held hands and did not quite meet his gaze. He could understand their apprehension. Meeting with a doctor to discuss the health and well being of a child was almost always stressful for the parents, but particularly so in this case. After all, young Daniel Balin wasn't an ordinary patient, or even an ordinary child.

"Jack, Mariel," Murasaka began, "we always knew there was a very good chance Daniel would develop some form of exceptional abilities. It appears those traits are beginning to manifest themselves, though in some ways they're quite different from your own capabilities, Jack."

Murasaka had been a licensed physician for nearly thirty years. Before the birth of Daniel Balin, he never offered medical care or advice to anyone who could be classified as an "enhanced human." He had initially resisted the idea, but Mariel Balin was a patient of his. Not Jack, of course.

After all, what kind of superhero needed a doctor?

Quite a large number of them, as it turned out, including a few living in central Florida rather than New York or other major cities where many of the more well-known "heroes" chose to make their homes. When Mariel, already the wife of "Hammer Jack" Balin and possessing as much fortitude as any enhanced human, became pregnant, Murasaka quickly found himself presiding over a superhero's unborn son.

That was five years ago, and the time since then had been anything but uneventful.

"How different?" Mariel asked. "Does he have Jack's strength?" Her husband had earned his moniker after demonstrating his superhuman physique for the first time in public while vacationing with Mariel in Washington, D.C. From what Murasaka had seen on cable news, Jack literally had punched through thirty meters of concrete, asphalt, rock and steel to reach people trapped underground after the collapse of a subway tunnel.

By the time other heroes had arrived on the scene, Jack's infravision abilities had helped him navigate to the buried subway train and locate its passengers. Everyone had survived the near disaster, and "Hammer Jack" was born. Many had likened his strength to that of popular comic book heroes, a comparison that the notably humble Jack had always eschewed. As Murasaka recalled, Jack even had refrained from choosing a more suitable nickname, deciding that the one bestowed upon him by an inventive journalist fit as well as any other.

Resting his forearms on his expensive mahogany desk, Murasaka answered Mariel, "In the tests I've run to date, Daniel exhibits some indications of enhanced physical strength. It's still quite limited, though that likely will improve to at least some degree as he grows older."

"You said there were differences," Jack said. "What do you mean?"

Murasaka cleared his throat. "We've talked about Daniel's eyesight before, when we learned about his extreme sensitivity to sunlight, and even the lesser illumination of interior lighting. As it turns out, what we thought was a problem is actually nothing of the sort. I checked for the presence of infravision abilities and in those tests, Daniel was able to see objects in the dark at distances of up to fifty meters."

This elicited expressions of surprise from both parents. "Only fifty?" Mariel asked. "Jack can see things in the dark up to three football fields away. Is there something wrong?"

Smiling, Murasaka shook his head. "It's possible that his range will increase as he gets older, but I'm not worried about that. I've run some other tests, and it seems that Daniel is capable of seeing in a wide variety of visual ranges. His effectiveness was limited during my first tests, but it's increasing all the time. Eventually, he may well be able to see across the entire electromagnetic spectrum. It's really quite extraordinary."

Now

The fire door was jammed shut, but it was child's play for Daniel to see through it and ensure the fire wasn't waiting for them on the other side. Holding his axe across his body, he shifted his weight and lashed out with his right foot. His heel slammed against the door just above the lock and Daniel felt the metal bolt bend from the strength of the kick, forcing the door to swing away and reveal more of the same smoke-filled hallway.

"You sure come in handy some times, you know?" Andrea said. "Your dad teach you that?"

"He would've just punched through it," Daniel replied. Though his visual abilities had continued to improve and broaden as he had grown older, his physical strength—though far superior to a normal person's—

remained but a fraction of that commanded by his father.

"We're through the south fire door," he called into his radio. "Should be coming up on the stairs now."

"*Roger that, Danny,*" Captain Leisner replied. "*Watch your ass in there.*"

"I would if I could see it," Andrea said.

Daniel smiled, though he said nothing. While he and other members of the crew had at first balked at the notion of women in what still largely was a male profession, Andrea had wasted no time demonstrating that she not only belonged in the department, but she also was better suited to the job than some of her male counterparts. If she was intimidated at being the only woman on the crew, she never showed it, often giving better than she got when it came to the usual antics—pranks, trash talking, crude stories and language—which often filled the quiet hours at the fire house. She and Daniel had been paired together for almost a year, and aside from a single misguided bout of drunken fumbling one night after the station Christmas party, their relationship had remained safely within the boundaries of friends and teammates.

Looking past the haze of gray smoke in the corridor before him, Daniel saw harsh white-yellow orbs surrounding the bulbs used in the light fixtures spaced at regular intervals down the length of the passageway. Dust and other particles rained down from the ceiling, looking to him like a light snowfall. Though they had passed through the area where the fire was burning on this floor, the smoke was getting thicker as they moved deeper into the building.

From behind him, Daniel felt Andrea tug on his respirator harness, which she had been holding in order to keep from getting separated as they moved about in the dark.

"You know," she said, "maybe we *should* have gone around."

Daniel shook his head at his partner's suggestion. "No time for that. Don't worry, I can see pretty good in here."

It was an understatement, of course. In truth, the smoke presented no obstacle to him, as he had learned long ago how to filter it from the visual maelstrom his eyes fed him. Power was out in the warehouse, which meant the elevators were useless. The building contained two stairwells, one of which had already been consumed by fire and ruled out as a point of approach. Given the choice of backing out of the warehouse and finding another entrance to get to the remaining stairwell or navigating through the smoke-clogged interior, he had argued for the second option. Captain Leisner, as always, wasn't thrilled with the idea, but knew from experience that getting his rather gifted young rookie firefighter into the thick of things was the surest way to ensure the victims' survival.

Sorting through "the soup," Daniel could distinguish the numerous discolorations and stains in the hallway's threadbare carpet, along with the grain in the cheap wood wall paneling buried beneath multiple layers of latex paint. Looking past all of that, he saw no sign of the fire here. How long might that last, given the building's age? It was an old one, constructed soon after World War II like many structures in this part of Tampa. Daniel knew it would burn like hay if the fire was left unchecked.

As they moved down the hallway, Daniel noted a break in the wall paneling ahead of them. It was a doorway. He saw a banister mounted to the wall at waist height and angling downward. They had reached the stairs.

He patted Andrea's arm. "Stay close. We're almost there."

"Screw those Pezheads downtown," Andrea replied. "I'll take you over one of those fancy thermal cams any day."

Despite their demonstrated value in finding trapped fire victims, state-of-the-art thermal imaging cameras were still a luxury item in the eyes of the Tampa city government, who so far had been able to secure funding for only four of the units to share between the city's twenty-two fire stations. Therefore, it was with no small amount of fanfare that Daniel Balin, probationary firefighter with powers of vision unrivaled by even the elite of the enhanced human community, was welcomed into the fold of Fire Station No. 3. There were many who might question his choice not to follow in the steps of his father, but none of them were backing him up on this fire right now.

Reaching the doorway, Daniel peered through the metal and wood forming the stairwell and got his initial look at the basement. Shipping crates were stacked everywhere, and cheap aluminum lockers lined the walls. Even the cavity created by the stairs beneath them was stuffed full of supplies, including one item in particular that earned Daniel's immediate attention: a tank of compressed oxygen.

Oh, wonderful, he thought, peering across the room and trying not to think too much about the fire playing across the floor, walls, and furniture near the stairs and the tank. Instead, he tried to filter through the dust, flames, and smoke as he searched for the missing employees.

"Can you see anybody?" Andrea asked.

Six Years Ago

"I can see them, damn it!" Daniel Balin shouted, pointing toward the burning dormitory building.

Lieutenant Jeff Summit's disbelieving expression looked as though it might be permanently etched on the firefighter's face. "Who the hell are you?" he asked, still holding the radio microphone in his hand. "Get away from here. I got people trapped inside and men trying to find them, and I don't have time for some wannabe psychic bullshit artist."

"It doesn't matter who I am," Daniel pleaded, pointing at the dorm again. "There are five people on the sixth floor, center break room."

"How the hell can you see that?" Summit snapped, genuine anger now clouding his features.

Ignoring the question, Daniel pressed, "Look, at least two of them are unconscious. Send your men to get them now!"

He found it almost effortless to see through the building's concrete and steel, having honed his abilities years earlier as just one of the countless exercises devised by Dr. Murasaka to help him learn to live with his superhuman eyes. Even with the doctor's guidance, it had taken much time and effort to master the art of focusing on a single aspect of the constant barrage of information his eyes received from across the width and breadth of the electromagnetic spectrum.

"What the hell are you talking about?" the firefighter asked, scowling.

Daniel pointed toward the building. "Four of your men are on that floor, heading toward the west stairwell at the opposite end of the hallway. One's carrying an axe. You've also got five men on the first floor, and three more on the second." Then, considering what else he might say to convince the man, he studied the firefighter himself, his eyes boring through protective clothing, skin, and muscle tissue. "Look, damn it; you've got a tattoo of a bulldog on your left arm, and a Marine Corps emblem on your chest. What else do I have to say to *convince* you?"

Eyes widening in surprise and disbelief, the other man's mouth actually fell open. "How in God's name do you *know that?*" Then, realization seemed to dawn, and his expression changed. "Wait. You're a—"

Cutting him off, Daniel gestured toward the building. "Tell them!"

He didn't know what finally convinced the firefighter to listen, whether it might be the force of his voice or the implication his words carried. All that mattered was that the man finally nodded, his expression a mix of confusion and suspicion but also laced with the faintest hint of hope.

"I hope you're right, kid," he said quietly before keying his radio and relaying new instructions to his people in the building.

Several minutes passed, with Lieutenant Summit coordinating the efforts of his firefighting crews as Daniel stood silent and doing his best to stay out of the way, before the speakers on the fire truck blared to life.

"We got 'em, Jeff. Five victims, two down for the count. We're taking them down the east stairwell."

His jaw slackened in shock, Summit turned back to Daniel. "How did you know?"

Shaking his head, Daniel replied. "I didn't know. I *saw*."

Now

At first, Daniel saw only the fire raging below them, close to the storage lockers containing the more dangerous chemicals and moving in that direction. He could discern that the flames burning toward the front of the building was hotter than if generated by wood or other naturally flammable materials. The air around them was inundated with the fumes of at least a dozen different chemical vapors, their colors swirling in and around each other in Daniel's vision.

Even if you manage not to roast, you'll probably still die of cancer.

He caught movement to his right and made out two figures, one male and one female, huddling within an enclosed space near the rear of the warehouse. The fire hadn't reached the office yet, but judging by its progress the flames wouldn't take long to get there. Daniel also saw the pale red auras surrounding both victims, signaling their rapidly elevating body temperatures.

"I see them, but we don't have all day." Keying his radio, he said, "Cap, we've got a bead on the victims. "They're in an office in the southwest corner of the basement level. I think we can get to them, but we're gonna need a way out."

"No sweat, Danny," Leisner replied. *"We'll be ready when you give the word."*

There were no windows in the basement, save for the small vent-type openings that were too small for a person to crawl through. With the north side of the building still on fire and the elevators useless, the stairwell was the only way out.

Shifting his position so that he could peer through the inner and outer walls separating him from the building's exterior, Daniel saw the figures, some running about in different directions while others stood near fire trucks and other support vehicles. Their deployment, along with the rest of the company as the situation continued to evolve and areas of the burning structure were brought under control, was much like a military formation preparing for an assault on an enemy position. It was an apt analogy, he thought, with him and Andrea playing the part of the advance scouts on a search and rescue mission, looking to free two prisoners from the clutches of an opposing force.

Glancing back to where Andrea waited behind him, Daniel indicated for her to follow him. "Let's go."

The fire cast flickering shadows on the walls of the stairwell as he stepped through the door and on to the first floor landing. *At least now Andrea's not blind*, he thought, also thankful that even the feeble light helped to combat the illusion that the corridor was closing in on him. Despite his ability to filter such distractions as darkness and smoke away from what he wanted to see, he had never figured out a way to distance himself from the uncomfortable sensations he experienced in these types of situations.

How does a guy who can see through walls get claustrophobia?

Daniel had decided long ago that he had fallen victim to a cruel joke; a penance exacted by fate in exchange for the gift it had seen fit to bestow upon him. Such an explanation lacked logic or even common sense, he knew, but it was good enough for him.

Below them, the fire continued to burn near the stairwell, and Daniel could see the telltale signs of damage to the landing between the first floor and the basement as well as the lower section of stairs. Heat blooms under the carpeting told him that the wood beneath was beginning to burn and weaken.

"Step where I step," he said, knowing the command was unnecessary. Andrea had followed him into enough burning buildings to know the drill.

Not worried about the upper flight of stairs, Daniel wasted no time descending to the next landing but paused before actually taking that last step. Beneath the platform, flames licked at the beams supporting the stairwell. Grabbing the railing to his right, he gingerly probed with his left foot, pressing down to test the platform's strength. He grimaced as the wood popped and cracked beneath his boot, but the floor held.

Good enough, he decided.

Then, everything went to hell.

Two Years Ago

"Lookin' pretty sharp, son."

Shaking hands with his father, Firefighter Candidate Daniel Balin offered a satisfied smile in reply to the compliment before taking a moment to smooth a nonexistent wrinkle from his uniform. As the student currently at the head of his class, he felt compelled to set the example in all areas of the candidates' training, and that included personal appearance. The creases in his shirt and trousers were sharp enough to draw blood, and his shoes were like mirrors reflecting the break room's overhead lighting. Other than the dark-lensed glasses he wore out of necessity, Daniel presented the recruiting poster image for the Tampa Fire Department.

Still, the effort he had put into his uniform did not seem to impress the man standing next to Jack Balin.

"Dan," said the elder Balin, "this is Special Agent Alex Gerardo from the Federal Bureau of Investigation. He's got a proposition for you."

With his dark blue suit and muted tie, Gerardo was the epitome of everything Daniel thought an FBI agent should look like. His jacket was tailored in that loose-fitting manner preferred by athletes but it did not quite succeed in hiding the small bulge along the agent's right hip.

Indicating a nearby table, Daniel took the seat directly across from Gerardo, with Jack opting for the chair to his son's left. To Daniel's surprise, the agent did not say anything even after all three men were seated, but instead regarded him in silence. The man's eyes were slate gray, unblinking, and boring straight into him.

"Your glasses," Gerardo said after several seconds, "do they help?"

Without thinking about it, Daniel reached up to adjust his sunglasses. Dr. Murasaka had developed the special eyewear with the assistance of colleagues from the medical center in New York City that specialized in the treatment of enhanced humans. The lenses, coated as they were with a special polymer, were similar to the faceplates designed for the helmets worn by astronauts to protect against the dangerous effects of direct sunlight in space. Acting as filters, the glasses were able to screen out the bulk of the electromagnetic spectrum and allowed Daniel periods of respite from the constant onslaught fed to him by his eyes.

"They do all right," he replied. Considering he didn't know the agent from a drunk on Nebraska Avenue, he thought the question rather unusual. Not that it mattered, really. The guy had to know the answer already, right? He pointed to the man's briefcase. "What, that's not in the file I'm sure you've got in there?"

As the child of a superhero, Daniel knew that his existence, like his father's and other enhanced humans, was of much interest to the various intelligence gathering organizations, both within and beyond the country's borders. Given Hammer Jack's prominence among other heroes, that curiosity remained even after his son's decision not to follow in his footsteps.

"Of course," Gerardo replied. "It's procedure, after all. Daniel, you know that the FBI feels your visual abilities would be an enormous asset. My superiors have expressed great interest in you, and the director's hoping you'll want to at least discuss the possibility of coming to work for us in some capacity. That's why I'm here."

Daniel rolled his eyes. "I've been over this with your people before, Mr. Gerardo. Let's face facts. Other than my eyes, I make a pretty substandard superhero."

Holding his hands before him in a gesture of supplication, Gerardo said, "I understand that you're reluctant to become an active participant in the superhero community, but many within the Bureau believe that there are other uses for a man of your particular talents."

"Look," Daniel snapped, no longer bothering with politeness, "it's not that I'm reluctant. I'm simply not interested." He cast a sidelong glance at his father, who still presented an imposing figure even without the trademark steel gray costume he had hung up a few years ago. "If I'd inherited my dad's strength, we might have something to talk about. As it happens, I've decided on a different approach."

Gerardo looked to Jack Balin as if seeking some measure of support, but the older man merely shook his head.

"It's his choice, Agent Gerardo. He's made it, and I stand by him one hundred percent."

The topic had been discussed several times, and Jack Balin had always supported his son's decision to pursue his dreams of being a writer, not a hero. For a time it seemed that was the path Daniel would take as he attended a notable Florida university in pursuit of his journalism degree.

Of course, all that had changed the day of that campus fire, when Daniel had realized that even without his father's super strength, he had discovered another means to share his own special gift with others.

"By joining the fire department," he said as the memories of that day replayed in his mind, "I can still help people, but I don't want to stand out when I'm doing it. I just don't need or want the attention that comes from wearing a costume." Glancing to his father, he smiled, "My dad always makes that part look easy, but it's never been my strong suit." He shrugged. "To make a long story short, Mr. Gerardo, I'm satisfied with the choice I made."

The agent nodded. "I appreciate your convictions, but fighting fire's a dangerous job. Considering what you have to offer, there are all sorts of ways to use your abilities without putting yourself at risk."

"It's no different from anyone else doing the job they volunteered for,"

Daniel replied. "I'm just going about it in my own way." Grinning at his father again, he added, "Besides, think of the book I'll be able to write some day."

Now

"Back! Get back!"

Daniel saw the contents of the oxygen tank igniting the instant before the tank exploded, drowning out the rest of his warning. Wood cracked and metal shrieked as he threw up his arms to protect his head and face. The stairwell trembled around them, the blast deafening in the confined space. Daniel fell backward in an attempt to dodge the brunt of the explosion, dropping to the stairs. Wood and metal debris hurled in all directions, some of it peppering his helmet and protective clothing. He felt the stairs sway beneath him, their support frame compromised by the force of the detonation.

Even as the echo faded Daniel's ears continued to ring, the constant buzz working to wash out the other sounds around him. Looking up from where he had crumpled into a ball to protect himself, Daniel saw that most of the landing and several stairs below it were gone.

What he did not see was his partner.

"Andrea!" he looked down and caught sight of her. She had been thrown clear of the stairwell and down to the basement's main level. Though the drop couldn't have been more than ten feet, the extra weight of her gear had probably thrown off her balance, causing her to fall badly onto the concrete floor below. The awkward angle of her left leg told him everything he needed to know, but it wasn't until he saw additional fractures in her hips that he understood the extent of her injuries.

"Hang on!" Daniel shouted as he navigated past the gaping maw in the stairwell and descended to the basement floor. Kneeling beside Andrea, Daniel saw that her respirator mask had been cracked by the fall.

"Don't move," he cautioned her as he checked her for other injuries and found none. "Is your mask still working?"

She gave a thumb's up in response before wiping her gloved hand across her damaged faceplate. "Yeah, but I'm losing air. My tank won't last that long now."

It wouldn't have to, he realized. All around them, the inferno raged, sweeping across the floor and walls as it consumed every flammable object in the room. The flames were much too close to the main chemical storage area. Daniel peered through the lockers and boxes into various bottles, vials and storage tanks and saw some of the liquid chemicals beginning to bubble.

Time to be someplace else.

Andrea knew it, too. "Danny," she began.

"Don't even think it," he said, trying to sound encouraging. "I'll get you out of here." Grasping her hand in his, he gave it a reassuring squeeze. "I need to move you, but it'll hurt like hell. Think you can handle it?"

Andrea forced a smile, which was quickly replaced with a wince. "Can't be giving the guys ammo against me, right?"

"You?" Daniel asked. "I'm the one with the girl for a partner."

Chuckling despite her pain, she said, "After we get out of here, remind me to smack you."

"No problem." Though he tried to be gentle, lifting Andrea from the floor still made her cry out in pain. Hoisting her over his shoulder was a simple task, and once he had her weight settled, he patted her good leg. "Sorry about that. Hang on, okay? We need to check on the others."

Daniel made his way across the floor of the cluttered basement, his enhanced strength making simple work of supporting the combined weight of Andrea and their gear. He was more concerned with maneuvering around desks, barrels, and storage crates, some of which were covered in flames. The smoke enveloping the room was thick, and his eyes distinguished the differing shades of gray and white owing to all manner of chemicals stored here.

"Cap!" he yelled into his radio. "Andrea's hurt. The south stairwell's gone, so I need another way out of here, and damned quick!"

"*We're on it, Danny,*" Leisner's voice came back. A minute later, the captain added, "*We're trying to get a ladder down the freight elevator shaft on the west side, but there's debris in the way. We should have it in three or four minutes.*"

"Make it less," Daniel replied as he continued forward. Able to peer though the obstacles separating him from the basement office, he saw that the trapped employees were wearing what looked to be surgical masks in an attempt to filter the worst of the smoke. The woman held a flashlight while the man aimed a fire extinguisher at flames beginning to lick the outside of the office wall.

"Thank God!" Daniel heard a voice, the woman's, yell as he emerged from the storage area. "You found us!" It was all she could get out before a fit of coughing overtook her.

She staggered back into the office and Daniel followed, taking the opportunity to place Andrea with as much care as possible on one of the desks before turning to the pair of employees. Both of them were sweat-streaked and covered with soot, their faces partially obscured by the surgical masks they had soaked with water or something to help block the smoke. Still, there was no mistaking the relief in their eyes at the sight of their rescuer.

"What's your name?" Daniel asked.

Between coughs, the woman replied, "Michelle." She pointed to her companion. "He's Roger."

Daniel nodded. "Are you okay to walk?"

"Yeah, I think so," Michelle said, rubbing sweat from her face.

"Good," Daniel replied. "Okay, listen up. You're gonna have to help each other. My partner's been wounded and I've got to carry her out of here. There's going to be a ladder coming down the west elevator shaft in a minute or two. When I give the word, you follow me. Got it?" Both employees acknowledged the instructions and Daniel nodded in satisfaction.

He keyed his radio. "Cap, where the hell's my ladder?"

"*Almost there, Danny,*" Leisner replied.

Daniel stared through the thick concrete wall forming the basement and saw the ghostly, thermal images of people moving frantically outside the building as they shifted gears to adapt to the new emergency. There was no mistaking the twisted wreckage clogging the elevator shaft from the basement to the loading dock on the warehouse's ground floor. Debris from higher up in the building had fallen during an earlier explosion and blocked the doorway. At least ten firefighters were working to clear enough of the blockage to drop a ladder down the shaft. How much time would that take?

Too long, he decided.

On the other side of the basement, the fire had surrounded the chemical storage area and was already eating at the wooden frame supporting the chain link fence enclosing the more volatile materials. Daniel peered inside the cage and into the bottles of combustible liquids, seeing their contents bubbling as the metal skin of tanks holding nitrous oxide, pure oxygen and other gases were rippling in the face of the mounting heat.

"Cap!" he yelled into his radio. "This place is gonna blow any second! Get everybody back *now!*"

Leisner said something in reply but Daniel ignored it. Looking around the room, his eyes fell on the huge steel structure at the back of the office, its door open and inviting.

"The vault!" he yelled. "Go! Now!"

Roger glared at him in disbelief. "Are you crazy?"

"Move!" Daniel shouted as he once again lifted Andrea, hating her cry of pain but forced to ignore it as he headed for the vault. Scrambling after Michelle and Roger, he tried to relay his hasty plan to Leisner, but couldn't tell if he'd been heard.

Following the two employees inside, Daniel tried to angle his body so that he could get Andrea inside without bumping her against anything along the way. He noted the tight fit for the four of them along with the vault's rows of filing cabinets and document storage boxes. With his free hand he began flinging anything he could reach out of their way in order to give them more room. It took some effort, but he still was able to send one bulky file cabinet sliding out of the vault, where it tipped over and crashed onto the basement floor.

"You're one of them, aren't you?" Michelle asked, but Daniel did not answer. Instead, he eyed the vault's door, happy to see that it could at least be opened from the inside.

Small favors.

Even as he set Andrea down on the floor and turned back to the door he was still arguing with himself over the sanity of this plan, trying not to think too hard about oxygen concerns inside the vault, when the decision was made for him. The first of the bottles in the chemical cage exploded, its contents igniting as it splashed over the rest of the surrounding area. Daniel was just pulling the vault door shut when the initial blast triggered a chain reaction that set off everything else in the basement.

Plunged into sudden darkness, everyone reached for something to hold onto as the shockwave rocked the vault, the explosion reverberating through the walls. Daniel stumbled and fell backward into a filing cabinet before sliding to the floor. Now lying on his back, he could look up through the vault's steel ceiling and flinched at the sight of metal beams, brick and wood cascading all around them. The sound of their impact on the basement's concrete floor reverberated through the tiny chamber.

"The building's collapsing!" Roger yelled.

It was true, but the bulk of the explosion being focused on the far side of the building had sent the collapsing structure tumbling in that direction. Daniel was able to see that most of the debris avalanche was falling away from the vault, though enough of it was piling up in front of the door that there was no way he'd be able to open it.

Several seconds passed before the commotion faded, and despite the darkness Daniel was able to make out Michelle and Roger hunkering down next to a heap of storage boxes, holding onto each other as they waited for whatever might happen next. Remembering his flashlight, he turned it on and removed his helmet, setting it on the floor. Next he pulled off his mask and closed his respirator's oxygen flow, knowing it might come in handy if they were to be here for a while.

"Now what?" Michelle asked, pulling down her surgical mask and brushing wisps of dirty blonde hair from her soiled face.

Activating his radio, Daniel called out, "Cap, can you hear me?" He received only static in response. That was to be expected, he decided, given the vault's steel construction.

"You think they know where we are?" Roger asked.

"I'm pretty sure Cap heard me," Daniel said, "but it might take them a while to get to us."

Coughing, Michelle wiped her mouth before looking to Daniel. "So, what do we do?"

Daniel wanted to tell her that everything would be fine. His crew knew they were in here and would be working to extract them as quickly as possible. The only question he had, and it was one he didn't want to ask aloud, was whether or not there was enough oxygen in here to last until Leisner and the others got to them. Shifting his position, he took stock of their surroundings. The wall behind the vault had collapsed, and he now stood almost eye level with the parking lot beyond the building. Wood, brick, and hunks of cement from the explosion littered the ground and those few cars which had not been evacuated from the lot had suffered smashed tops and broken windshields from falling debris. The vault was surrounded by enough wreckage that Daniel knew extrication could take an hour or more, and that was without waiting on a bulldozer or other heavy equipment to help move rubble out of the way. It would take less time, he decided, for four people to consume the vault's remaining oxygen.

"What's the plan, Danny?" Andrea asked, her voice weak and slurred; a sure sign she was going into shock.

Roger said, "Can't you get us out?" He gestured toward the vault's door and one of the remaining file cabinets. "I mean, after what you did before...."

"I'm a little light in that department," Daniel said, shaking his head as he continued to watch the fire fighters and other people moving about beyond the collapsed building. The vault's walls acted like a translucent veil, casting a pale gray pall over everything, highlighted by a dull red or pale white along some of the rivets and seams joining the container's walls and joints.

Wait.

"How old is this vault?" he asked, rising to his feet.

"Thirty or forty years, I suppose," Roger answered. "Why?"

Daniel nodded as he ran his hand along the vault's low ceiling. Thirty or forty years. What might humidity and prolonged exposure to salt air do with that kind of time to work with? He could see variations in the metal where corrosion had weakened some areas.

Worth a shot, he decided.

The vault's roof reverberated as Daniel punched it with his right fist, and while he felt no pain, there was a tingle. Could he punch through before he broke his hand? There was one way to find out.

He punched the roof again, and this time he saw the dent he had made in the aged steel. Pausing just long enough to cast a reassuring smile at his three companions, Daniel drew a deep breath before throwing all of his strength into a third punch. This time, he felt a jolt of pain shoot through his hand, but he also sensed the roof buckling just the slightest bit. Above his head, a gap of dim light appeared near the vault's back corner.

"See?" Andrea said behind him, her voice weak but carrying an unmistakable tone of relief. "I said you came in handy once in a while."

Once the roof had yielded, bending a section up and out of the way was easy. With oxygen no longer an issue, Daniel could assist with the extraction as members of his crew cleared away debris and maneuvered a ladder into position. It took only minutes for paramedics to get Andrea as well as Roger and Michelle, who were suffering from smoke inhalation, to an ambulance bound for Tampa General Hospital. The fire was almost completely out, and crews were dousing the remaining suspect areas with water just to be sure. Other members of Daniel's company were returning equipment to their trucks, leaving him to sit on an unoccupied section of curb along the opposite side of the street, ordered by Captain Leisner to take a well-earned breather.

"Nice job, son," a voice said, and Daniel looked up to see his father walking toward him. Though Jack Balin was dressed in civilian clothes, Daniel noted the gestures and smiles of nearby onlookers who had not failed to recognize "Hammer Jack's" familiar visage. His once jet black hair had gone gray and his chiseled jaw had softened with age, but his piercing blue eyes still gleamed with the same strength embodied by his alter ego.

"What are you doing here?" Daniel asked.

The elder Balin replied, "Saw the fire on the news. One of the cameras showed a close up of your station's truck. When the building collapsed, they weren't ready to deal with trying to get you out, so I offered to help." Then, he smiled. "It was either this, or the weekly Dominoes tournament. At least next week, I'll have something new to talk about."

Unable to resist a smile, Daniel said, "Don't worry, I'm not looking to cramp your style." He flexed his right hand, feeling a residual numbness from his bout with the vault, though a look through the skin showed no fractures. The slight pain he'd earlier felt was now all but gone.

"I'll be damned," he said.

Jack gestured toward Daniel's hand. "It's healing?"

"Feels like it." Daniel recalled the stories his father had told him about discovering his own abilities and how they had improved over time. In the beginning, Jack Balin had suffered from bruises, muscle sprains, and other minor injuries as a result of his superhuman feats of strength, only to find his body healing with ever-greater speed to the point where he rarely incurred any damage at all except in the most extreme circumstances. It appeared that in addition to at least some of Hammer Jack's physical strength, Daniel had inherited a portion of his father's recuperative abilities, as well.

"That'll come in handy," Jack said, before turning and pointing to where the trucks from Daniel's engine company were parked on the street. "Your captain tells me Andrea's in rough shape, but she should be okay. What about you? How are you holding up? Other than the hand, I mean."

Daniel nodded. "I'm fine, thanks."

His father grinned. "I always knew you had it in you."

"All part of the job, Dad," Daniel replied. "You know the deal."

"Yeah, I know the deal," Jack replied, his mouth curling into a mischievous grin. "You know, I could be talked into coming out of retirement, and it'd be fun to have a partner, if you ever feel like changing jobs."

Daniel chuckled. "Thanks, but I like the job I have now." If anything, today had only served to reinforce the conviction which had guided him to the path he'd chosen.

As he had until now, he would continue to go his own way.

Identity Crisis

Lisa Gail Green

MY SISTER HAS a habit of ticking me off. It's Miranda's fault that I'm stuck in a dark alley as the freezing cold rain beats down on my thin jacket. My teeth chatter uncontrollably, and I'm surprised she hasn't heard me in my hiding place behind the beat-up dumpster. I'm starting to get used to the rancid meat smell, but when a rat the size of Delaware scuttles over my foot, I bite down on my lower lip to make sure I don't scream.

Miranda's pacing now, and she checks her cell phone for the fifteenth time in the last ten minutes. Whatever it is we're waiting for, I wish it would hurry up, because this is miserable. Sure, I want to catch little Miss Perfect up to something nefarious for once, and this side trip to the worst part of Los Angeles has "busted" written all over it. But I'm obviously not cut out for this kind of secret-agent crap. At the very least I need to remember to bring along some essential tools next time—like an umbrella.

Wait. She's finally doing something. What the hell? She's changing clothes right here in the middle of the alley. Thank goodness the only light available is coming from the flashing neon sign over the Chinese restaurant. I hate the idea of her getting naked because it's like watching myself, which is just plain awkward. Having an identical twin is freaky. It's sort of like an out-of-body experience. At least she's fast about opening her black backpack and pulling out the—

What kind of outfit is that? Why is my sister dressing up like *SolarFlare*, Los Angeles' real life, flame-throwing superhero? Halloween isn't for another ten months.

Miranda stands there dressed in skin-tight leather from head to toe, red-gloved hands on her hips. Where did she even get an outfit like that? I know we're identical, but I have a hard time believing I'd be able to pull off that look: low-cut black bodysuit, scarlet gloves, yellow eye mask, red and yellow doublewide belt with a two-inch stone of yellow topaz embedded in the center, and boots that end mid thigh.

No way! No freaking way. Miranda may be annoyingly perfect, but she's no superhero. Unless...I know she's been gone a lot at nights lately, but I just assumed she didn't want me interrupting her time with her current flame, Daniel. No. This has to be some kind of joke. She must know I'm here, and she's trying to get back at me. Or maybe she's going to some kind of costume party after all.

Speak of the devil, Daniel Bauer walks around the corner of the alley, looking way too hot to be real with the rain sliding off his jet-black hair and making his tan t-shirt cling to his chest.

They're talking. I scoot around the corner of the dumpster so I can get a better vantage point.

"You're sure Mayhem is going to show?" Miranda asks.

Daniel reads something on his phone. "Yes. According to all the anonymous tips on the hotline I set up, he's going after the pawnshop across the street. It is an easy target."

Oh. My. God. I can't believe this! My sister *is* a superhero?

My sister is a superhero.

Oh, this just isn't fair!

Acing all her university classes while I balance precariously at the no man's land of C minus is bad enough. So is being queen of the extracurriculars while I stay home and surf the net. And dating every guy I've ever even been remotely interested in, including Daniel. But did she have to go this extra step? There's no way I'll ever reach her pedestal now.

"Daniel, I want you to know I really appreciate you helping me out like this," she says.

"Are you kidding? I'd do anything to help." He moves toward Miranda—excuse me, *SolarFlare*—and lays a hand on her shoulder, rubbing his thumb back and forth over her collarbone. "Still, you shouldn't have come in person. You've only been a superhero for a few months and Mayhem is dangerous. He's completely unbalanced. This isn't a movie."

She rests her palm against his cheek, and he closes his eyes.

I fight off a twinge of jealousy I feel at the simple gesture. They share the type of closeness that looks so effortless but never seems easy for me.

"I have to act when we get tips like these," Miranda says, squeezing her hands into fists. "If I'm going to be a superhero I have to do everything I can to stop creeps like Mayhem."

"Just be careful," Daniel says, tucking a stray hair back behind her ear.

Miranda straightens. "It's almost midnight. I better get out there."

"I'll take your stuff back to the car," Daniel says.

"Thanks."

This time they really do kiss. And I'm not talking a quick peck either. I'm talking get-a-room, spit-swapping, hands-everywhere kissing. My chest constricts, and I reach for my inhaler, drawing out two puffs.

I wait for Miranda to dart out of the alley, and Daniel to head after her. Finally I can step out into the open, relieved to stretch my neck and back.

I'm about to try my luck at slipping inside the Chinese restaurant so I can call my friend Pete to come pick me up, when Daniel appears in the mouth of the alley. I jump and let out a little yelp.

"Leslie?" he asks. Lightening flashes from above, highlighting his shocked expression.

"Hi," is all I can think to say. And it's pretty weak as I wiggle my fingers at him in greeting. By this point we're both soaked to the bone, and I wish I could carry myself the way my sister does. Then I'd feel less like a half-drowned cat.

"What are you...? Did you see...? How did you get here?" Daniel finally manages, stepping forward to pick up my sister's backpack and clothing.

"I sort of stowed away in Mir's back seat under the emergency blanket," I say, trying to look anywhere but at him. The heat rises up the back of my neck despite the weather. "I thought I might catch her up to something, but I never could have imagined this. I can't believe she'd keep it a secret from me." Not something this big.

"It's dangerous for anyone to know about her true identity," Daniel says, taking another step toward me. "Dangerous for you and your family. If someone like Mayhem were to find out who SolarFlare cares about, he wouldn't hesitate to use it against her."

"Uh huh," I say. "But it's okay to tell her boyfriend." I push away the old childish envy and fight the tears even though I doubt Daniel would be able to tell in the rain.

"She probably wouldn't have told me either," he says, "but I was with her when she found the stone."

Like that makes any sense.

"Oh, my God. You don't know about the stone do you?" he asks, burying his head in his hand.

"Are you talking about the one in her belt?" I ask. "It's very pretty. But what does that have to do with it? How can she start fires with her mind? I mean how'd she get the cool power?"

If it's genetic, where are my powers? I deserve some powers too.

Daniel peeks out from between his fingers and then shakes his head.

"Les, the topaz is what *gives* her the powers. Look—" he begins. But whatever he's going to say is drowned out by the sirens coming from the street.

We both freeze at the call back to reality, stare at each other for a second, and then tear out toward the front.

"Here." Daniel rummages in Miranda's bag and pulls out a baseball cap. "Put this on, and try to stay out of sight. The last thing Mir needs is to see you and get distracted when she's fighting Mayhem."

I stuff the rest of my stringy wet hair up under the cap as we make our way toward the rapidly gathering crowd in front of the restaurant. I stand on tiptoe trying to see over the shoulders of the three rows of people in front of me. Thankfully, the rain is finally starting to let up. Two nervous-looking police officers rush forward. I assume they're trying to keep the crowd as far from the maniac as possible, while SolarFlare tries to draw Mayhem's attention away from the innocent bystanders by placing herself at the far end of the street.

Mayhem looks more menacing in person than on TV. His black cape billows behind him, making a whooshing sound, and his thick black body armor bristles with hooks holding the kind of gadgets that give me the shivers if I think about them too long. Things with spikes like metal teeth, and other objects that look like they belong in a Sci-fi flick. According to news reports, he's some kind of evil inventor, so I'm sure they're even worse than they look. His crime spree started about six months ago and he's hit everything from jewelry stores to museums. So far, in the course of his burglaries, he's killed two security guards, one bank-teller, and a policeman. I don't blame the guys in uniform for being frightened.

"Give up, Mayhem!" Miranda shouts from the far end of the street.

Does she really think he's going to listen? Come on, Mir, you have better distraction techniques than that at your disposal. As if she hears my thoughts, a column of flame like a solar flare shoots into the sky from the stone in her belt. Guess that's where she got her name. No way Mayhem can miss it.

Mayhem rises above the crowd with his massive antigrav boots. If I were my sister I'd just blast them off his stupid feet and be done with it.

He pulls a large, blue gun from beneath his cape, and points it at the inferno before him. A high-pitched *whirr* makes me and everyone else in the crowd throw our hands up over our ears as the weapon goes off, creating a wall of ice directly in front of the flames. Crystal icicles hang from the sides, reflecting the blinking lights of the Chinese restaurant's flashing neon sign.

"A freeze ray!" someone from the audience shouts.

"And now I'll show you how it works on a human being," Mayhem says in a voice colder than the frozen wall before him.

"Get out of there, SolarFlare!" I scream.

The crowd around me, including the cops, bolts as I press forward, my only thought to get to my sister. But I would be a pancake thanks to the stampede of fleeing onlookers if Daniel didn't grab me by the arm and pull me to the side.

"We have to get to Mir," I cry, as he squashes me to the side of a brick building with his body.

But just as he opens his mouth to answer, I hear the same high-pitched sound, and begin to shiver as the ice spreads over Daniel's shoulders, face, and stomach like a creeping shadow. His hands, pressed against the wall on either side of my head, harden, icicles forming along the undersides of his arms. His eyes meet mine, pure terror written on his face, a silent plea for help.

And I scream.

"No!" Miranda cries.

I rip my eyes away from Daniel's frozen face to find my sister's expression a mixture of pain and anger. Her eyes ask the silent question, *What are you doing here?*

"What's the matter, SolarFlare? Too cold for you?" Mayhem taunts.

I come to my senses enough to duck beneath Daniel's outstretched arms and find Mayhem's freeze gun pointed at me, and even from twenty feet away I know I'm in trouble.

My sister sees it too and runs toward me. Damn her! I know exactly what she's going to do—jump between the weapon and me like the heroic idiot she is. Without even thinking, I yank one of Daniel's icicles off and hurl it like a javelin at the bastard, Mayhem. It hits his wrist as he squeezes the trigger and knocks off his aim just enough to put the neon sign on ice.

"Get into the alley!" Miranda screams, shoving me toward safety.

Her face is so strained even under the mask that I do what she says. I tuck and roll like some stupid kid's kung fu game and come up just around the corner in the alley.

I poke my nose around the side of the wall to find SolarFlare facing off against Mayhem. They're both on the ground now, and circling each other while SolarFlare shoots fire directly into the freeze ray bursting from the gun.

I throw my hands over my ears at the sound and scream, "SolarFlare!"

trying to get her attention. But I don't think she can hear me over the screeching of Mayhem's weapon.

From my point of view, it seems obvious what Mayhem's up to. He's backing her away while he moves closer to Daniel. He fires a continuous stream of ice at SolarFlare. But she's so focused on shooting flames into the freeze ray to counter it, she doesn't see what he's doing.

I debate rushing out again, but I don't want to make things worse. That's what I've always done for Miranda. Hold her back. She can handle this better than I ever could.

"Go, SolarFlare!" I shout, stepping onto the sidewalk just in front of the alley. The cowardly crowd's gone, so maybe I can offer moral support.

She's looking frazzled, and I don't think it's the reflection of the flame on her face. I know she's worried about Daniel. Suddenly, I wonder if the power in the topaz is unlimited. Will it keep working or will it suddenly burn out like a light bulb?

Mayhem lunges for Daniel and grabs him around the waist. Miranda lets her hands fall at her sides. Even from here, I see the exhaustion on her face and in the brace of her shoulders. Or maybe it's just that I've always been able to sense her feelings.

One of those weird twin things.

"Give up now, SolarFlare," Mayhem warns. "Or this innocent citizen loses his life."

Thank goodness. That means Daniel is still alive in there.

Mayhem's freeze ray makes that awful whirring sound again as he presses it to Daniel's icy temple, only this time it fades to a whine, sputters, and falls silent. He gives the thing a little shake.

"You're the one who needs to give up, Mayhem," Mir says. "Looks like your power supply is out, and I'm just getting warmed up."

Mayhem shifts uncomfortably behind Daniel. I think Mir's got him!

"I have plenty more weapons at my disposal," Mayhem says. He'll be dead in a second if you come any closer. Surrender now!"

"No way," Mir says. "Take the time to kill him, and I've got *you*."

I hope *I'm* the only one who can hear the tremble in her voice.

"You won't attack while an innocent life hangs in the balance, so it seems we are at an impasse, SolarFlare," Mayhem says. "If you want him alive, you will meet me at the Santa Monica Pier tomorrow night at 3:00 AM. The Ferris wheel. It has to be you, and you alone, or I'll drop him from the top, and you can clean up the shards left over."

I picture Daniel shattering into a billion pieces on the ground. I stumble backward on the sidewalk slipping in a puddle of icy water, and fall. My head bounces against the pavement, my body hanging half in the street. Not only am I seeing double, I've also managed to attract the attention of both SolarFlare and Mayhem.

Mayhem's eyes bounce to Miranda. He moves in what looks like slow motion, one hand clutching Daniel's waist, the other pulling out another gadget, a purple gun. Miranda doesn't see it—her eyes are on me, her clumsy sister. I call out in warning, but it's too late, he's fired the weapon.

The purple lightening bolt hits her square in the back, and I watch stunned as her face contorts with pain. She falls forward and rolls onto her back. I panic when I see Mayhem reach for her. The next thing I know a blast of fire streams from her belt. It forces Mayhem to back off to avoid being barbecued. I don't know if it was activated when she hit the ground, or if it's some sort of automatic defense system. Either way, it keeps him at bay.

Scowling, Mayhem launches into the sky dragging Daniel with him. By the time I scramble to Miranda's side, both Mayhem and Daniel are gone from view.

"Oh, my God. Oh, my God. Miranda!" I scream as Miranda's eyes roll up into her head. I shake her shoulders. "Please don't be dead. Oh, God. Please don't be dead."

A low moan escapes her lips, and I sit back on my heels. I think I might faint, but her hand shoots up, grabbing my arm so hard I wince. Her mouth is moving, and I lean down so I can hear her.

She squeezes harder. "I can't move my legs, Les." She sounds like a scared little girl.

"You're going to be okay," I say. She doesn't answer. "Look, Mir, I'm sorry. Okay? I'm sorry I followed you here. I'm sorry I screwed everything up. This is all my fault."

"No, it isn't," she says, finally loosening her grasp. "I should have told you. I was selfish to keep it to myself. You would have told me if things were reversed. I'm sorry."

"Stop apologizing, Mir! You already win the gold medal for goodness, okay?" My teasing sounds strained even to my ears. I try a different tactic. "You have to get better," I say. "You have to go save Daniel tomorrow."

"That was an EPG," she says.

I blink. "A what?"

"An Electro-Pulse Gun. I'm lucky it didn't hit my head; it would've disrupted all brain activity. But there's no way I'll be able to make the meet-

70

ing tomorrow night."

"No. Daniel." It's all I can get out because my throat is closing up; my lungs feel like they're being squeezed by a massive fist. I pull out my inhaler and take a puff. I know it hasn't been four hours yet, but it's an emergency inhaler, and if this isn't an emergency I don't know what is.

"You have to get us both home before someone shows up and finds us here," Mir says.

She's right. It takes all my strength to get her to the car and in the backseat. The moment I get behind the wheel, she starts talking again.

"You're going to have to save Daniel, Les. You have to go instead of me," she says.

There's silence for a moment, and then I'm laughing like a lunatic. "I think that thing really did get your brain," I say. "You're the superhero, not me."

Mir's hand finds my shoulder and squeezes. "You can wear the outfit. You look exactly like me. You can save him, Les."

"It isn't the outfit, Mir. It's you." I glance in the rearview mirror so I can see her face.

She looks like she'd like to slap me, but that's nothing new. "You can do this, Les! You have to."

"Mir, this isn't fifth grade, okay? We aren't just switching classes because it's funny. I'm not you. I'm not SolarFlare. I can't do any of the stuff you can."

"You're Daniel's only chance, Leslie. If you don't do this, he'll die." She leans back against the seat, exhausted no doubt.

I gun the engine and head toward home. I have nothing more to say because as much as I hate to admit it, she's right again.

It's Saturday morning at nine, and I'm stuck in bed staring at my ceiling because it hurts to move. Every muscle in my body is in pain. Even the ones in my pinkie finger that I never knew existed.

I should really get a medal. Not only did I manage to get my sister's dead weight to the car unnoticed and drive home through LA traffic, I then got her leather-clad butt all the way upstairs to our tiny apartment, put her in pajamas, and tucked her into her bed. Finally, I took the longest, hottest shower of my life.

I tried to sleep, but every time I'd close my eyes I'd feel Daniel's strong arms pushing me to safety. Watch his horror-stricken face turn to ice inches from mine. Hear Mayhem's threat to push Daniel to his death.

He's been frozen and kidnapped by an insane man, and it's all my fault.

I groan as I pull myself out of bed and stumble into the kitchenette. Coffee and ibuprofen: the perfect cocktail. Then I throw a muffin on a plate and take Miranda breakfast. She is still asleep. I'm not surprised after what she went through last night.

I return to my own room and pick up the SolarFlare costume from the floor where I dropped it last night. It's stiff and caked with mud, so I heave a sigh and set to work in the shower scrubbing it clean. Then I roll it into a big towel and stomp it as dry as I can. Finally, an hour later, I'm standing in front of my full-length mirror dressed like a superhero.

I knew it. I look like a total fake, like I really *am* dressing up for Halloween. Then I think of Daniel. Now I look like a worried fake. I have to try something else. I put my hands on my hips, widen my stance, and stick out my chin. Huh. Better. I mean, Miranda and I do look identical to most people. I wish the costume didn't show so much cleavage though. I'm surprised Miranda didn't name herself *The Rack* instead of *SolarFlare*.

I'm not used to these boots either. The whole ensemble feels kind of rigid and suffocating. I guess it's so thick for protection. Miranda moves so gracefully in it. She makes all the fighting and stuff look easy. I suddenly wish I'd taken gymnastics and Tae Kwon Do with my sister instead of staying home with my nose buried in video games.

Right. Down to business. Now I just need to figure out how to use the *magical* topaz stone in the belt.

Five hours later, and I've set fire to my carpet with the topaz twice, just barely managing to put it out before the fire alarm went off. The masked girl in the mirror looks pretty beaten down, and this outfit is making me sweat in places I didn't know could sweat. At least I've gotten pretty used to moving in it.

I change into a t-shirt and jeans, and fix sandwiches and drinks for Miranda and me. When I enter her room, she's propped up on pillows watching cell phone footage someone must have taken of her battle last night. I set the tray on her lap and scoot in next to her.

Even without the red, puffy eyes, it would be impossible to miss the worry on her face. I'm pretty nervous too. I have to try and get her mind off of Daniel.

"I have to admit you look pretty cool," I say.

"I just make it look that way. The truth is, most of the time I'm like a scared rabbit." She lowers her head, letting her still-tangled blond hair fall like a curtain over her face.

I nudge her a little in the shoulder, and she peeks out. "You're getting hair in our food," I tell her.

She shoves me back hard enough that I almost topple off the bed. The girl's got some serious muscle on her.

"Honestly, Mir. I'm really impressed. I don't know what made you decide to do this whole superhero thing, but it's—"

"Dangerous? Stupid?" she asks.

"I was going to say 'cool' again."

"I thought so too, at first. Then I started fighting guys like Mayhem, and I realized I'm kind of in over my head. Even with the stone."

"How'd you get it, anyway?" I ask.

"A couple of months ago I was in an antique store in Old Town Monrovia with Daniel. I saw it in a pendant and I just had to try to it on, you know? Well, I looked over at some candles that were sitting in these intricate silver holders on a table. I remember thinking how romantic it would look with the candles lit. The stone in the pendant glowed, and both candles flared like I'd held an invisible match to them."

"And you didn't get kicked out for starting a fire?" I ask, because that's probably what would have happened to me.

"Daniel put them out before anyone noticed, and I bought the pendant, even though it took some time before I really believed the stone was responsible. Then I kept seeing bad guys like Mayhem on the news and wanted to do something so bad. I realized I could use the stone's power to help others, so I created SolarFlare. But it will take years to really understand all the topaz can do. I'm discovering new techniques all the time."

"Wait a minute!" I'm up so fast my head spins. "I don't have years to learn how to use that thing."

"I did figure out how to operate it pretty quickly," she says. "But that doesn't mean I really understand everything it can do. Or how and when to best utilize its power. But *you* may be able to, Les. You've always been the smart one."

Okay, did my perfect sister actually just call me the smart one? Mayhem's purple lightening ray hit her harder than I thought.

"I'm serious," she says. "I might be good at calculus and chemistry, but you've got *street* smarts. You think fast under pressure."

"Yeah, that's why I got both you and Daniel hurt last night, and why he's probably going to die." My usual sarcasm breaks at the last word. I know my feelings for Daniel are no more than a silly crush, but Mir actually loves him, and I can't be responsible for her losing him. That's why I already know I'm going to go through with this.

"Hey." Miranda puts a hand on my shoulder and waits until I look at her. "I know I'm asking a lot. It is dangerous. But Daniel—he doesn't deserve this, and...and...and none of this is your fault, Leslie. It's mine. I'm supposed to be the superhero."

I've never seen Miranda look so broken. If I say one more word, I'll just burst out crying because I feel like I've made such a mess of everything. So I turn around and head straight for the door.

"Leslie?"

"I have some practicing to do."

***

I pause on the boardwalk and stare through the darkness toward the Santa Monica Pier. The wind whips my hair around behind me, and the only sound is the water crashing onto the shore. Something feels wrong. Maybe it's because even in the middle of the night the Pier should be lit. I shiver.

I remember the Pier being a fun, happening place, a little amusement park with music and tons of souvenir carts dotting the length of it. Tonight it feels more like a sinister ghost town, filled with dark shadows and millions of places where someone can hide, ready to attack.

My eyes are glued to the hulking form of the Ferris wheel so close to the end of the Pier. The outline is obvious from any vantage point, even through the darkness. It looms over everything else like a monster waiting to strike.

My body is still sore from lugging Mir up the stairs yesterday, despite all the caffeine and ibuprofen I chugged before leaving the apartment. *You can do this*, I repeat to myself as I make my way past the refreshment stands and kiddy rides, my hands tucked inside my coat pockets.

It's only thirty minutes until Mayhem shows up and I'm still trying to figure out my next move. Plan A? Try not to get Daniel or myself killed. Plan B? Oh, who am I kidding? I don't have a plan. So I guess I'll just have to improvise.

The closer I get to my destination, the more I desperately want to call the police to help handle this. But I remember Mayhem telling Miranda to come alone, so the phone stays in my pocket.

At least it isn't raining tonight, although the wind carries an icy chill that penetrates even through the leather suit. As I work my way down past the carousel, I catch the faint scent of cinnamon and sugar that makes me think of the funnel cake I ate last time I visited. Of course that was in broad daylight when the biggest thing at stake was whether I'd ruin my appetite for dinner.

I long to hear the usual chatter of a thousand visitors around me. It would help break the eerie silence. My boots don't make much sound, but every soft thud makes me feel like I'm screaming, "I'm over here!"

I stop directly beneath the Ferris wheel. The cars creak, swaying in the breeze, but nothing turns. I swallow hard and my chest constricts. I fumble for the inhaler in my coat pocket and take two quick puffs. I crane my neck back. It's a lot higher than it looked a minute ago.

I need to get a better vantage point. If Mayhem's planning to throw Daniel from the top—well, I better get up there somehow. Good thing

I'm not afraid of heights. I climb carefully from car to car working my way toward the highest one. I use the spokes as hand and footholds, hoisting myself upward.

About two-thirds of the way up, bright lights and carnival music erupts all around me. It scares the hell out of me and I almost lose my grip.

Someone turned on the Ferris wheel!

I squint against the blinding flashes. Then my boot slips against the side of the nearest car when the wheel begins to move. I scramble inside and plop into the seat.

Mayhem's laugh echoes all around me in time to the creepy music.

Tugging off my coat, I brace myself against the sides and focus all my energy on the topaz, firing it up—so to speak. I never did manage to figure out half the cool moves I've seen Miranda pull off on TV, but I did spend quite a bit of time practicing the most important one.

Now if only I can get a chance to use it....

The Ferris wheel grinds to a halt with my car almost at the top. Mayhem leans over the car above me, holding what looks like a remote control.

"Enjoying the ride?" he asks.

He wears an awful smirk that I desperately want to wipe off with my fist, only he's about twice my size and has far too many scary gadgets. So I stay still, praying my wobbly knees aren't too obvious. I plant my hands firmly on my hips like I practiced, but it's mostly to stop the trembling.

"I've always loved the Ferris wheel," I say. My voice comes out breathy, but I think it sounds pretty good. He doesn't need to know it's because of my asthma.

"So glad you like it," he says, tugging the still-frozen Daniel into view. He props Daniel precariously against the rail of the car. One good shove and down he'll go.

I need to somehow get up there, and force Mayhem away. Yeah, *that'll* be a piece of cake.

"So I'm here," I say, stepping out onto the spokes. I can do this. "What is it you want? I'm a very busy girl you know. You aren't the only bad guy around Los Angeles."

He jerks his head back like he's actually offended. "You think there are greater threats to this city?" he asks in a low, menacing voice. He climbs onto the scaffolding, leaving the car swinging with Daniel still perched on the edge.

Uh, oh, maybe I shouldn't be making him mad.

"Duh," I say, picking a piece of imaginary lint from my glove. After all,

I've already kind of committed to a pseudo blasé approach. In the comics, it always throws the villain off-balance. "There've probably already been like ten murders while you've kept me here chit-chatting."

I edge as close to the inside of the wheel as I can, and brace myself against the metal strut above with one arm while trying to look casual. Well, as casual as possible, considering I'm on one of the highest spokes of a Ferris wheel.

Mayhem drops to the far end of my beam, making the whole thing creak. His cape billows out behind him.

I've never been this close to him before, but now I see how ripped the guy is. And tall. In what universe is it fair that he's a genius inventor *and* a body-builder? I do my best to ignore the fact that he could probably push me off the edge with one tap.

"So what's up?" I ask, and I'm really proud that my voice doesn't crack.

"*What's up?*" he asks with a sneer. In the bright lights of the ride, his features harden into deep lines of black against his sallow skin. His shaven head and eye-mask twist his face into a freakish image, something like a broken skull. "What's up, SolarFlare, is that the young man in the car above us is about to take a nose dive off this Ferris wheel and shatter into a million tiny fragments all over the Pier."

My lungs compress, and I try to breathe through it. I want to laugh at his comment, but I'm too afraid I'll end up in a coughing fit and fall off all by myself.

I shrug. "It's not like he's my boyfriend," I say instead.

"So you don't care if I just kill an innocent man?" he asks, and he sounds genuinely confused.

"Of course I'd rather you didn't. But to tell the truth, I was kind of considering turning to the dark side myself. So I guess now's as good a time as any." The plan just pops in my head, but I decide to go with it. It's just crazy enough to actually work.

"*Wait.*" Mayhem shifts uncomfortably making the metal creak beneath us. "You mean you want to become a villain?"

I nod, pretending my stomach isn't dropping out from under me.

"You want to join me?" he asks, crossing his arms over his chest.

"Actually I was thinking I'd branch out on my own," I say, wrinkling my nose. "You know, do it *right*."

His mouth twists into an ugly sneer, and I wonder if I've gone too far. Okay, time to act.

I focus on the stone in the belt and watch as a thin stream of fire connects with Mayhem's antigrav boots. The sound is something like fire-crackers as they spark and pop. Mayhem actually yelps and stamps his feet to smother the flames, and I dive down the metal beam toward him like I'm sliding into home plate. He definitely isn't expecting that, and he fumbles at one of his hooks to release some kind of weapon. Perfect. He isn't paying attention to the thing I'm after—the thing that could've been my downfall if he'd reacted differently.

My feet collide with his legs, and we end up in a tangle of limbs. I pry the remote from his hand and start pushing buttons. The whole ride jolts into action again, and I wrap my legs around the girder. Mayhem slips off the side, but I can't do anything about it because I'm focused on Daniel, who's about to tumble over the edge of the car directly above.

I scramble up as fast as I can and somehow manage to get high enough to grab hold before Daniel goes completely over. He's cold and slippery, but knowing what will happen if I let him fall keeps me focused as I shove him back inside the car. I feel like a circus act, clinging to the edge of the car with my knees, and holding a frozen guy steady so he won't fall out. But I stay put until our car brushes the ground.

I slide off the ride, and tumble to solid ground along with Daniel. I press my eyes closed momentarily while the world stops spinning, then struggle to my shaky feet.

At first I see no sign of Mayhem. Then I look up. He must have caught one of the spokes on the wheel after he fell, and now he's started climbing. I punch at the remote still clutched tightly in my hand, and move the Ferris wheel until Mayhem's hanging vertically from the topmost spoke. Then I stop it again, shiver, and haul Daniel to his frozen feet.

Time to see if my single day of training with the topaz pays off. I practiced this maneuver on every frozen treat and ice cube in our freezer, but this is Daniel. Not an ice cube.

You can do this, I repeat. An orange glow seeps from the stone in my belt and surrounds Daniel's entire body. Moments later, water begins to drip to the cement. I turn up the heat, but not too high, and now I can see some skin and clothing poking through the ice in spots.

Come on. Hurry up.

Daniel's moving now, shaking from the cold. Then he's sucking in huge gulps of air with a terrible wheezing sound. He falls to his knees, and I crouch alongside, keeping my hands on his shoulders to steady him as the last of the slush and water fall away.

"Daniel?" I ask softly, afraid he's suffered brain damage. But he looks up at me when I say his name. His eyes are sharp. They make *me* want to melt even though he's the one who's been encased in ice. I shrug it off, and remind myself that it's Mir he loves. Mir who deserves him.

"I knew you'd save me," he says, crushing me to him.

I stiffen in his embrace, and then pull away. "Mayhem's trapped on the scaffolding," I say.

"*Leslie*, is that you? Where's Miranda? What happened? Is she...she can't be...she's okay, right?" His voice grows higher with each question.

I nod and shrug my shoulders a little. "She's going to be fine. She was just temporarily incapacitated, so I kind of had to take over."

His expression tells me he isn't exactly full of confidence. He swallows and stands. I follow, reaching for him. I have to do a better job explaining what happened. But before I can open my mouth, I hear the whoosh of a cape behind me.

I spin to find Mayhem inches away, pointing his purple electro-pulse gun at my head. I quickly shove Daniel behind my back as best I can.

"Were you distracted by a pretty face?" he asks with another leer.

God, I am an idiot. I'm not used to this superhero thing. This guy is better than I gave him credit for. I should have made sure he was secure before fixing Daniel.

"I thought you said he wasn't your boyfriend," Mayhem adds, clearly taking my silence for the wrong kind of embarrassment.

"He isn't. But I *was* lying about the whole turning to the dark side thing," I say, a grin spreading over my face.

"Still cocky, eh? Great act, little girl, but now it's time to pay the price for playing dress up." Mayhem gestures with the gun for me to move aside. "I'm going to make you suffer by watching lover-boy die first."

If only he knew how dead-on his comment is. I am just playing dress up, and now Daniel's going to pay. But Mayhem will still have to go through me to get to him.

Unfortunately, Daniel picks this moment to try and act the hero. He pushes me aside and steps in front, still dripping wet and shivering.

Something inside of me sparks. I am not going to let Daniel—or anyone else—die when I could have stopped it.

Mayhem smiles, giving me the split second I need. The hair on the back of my neck and arms stands at attention from the electric blast that flies over us while I tackle Daniel. We're like a row of dominoes—I knock Daniel down, and he knocks Mayhem right in the knees.

I crawl forward, right over Daniel, and pry the gun from Mayhem's fist. By the time he's righted himself, I'm pointing it in his face.

"You wouldn't kill me," he says. But his voice shakes like he isn't sure.

"You'd be surprised what I'm capable of," I say.

"I knew you were going to be a threat the moment you showed up yesterday," Mayhem snarls. "I set this meeting up on my terms, and it wasn't supposed to end like this! I was up all night, studying your behavior using footage off the Internet. I know every one of your moves, and you've never gone for the obvious physical grab when you could have used your fire. I spent hours fire-proofing my suit!"

"You can stop whining now," I say.

Daniel uses my cell to dial 9-1-1. Mayhem's eyes narrow, and he clenches his fists so tight they shake. I should really learn to keep my mouth shut.

"The police are on their way," Daniel says.

I turn when I hear his voice, and the next thing I know Mayhem is pulling the gun from my hand.

"Oh no, you don't!" I yell as he aims for Daniel again.

Fire blasts from the stone in my belt, engulfing the gun. Mayhem screams, falling to his knees and clutching his burned hand.

"Guess you forgot to fireproof your weapons," I say, kicking the smoking gun out of reach. Sirens blare behind me, but I don't take my eyes off of Mayhem until after the police arrive and he's handcuffed.

"Well, I better get this innocent citizen home," I say to the cop making notes.

The guy in uniform looks a bit confused. "He's gonna need to come in to finish this statement like they usually do, SolarFlare."

"Let me just thank our hero," Daniel says, pulling me aside.

"Sorry," I whisper, peering around to make sure no one's paying attention. "I didn't know the protocol."

"Don't be sorry," Daniel says. "You were amazing. Mir couldn't have done any better. Actually it sounds like he was ready to take her down tonight. What he wasn't counting on was you, Les."

"I just acted without thinking it through," I say.

"Exactly. Sometimes that's what you have to do. Look I have to go. Tell Miranda I'll call her in the morning. And Les?"

"Yeah?"

"Thank you for saving me."

I'm not thrilled about facing Miranda. No matter what Daniel says, I still feel like I really screwed up. I get dizzy whenever I think about how close I came to getting us both killed.

My stomach roils as I climb the stairs to our apartment. I find her propped up in bed watching the news. I pull my crumpled gloves and mask from my tench coat pocket, toss them on the nightstand, and crawl in next to her. Now I can stare at the screen instead of her beaming face.

"I knew you had it in you," she says, throwing her arms around me.

"Um....," I say.

"You not only saved Daniel, you actually got Mayhem arrested!"

"It was a fluke," I say, picking at a loose thread on the comforter.

"Hey, stop being so modest," she says.

"I'm not!" I turn to look at her. "I was scared. I didn't know what to do, and I nearly got both of us killed. I'm not you."

"Les," she says, taking my shoulders in her hands. "I was terrified every time I put on that costume. All I ever thought was that you'd make a better SolarFlare than I ever could. But *I* wanted to be the hero. I was greedy, and I made myself believe the stone was meant for me. Until yesterday."

"What happened then?" I ask, confused.

"You happened. You were there. You saw how the mistakes I made almost cost us all our lives."

I open my mouth to protest but realize she's right. I remember thinking how she should have taken advantage of Mayhem's slowness. Should have realized he was forcing her away from Daniel's frozen body. Even how I saved her life by throwing that icicle.

"Still—" I start to protest.

"I let myself get distracted when I saw Daniel push you against that wall. That's why I didn't stop Mayhem from freezing him. I was jealous."

My mouth is suddenly very dry. "You were jealous of *me*?"

"Yeah. I'm so sorry. It's stupid and childish. I mean, I know Daniel loves me, and I know you would never do anything, but seeing him protect you like that...."

"I'm sorry, too," I admit. "I owe you an apology."

"For what?" she asks.

"For hating you for being so good at everything and having everything I don't. But if it makes you feel any better, I think you and Daniel are really good together. He's a pretty cool guy, and he really does love you."

"Wow." Miranda leans back against the headboard and stares straight ahead for a minute. Then I settle back against the headboard again.

"So what are we going to do about SolarFlare?" I ask.

Miranda's eyes trail over my outfit, and we both say, "I think *you* should do it."

We stare at each other for a few minutes.

"This city sure needs SolarFlare," she says, flipping off the TV.

"Maybe we can be her together," I suggest. "Like equal partners."

"Yeah," Miranda says. "I like that."

Being SolarFlare *was* kind of fun. And I guess I really wasn't half bad at it after all.

The next thing I know, I'm hugging my sister tighter than I have in a decade. This superhero thing might just be all right.

Blunt Force Trauma

Kevin Hosey

PSYKORE'S CLENCHED FIST completed its tight arc and smashed hard against the kidnapper's chin. Even through the thick padding in his glove, PsyKore could feel the bones in the man's jaw pop, crack and crunch like thin ice.

And it felt fantastic.

A fine mist of blood spewed from the mouth of Bobby Lee Reardon, kidnapper, sexual predator and murderer, as his head snapped back. The force of the blow carried him across the room until he slammed against a concrete support column. His body seemed to pause there a moment, defying gravity, as if he had struck the pillar so hard his body embedded in it. Then he finally crumpled to the floor and lay there like a pile of rags.

((behind you))

The mental warning from PsyKore's psionic sense pinged through his mind. He spun to face Reardon's partner, Leon Murphy, who must have just entered the room.

"Son of a bitch!" the massive bull of a man yelled as he hurtled at PsyKore. Rage reddened his eyes and rabid spittle spewed from his lips. "I'll kill you!"

((right punch))

PsyKore instantly reacted to the second mental alarm by deflecting the swing of Murphy's bulging right arm.

((left punch))

He avoided Murphy's left strike just as easily, and countered with a sledgehammer blow to the bastard's right ribs, cracking them. Though PsyKore would have enjoyed hearing the inevitable scream of agony, he didn't give him the opportunity. He smashed his forearm into Murphy's face, shattering his nose and dropping him like a 300-pound bag of shit.

Dispatching the scumbag wasn't difficult—his type rarely were—especially with PsyKore's ability to psionically sense his opponents' every move

83

seconds before they made it. That power was his advantage in his fight against crime, and it never failed him.

PsyKore wanted to continue beating both the Satan-worshipping sons-of-bitches until all that was left were deflated bags of skin filled with bloody pulp and crushed bone fragments. But he fought the urge. Sometimes it was so damn hard to remain faithful to his "no kill" policy.

Three days. It had taken three days to track Reardon and Murphy after they abducted five-year old Cynthia Dunham. Most kidnapped children don't survive past the first forty-eight hours.

Praying he wasn't too late to save her, PsyKore moved swiftly across the basement floor toward a heavy wooden door covered in black painted occult symbols. It was sealed shut by an industrial-sized padlock. He didn't stop to search the two animals for the key. Instead, he summoned the primal anger and frustration that had been festering inside him for days, and kicked the entry right off its hinges.

That's when the bomb exploded….

Frank Offutt's eyes never wavered from the flames flickering in the fireplace in his den. It was four in the morning. He'd been awake for over fifteen minutes, ever since the recurring nightmare dragged him from his sleep—once again.

Sighing with exhaustion, he picked up a nearly empty glass of whiskey sitting on the lamp table next to an open bottle of painkillers. They were the only two things that helped alleviate the chronic pain in his leg. He took a sip and winced as the amber liquid burned its way through his chest.

The siren call of the fire held his gaze. Shimmering arms of crackling heat danced across the logs inside the wide brick chamber. And as he watched, his mind drifted back.

Flames…heat…burning…agony…screams…his *own* screams….

He pulled his eyes away and shook the images out of his head.

The nightmare had returned and it was worse than ever. The explosion…the pain….

But why now? He still felt the ache of his injuries, but he thought he had suppressed the nightmares years ago.

Frank drained his glass. As he moved to pour another, his cell phone rang. He picked it up and frowned at the blinking number. Who would be calling this late?

Ice shot through his veins. The area code was for Chicago. Certainly it wasn't….

"Hello?" he answered.

Silence on the other end greeted him. Then a raspy voice replied, and the ice in Frank's veins hardened. "*Frank?*"

Jesus. "Shamus?" Frank whispered. "Is that you?" He recognized the heavy Irish brogue of his ex-partner, though he hadn't heard it in almost two decades. It seemed the explosion wasn't the only bad memory that had resurfaced.

He was even more shocked to realize Shamus was crying. In all the time they fought crime together, Frank never heard his former mentor cry, even when the man who used to be called SlamRock failed to stop a busload of school kids from plummeting off a bridge.

"*She's dead, Frank.*"

"What—?"

"*Sylphe is dead.*"

At first Frank thought he had misheard. But then the meaning and impact of the words hit him like a spiked gauntlet. "What?" he breathed into the receiver.

"*My daughter is dead,*" the husky voice cracked through suppressed sobs. "*She was murdered, Frank. My baby is gone.*"

"Caitlin...? Jesus!" was all Frank could manage. The fatigued fog in his head evaporated. "I'm sorry, Shamus. What happened?"

"*Someone beat her...then shot her in the head.*"

Frank buried his face in his hand. "God...." He felt lightheaded. No, he felt sick. "Do they know who did it?"

Except for an occasional sob, heavy silence filled the other end of the line. Frank waited patiently for Shamus to compose himself.

"*That's not why I called you, boyo.*"

"Then...why—?"

"*I...I had no one....*" The voice faltered again, then suddenly took on a harsher tone. "*It doesn't matter why.*"

"Shamus, I'm coming to Chica—"

"*No! You're not welcome here.*"

"You need me there. You need someone there. I'm—"

"*I shouldn't have called. Not you.*"

The phone fumbled on the other end and disconnected.

Stubborn son-of-a-bitch, Frank thought. Tears welled in his eyes; tears for a girl he hadn't seen since she was a baby.

Maria's baby.

Maria.

He couldn't believe it. Caitlin was dead.

Sylphe was dead. That's what Shamus said. Frank found it odd that he referred to her by her hero name rather than her true identity. But his former friend was distraught. No telling how a father might react after the death of his only child.

Well, no longer a child. She was twenty-one. Still....

Frank realized he hadn't hung up his cell. He flipped it shut, but then opened it again.

Shamus didn't want him there, but Maria....Frank wanted to be there for her.

Wiping tears from his face, he dialed the airlines, and glanced again at the flames. As he waited for an answer, he fought back the resurfaced images of the explosion that had ended his career as PsyKore.

And focused on the tragedy he was about to confront.

Twenty minutes after his plane touched down at O'Hare, Frank rented a car and aimed it toward the memorial service. He hadn't spoken to Shamus since the call three days before. And Frank had no doubt his old partner was *not* going to be happy to see him.

He drove in grim silence as he listened to the chatter on talk radio. A self-proclaimed pundit railed against the Mask Act going before Congress. The act, if signed into law, would significantly expand the range of evidence obtained by masked heroes that could be admissible in court cases. The radio host was enraged. She considered "costumed vigilantes" to be no better than common criminals.

Though he no longer wore a mask, Frank still kept abreast of matters affecting the hero community. He knew that Congressman Briggs, the man who created the bill, was an ex-costumed hero himself, though that was unknown to the public. The passing of the act would be a boon to those few heroes who still fought the good fight. Yet it was still far less support than they hoped it would bring.

Reaching the massive Catholic church, Frank slipped on his black suit jacket and limped up the stone steps and through the wide doors. Inside, he was surprised to find the place empty. For a moment, he feared he had the wrong day. Then he spotted a small wooden marquee that carried Caitlin's name and today's date in small white plastic letters.

Sighing, he felt he knew why there were no mourners. Caitlin and Shamus had no other family and probably very few friends. It was the curse of dedicating one's existence to serving the ravenous gods of justice.

No time for a private life. And even those who did have time avoided making civilian friends and almost never started families, since they could be used as leverage against them.

In fact, the only reason Shamus had married his wife, Maria, was because he got her pregnant. Unfortunately, she had miscarried soon after. Yet they had remained married due to their Catholic faith, and three years later, they were blessed with Caitlin.

Frank walked solemnly down the aisle toward the chancel. He had been at that church before, when Shamus married Maria and when Caitlin had been baptized. Frank felt a pang of sorrow when he realized he had been there only at her birth...and now her death.

Caitlin's elegant mahogany casket sat at the foot of the steps leading to the alter. Not surprisingly, the lid was closed. Frank grimaced. According to the medical examiner's report he uncovered when he hacked into the police department server, her death had been brutal. The details of her attack had sliced him like a cold knife. Damage to her face and skull was so severe, no amount of funeral parlor tricks would have concealed it.

A shiver encircled him as he brushed away the mental image.

Luckily, her true identity hadn't been revealed. Whenever a masked hero was killed, a specialized police group recovered the body quickly in order to maintain their secret. It was one of the first programs Congressman Briggs had set into place after taking office.

A generous floral arrangement of delicate white roses adorned the top of the casket. It must have been placed recently, because there was still a fine mist of water on the petals. Nestled against the flowers, a silver frame held a color photo of a smiling Caitlin. She had been so stunning. The dark hair, olive skin and radiant brown eyes gave her an exotic beauty that must have melted men's hearts. They were all traits she inherited from her Greek mother.

Though he hadn't seen her since her baptism, Frank had followed Caitlin's life through letters from Maria. Later, when Caitlin turned eighteen and chose to follow in her father's footsteps, Frank kept track of her exploits in the news. Donning a costume, she quickly made a name for herself as Sylphe. She had a black belt in every martial art ever created. The media dubbed her "an unstoppable teenage force of nature."

A tear welled in Frank's eye. Apparently, someone finally figured out *how* to stop her.

"What the *hell* are you doing here?"

Turning at the sudden sound of his ex-partner's sharp voice behind him, Frank found the much older man storming his way from the rear of the church. And Frank had guessed right, he was *not* happy.

Shamus Riley hadn't changed much since the last time Frank saw him. Even in his late seventies, his hair was dark red. He was still fit, too, one of the side effects of the secret radioactive formula he accidentally drank in the Army.

The man who used to be SlamRock, the Irish Defender, stopped two inches from Frank and pushed a finger against his chest. "I asked what the hell you're doing here, Offutt?" His bright red hair still seemed to darken when Shamus was angry, as if it were about to burst into flames. "I told you not to come. You're not welcome. Not after what you did to me!"

"Now isn't the time for this discussion, Shamus," Frank said in a hushed tone as he glanced toward an old priest looking their way.

Fortunately, Shamus followed his gaze and fell silent after seeing the cleric's stern expression. But when he turned back to Frank, volcanic fury burned in his eyes. His hair-trigger temper had obviously not mellowed in his old age. Unfortunate, since it was one of the main reasons for the rift between them.

After taking a deep, slow breath, Shamus leaned closer. "Get the hell out of here."

"I've come to pay my respects to—"

"*Now.*"

"Please, I can help you. I've already begun searching for—"

When Shamus turned to leave, Frank gently touched his shoulder. "Please, I can help you. I've already begun searching for—"

"*No!*" his former mentor cut in, not bothering to face him. "I needed you years ago, boyo. But you abandoned me. I don't need your damn help now. Leave...before I throw you out." Then his voice tightened like a funeral drum. "And Frank...if I see you anywhere after today, trust me...you won't like what happens."

Frank Offutt watched his ex-partner walk away, and then glanced back at the casket. He longed to stay, but decided against it out of respect for Caitlin. But, though he'd leave the church, he wouldn't leave Chicago. Not until he tracked down her killer, one way or another.

He owed that to Maria.

Rubbing the ache in his leg, Frank Offutt leaned back from his laptop and took a sip of very strong, very cold coffee. Outside his hotel curtains, the sun had vanished long ago.

He had spent the afternoon and evening following up on the extensive research he had done before leaving Houston. He had dissected every public, private and classified database—of law enforcement and criminal organizations—he could access. Like a dull razor shaving layers of metal away one millimeter at a time, he tracked current, past and future illegal activities in Chicago. By doing so, he determined to uncover the identity of Caitlin Riley's murderer. Or rather, Sylphe's.

Diving back into his search, Frank mused on how vastly different it was now than when he wore a mask. These days, he could do most of the "leg work" sitting in a chair. Thankfully, he had spent the time since his *involuntary* retirement acquiring exceptional computer skills rather than sitting on his ass lamenting his predicament. Now there were very few networks he couldn't pry open.

Killing a costumed hero was a huge deal. Whatever shit stain committed the murder would undoubtedly brag about it, or someone else would get wind of it and pass on the news. Once the media reported that a hero had been eliminated, the other criminal insects always wanted to know who did it, usually to reward them.

In all the winding electronic trails Frank had followed, one name kept popping up: HeadShot. Considering what happened to Caitlin, the name alone put him at the top of Frank's suspect list. But it wasn't enough. So Frank kept digging.

After another hour he uncovered more about HeadShot's life than the man himself probably knew. His true identity was William Portaine. At least, that's what it was now. He had changed it twelve years ago after his father was imprisoned. Frank grunted when he discovered who the father was. Miguel Baltasar, aka Prof. Meko Nebulous, one of the most vile and psychotic villains Shamus had ever fought.

Check that, it *had* been his father's name. Baltasar had died from colon cancer in prison last year. No loss to society, but Portaine probably felt otherwise. His father's slow excruciating death may have emotionally traumatized him. Even some hardcore criminals had a soft spot for family.

It also gave Portaine motive for the murder of Sylphe. Perhaps he had discovered her relationship to SlamRock. Why kill SlamRock for the imprisonment of Nebulous when you could make him suffer more by killing someone he loved?

Revenge made sense. According to the coroner's report, Caitlin had died from severe blunt force trauma. The bullet in her skull—HeadShot's signature—had been delivered postmortem. Whoever killed Sylphe was extremely angry at her. The murder was very personal.

Frank decided to pay William Portaine a visit. And based on a location map he had comprised of HeadShot's considerable crimes, as well as a few calls to informants he still knew, Frank had a pretty good idea where

Portaine's base of operations might be. Following the "paper" trail, he had discovered that Cyrus Commercial Realty, a shell company owned by

Portaine, managed a deserted industrial warehouse park on the other side of Chicago.

That was where Frank would begin his search.

But first, he had to make a stop on the way.

"May you see God's light on the path ahead."

Frank softly recited the freshly engraved inscription adorning the marble headstone. Below the blessing, it also read "Caitlin Riley, Beloved Daughter, Valiant Heart, Heroic Spirit."

Sighing, he whispered mournfully, "You deserved so much better than this, Caitlin."

Above him, the moon nudged silently across the star-speckled sky, and cast a solemn silver light across the freshly packed dirt at his feet. Since Shamus had forced him to leave the church, he had come to the cemetery to pay his respects to Maria's daughter.

No one should ever die that young, or in such a horrible way. She should have had a normal life, with friends, school...marriage. But when you're the daughter of one of the greatest crime fighters ever, destiny usually has other plans for you.

And she had been a damn natural, too. Even though Sylphe never inherited SlamRock's artificial speed or strength, she was still a force to be feared. Caitlin had held her own against villains other heroes would avoid.

So how the hell did someone manage to kill her, especially a mid-league dirt bag like HeadShot?

No, not just kill...utterly *destroy* her.

The injuries she had suffered dredged up memories of the day Frank had almost died. Even after eighteen years, he could still feel the searing heat of the explosion tearing into his skin. If not for the full face mask and Kevlar-padded uniform he wore as PsyKore, he wouldn't have survived. But he had not emerged unscathed. The scars across the side of his face, torso and right leg reminded him of that every time he looked in a mirror. And the muscle damage in his leg meant he would always walk with a noticeable limp.

But worst of all, he had lost the power that made him unique: the psionic sense that enabled him to hold his own against any foe he fought. That and his other injuries had forced him to reluctantly hang up his mask.

He had survived...but Caitlin hadn't. It just wasn't fair.

But if her death was affecting *him* this much, imagine how much worse it must be for her father. A child should never die before a parent.

Frank wished Shamus would give up his intense grudge against him. They should be working together to find the identity of Caitlin's killer, not fighting each other.

He and Shamus had once been close. *Very* close. They were partners in the seventies; the perfect crime fighting team. At the time, Frank, barely in his twenties, was known as Kid SlamRock, the "Psychic Sidekick." He had hated the ridiculous name. But he idolized Shamus so much he would have called himself *Baby* SlamRock just so he could fight by his side.

He had even ignored the usual innuendos that he and Shamus were lovers. That idiotic allegation was always circulated about every same-sex crime-fighting duo, especially when one member was so much younger. Every team just ignored them, even though, in some cases, it was true.

But as Frank grew older, his respect for SlamRock slowly waned. He began to realize that the rage that dwelled within Shamus was slowly growing worse. More than once, Frank had pulled him off some villain he had almost beaten to death. Eventually, Frank was spending more time protecting the villains from SlamRock than protecting civilians.

Frank had suspected the formula that gave Shamus his powers was beginning to affect his mind. But when he confessed his fears to his partner, Riley had warned him to mind his own business. Desperate, Frank had asked Maria to try and convince her husband he needed help. When Shamus found out, he had gone ballistic. He had accused both of them of betraying him and almost broke Frank's jaw with one punch.

So Frank had left the team and moved to Houston, where he became PsyKore. To this day, Shamus still accused Frank of abandoning him when he needed him most.

Shamus's rage grew even worse when Maria died five years later. She was no longer there to quell his seething anger.

Maria. *Damn.* Not a hero, just a normal woman.

And the only woman Frank had ever loved.

Releasing his pent-up breath, he forced himself to do something he had avoided since arriving at Caitlin's gravesite. He turned to face Maria's headstone next to it. Emotion overwhelmed him as he placed a hand on the cold, hard marble.

"I'm so sorry, Maria." He spoke to her softly, gently, intimately, like he used to years ago during the few times they were....

She was seven years older than him, and thirteen years younger than Riley. And her beauty had been unimaginable. The same beauty Frank saw reflected in Caitlin's photo.

Unknown to Shamus, Frank had visited her grave occasionally following the house fire that claimed her life. But it finally became too difficult, so he had stopped.

The fire. To the world, it was just a small item in the daily paper. To Shamus, it had been his entire world collapsing. He discovered it had been set deliberately, and he didn't rest until he tracked down the man responsible. Frank had learned through police reports that the arsonist had been some smalltime villain named Weaseler trying to make a name for himself. The man had died while trying to escape from Shamus. The police investigation had ruled the death accidental.

It was a miracle Caitlin hadn't been home when the fire started. She had been at her grandparents' house for the weekend.

But fate had finally caught up with her.

Bowing his head, Frank swore again to Maria that he would find Caitlin's killer. And he needed to do it before Shamus. Frank knew his old partner would also go after the person responsible. But in his current state of mind, Shamus might kill the culprit. And with everything else the man had suffered, Frank didn't want Shamus going to prison as well.

After one final look at Caitlin and Maria's graves, Frank turned and walked away. As he did, he reached for the face mask he'd removed when he arrived, and pulled it back onto his head. The specially-designed lenses instantly shifted to night mode. Mask in place, his uniform was complete. He was once again PsyKore for the first time since the explosion.

He referred to it as a uniform, though the standard term used by other masked heroes was "costume." Frank hated that word. Costumes were what children wore at Halloween.

Frank had always considered the concept of heroes wearing costumes to be silly, as if they were all part of some flamboyant professional wrestling group. For his uniform, Frank wore a less gaudy—and more protective—outfit of black leather and Kevlar. He had brought the extra uniform with him to Chicago, knowing he would need it. The obsidian full-body suit, mask, gloves and boots helped him blend into the night.

And stealth was an asset he definitely needed. For without his psionic sense to fight off an attack, taking Caitlin's killer by surprise might be Frank's only option of succeeding...and surviving.

At 3:20 AM, Frank exited the fourth of six derelict warehouses in the Cyrus Realty industrial park. Except for a few drug addicts gradually killing themselves to satisfy their addictions, and malnourished hookers plying their trade in parked cars or alleys, the warehouses were empty. In fact, they didn't appear to have been used for any type of business—legal or otherwise—in quite some time.

Frank pulled in a deep breath through the porous fabric of his mask. Even though he was just skulking about abandoned buildings, he hadn't felt so alive in years. Funny how quickly he got back into it, too, as if he had never stopped fighting for justice.

Of course, he wouldn't be slipping into his old routines as smoothly if not for the two painkillers he had swallowed earlier. They were specially crafted by Dr. Smith Jonas, a physician who aided the masked community. The pills, which, like most of his medicinal inventory, weren't approved by the FDA, helped alleviate the pain in Frank's leg without making him drowsy or dulling his senses.

The analgesics would help when he confronted his quarry. He had maintained a regiment of exercise and martial arts training on the likely chance some past enemy might uncover his identity and come for him. But facing sparring partners wasn't the same as fighting for your life. When the time came, he needed to be in prime physical condition, but also maintain peak mental efficiency. He knew more heroes who had been defeated by a weak mind than a weak body.

Frank approached the fifth warehouse cautiously. He climbed the rusted metal ladder on the side and entered though an open window about thirty feet above the alley. Instantly, he sensed something was wrong. The building reeked with the familiar stench of death.

His eye lenses cast the warehouse in a dark green glow. He searched the interior from his perch on a rusty catwalk high above the concrete floor. Nothing moved among the various size crates cluttering the main area below. Frank increased the aural sensitivity on the earpieces in his mask. All he heard were scratches of rats scurrying within the walls and shadows.

Vermin, but not the type he hunted.

He allowed a few moments to pass, and then made his way to a narrow stairway. The thick rubber soles on his boots muffled his steps. Even if the warehouse was occupied, no one would hear him approaching.

Stepping onto the main floor, he paused. The stench was stronger. Whatever had died was close by. He scanned the entire area, but it was still clear; only crates and a large tarpaulin covering some sort of vehicle on the other end of the warehouse.

His adrenaline was working overtime. He fought to take control of his rising heart rate so he could concentrate. In his prime, he had been able to maintain an unearthly calm in any situation. But that was long ago, *before* he lost his powers. Back then, suppressing fear had been simple when you knew what your target was going to do almost before *they* did.

Frank took a step—then stopped.

There wasn't any dust on the floor. In the other buildings, his footsteps left trails in the layers of particles left by years of neglect. Not in this one. The crates were the same. Everything was cleaned and maintained. That meant this warehouse was in use on a regular basis.

He examined some of the metal crates. All of them were unmarked and sealed shut. He'd need a jackhammer to pry them open. Whatever cargo they held would have to wait.

So he focused on the tarp instead.

The closer he got, the more powerful the stench became. Whatever had died was under the heavy covering. The tarp hadn't been secured to the ground, so Frank grabbed the edge firmly and yanked it away, ready to confront any danger it might conceal.

His breath froze in his chest at the horror that lay beneath.

It was Shamus—or what was left of him. He was strung up by chains on the back of a small semi-truck. His arms were outstretched as if he was being crucified. And he was wearing his SlamRock costume.

But his face—almost his entire head, mask and all—was a bloody pulp. Someone had beaten him to death. Exactly like Caitlin.

Fury erupted inside Frank; a rage so powerful it literally sent pain through his chest. He felt the bones in his hands stretch to the point of breaking as he slowly clenched his fists.

As Frank had feared, Shamus had donned his costume and gone after Caitlin's killer himself.

Why the hell didn't you work with me, Riley? Frank thought as his anguish and anger threatened to engulf him. Even with his increased abilities, Shamus was too damn old to be operating alone.

Now he had paid for it. One of the greatest champions the world had ever known, and he had been hung up like a side of beef by some gutless mother—

Smething slammed against the back of Frank's head. *Hard.*

He dropped to his knees, stars exploding across his vision and nausea rising in his throat. Even with the thin layer of Kevlar lining his mask, the impact felt almost as if it caved in his skull. Frank damned himself for being so stupid. He no longer had his power, so he should have been more alert. Instead, he was so distracted by Shamus's body, he had let someone walk right up and blindside him like a rank amateur.

"What the *hell* is this?" A strange male voice behind him pierced through the roar of the blood rushing into Frank's ears. "Senior night? First that old fossil in the green costume shows up, and now you?"

Inhaling deeply, Frank managed to clear most of his vision. His head still hurt like hell, but it could have been worse. Luckily, the pills he took suppressed most of the pain. But he felt something wet against his skin under his mask. Blood.

"I recognize you." The man snapped his fingers. "What was your name again? Oh, right...*PsyKore*. My old man used to talk about you."

Frank managed to turn slightly. In the green hue of his lenses, he found his assailant. The son-of-a-bitch was wearing a Kevlar-padded suit similar to his, but his head was draped in a half mask with a large white crosshairs painted on it. He also wore two shoulder holsters with semi-automatic revolvers. And in his gloved right hand was the thick lead pipe...covered in blood. Shamus's blood.

William Portaine. "HeadShot," Frank said, his voice strained.

"So you know who I am, eh? I'll bet it's a big thrill for an old pisser like you to locate someone of my reputation. So did you two leave the heroes' nursing home just to come after me? I'm honored."

Pain once again at an endurable level, Frank rose to his feet. "I'm not *that* old, you son-of-a-bitch."

The scumbag laughed. "Really? Truth be told, PsyKore, I thought you were dead. Guess not." His lips pulled back against his teeth in a humorless grin. "But I can remedy that."

((*lead pipe*))

On blind instinct, PsyKore reacted to the sudden warning in his head. He rammed his extended fingers into HeadShot's right arm, gouging a pressure point. Portaine cried out as his limb went limp. The pipe popped loose and scattered across the warehouse floor, leaving a bloody trail like tiny footprints.

"What the *hell?*" HeadShot muttered, his eyes wide in shock.

But not anywhere near as shocked as Frank felt.

The blow to his head. It must have—

((*left gun*))

This time Frank slammed the flat of his palm against HeadShot's right hand before he could reach the gun in the left holster. Frank felt the bones in the Portaine's hand shatter, and the man screamed in pain. He staggered back, but Frank pressed his attack.

For some miraculous reason, his psionic sense had returned. But he didn't need it. This time he allowed his adrenaline to erupt. Between it and his unbridled rage at what the animal had done to Shamus and Caitlin, Frank's assault was so brutal the bastard never had a chance to defend himself. In mere moments, a series of practiced punches and kicks, each with the purpose of inflicting the most pain possible, dropped HeadShot to the floor in an unconscious heap.

Once satisfied he wasn't going to get up again, Frank removed Portaine's other revolver and cuffed his wrists and ankles with two plastic restraints he carried in a belt compartment. He then kicked him in the head once more for good measure, and left him trussed up like a branded calf.

Pulling out a disposable cell phone, Frank dialed 9-1-1. After giving the dispatcher the address, he notified them that a murder had been committed and that they would find the killer unconscious on the floor. When asked for his name, Frank closed the phone and tossed it away so they couldn't track him later.

An intense twinge of pain hit him above the right temple. The painkillers were wearing off. After one more anguished glance at Shamus, Frank started toward the exit. He needed to leave before the police arrived with too many questions he didn't want to answer.

But his wound must have been more serious than he feared. Dizziness pulled his legs out from under him. Room spinning, he collapsed to his knees with such force they would have cracked if they weren't protected by Kevlar padding. Another wave of vertigo swelled over him, and he fell forward onto the concrete.

In the distance, he heard the mournful sound of police sirens. But only for a moment.

Then he blacked out.

"Frank Offutt? My name is Detective Eli Hoyt of the Chicago Police Department...and you are under arrest."

"*What?*" Frank sputtered as he almost choked on a mouthful of ice chips. "Arrest for what?"

"The murder of Shamus Riley."

Less than an hour before, Frank had finally regained consciousness to find himself in a hospital bed. His head was wrapped in bandages and his arm hooked to an IV. His uniform was also missing. A young blonde doctor informed him he had been in a coma for almost two days. He suffered a severe concussion, but his condition was stable. Frank had asked how he arrived at the hospital, and what happened to the other two people in the warehouse. But all the doctor said was that someone else would be in shortly to discuss it with him.

As soon as the physician left, the detective walked in, closed the door and flashed his badge. During his forty-eight hours of comatose slumber, Frank had experienced a rash of horrific and truly bizarre nightmares. But none were as utterly surreal as the words Hoyt just pronounced.

"Shamus?" Frank's hand trembled as he set his cup of ice the table next to his bed. He tried to sit straighter, but a spasm of pain prevented it. "No...no...he was killed by William Portaine...."

"Who?"

More pain impeded Frank's ability to think. "Wait...it's *Baltasar*. His name is Baltasar."

"So which is it?"

"Both. He's a low-life scumbag who calls himself *HeadShot*."

Frowning, Hoyt flipped open a small notepad. "I have no idea who that is, Mr. Offutt. What I do know is that we received a call from an anonymous source that a murder had been committed and we would find the perpetrator unconscious when we arrived."

"That was *me*. I made that call—"

"The only person we found unconscious was *you*. You were lying less than ten feet from the severely beaten body of Shamus Riley. His body was so traumatized we had to identify him by the few teeth left in his head. We also discovered his blood on the mask you were wearing."

"Blood?" Frank paused to think. His head hurt so badly he could barely see. He wished he had more of Jonas's painkillers. "The blood...it must have come off the iron bar when HeadShot hit *me*."

"We did locate an iron bar...."

"Good, it—"

"But it only had *your* fingerprints."

"*No*. That's...that's not possible. I was wearing gloves...."

"No you weren't."

"I...*what?* I always wear gloves...it's part of my uniform." Frank closed his eyes and took a deep breath. He sounded insane. No, worse, he sounded guilty.

"Here's the way I see it, Mr. Offutt..." Hoyt lowered his pad. "We know that you and Mr. Riley used to be superheroes back in the day. I did some research and it turns out you had a very public breakup of your partnership. I imagine that left some substantial ill will between you two, something that may have festered since then. So, perhaps, for whatever reason, you two finally went head-to-head two days ago...and you killed him."

"No...no...I came here for the funeral of *Caitlin* Riley...."

"About that." The detective referred to his pad again. "A priest at St. Michael's said he saw you and Riley arguing. According to him, Riley was very upset and told you to leave. The Father was afraid you two were about to come to blows right there in the church."

Gritting through the throbbing pain, Frank shook his head adamantly. "It wasn't that way...."

"He didn't ask you to leave?"

"Yes, but...." Frank sighed and closed his eyes. He needed to think. Then a flash of insight popped into his head. Facing Hoyt, he said, "Portaine. He must have gotten loose from his cuffs and left before you arrived. HeadShot set me up."

"HeadShot set you up," repeated Hoyt in a skeptical tone as if Frank had suggested Santa Claus had framed him. "I don't buy it. The scenario I suggested makes much more sense. A long history of hatred between two ex-partners finally comes to a violent, bloody end. Or maybe *you* had something to do with the murder of Riley's daughter, and he—"

"*Bullshit!*"

"Maybe, maybe not. Make it easier for yourself, Offutt. Confess right now and I can—"

"*No*," Frank said as his entire body deflated in exhaustion. "I...I think it's time I spoke to my lawyer."

"Fine," Hoyt said after an extended pause. "And for your sake, Offutt, I hope he's a damn good one."

Frank Offutt's lawyer *was* a damn good one. Just not good enough.

With all the evidence against Frank, even though much of it was circumstantial, the best his attorney could do was avoid the death penalty. So, ultimately convicted, Frank was placed in the Illinois Tamms Supermax prison with the rest of the general population.

As he expected, several attempts were made on Frank's life during the first few months. He hadn't put many of the current penal residents away himself, but being an ex-masked hero still qualified him for their hit list. Fortunately, his restored psionic sense helped him avoid being shanked, drowned, burned and various other nasty forms of homicide. After a while, the other inmates finally gave up.

Meanwhile, his lawyer filed appeal after appeal, but to no avail. Finally,

Frank's money ran out, and so did his lawyer. But Frank refused to surrender. Virtually penniless, his only legal recourse was the aid of a public defender. It wasn't an avenue he put much faith in, but it was worth a try.

"Your lawyer's here, Offutt."

Frank nodded to the guard standing in the narrow doorway of the small, windowless conference room. As the uniformed sentry stepped away to let in the visitor, Frank stared at his cuffed hands resting on the cold gray metal table. A million thoughts ramped through his mind as he heard the heavy door close. All of them, as always, focused on proving his innocence so he could be freed to hunt down HeadSho—

"How's it going, boyo?"

Frank's breath seized. He suddenly felt as if someone had plunged his entire nervous system in an arctic ocean.

That voice. It *couldn't* be.

Still holding a stunned gasp tight in his throat, he looked up into the deep emerald eyes of—

"Shamus?"

Frank's former partner nodded at him with a slight grin. His hair...it was brown rather than red. And he had shaved his mustache. But it was him. For a fleeting moment, Frank thought he was hallucinating, perhaps losing his mind from the strain of his years in prison.

"What...?" he whispered. "*How...?*"

"Am I still alive?" Shamus finished.

A nod was all Frank could manage.

"Simple, kid...I never died."

"I...don't understand. I saw your *body*...."

"You saw *a* body. It wasn't me."

"But...your costume..."

Shamus leaned back in his chair, his dark suit jacket and tie tightening around his fit physique. "Come now, boyo. I always suspected you were a little dense, but even you can't deduce that I *faked* my death?"

"Faked...?"

Raising his hands like a magician after a successful ruse, Shamus flashed a huge grin. "Tada!"

"*Why*? Shamus, why are you here?"

"So I can tell you why *you're* here, Frank."

"Because they think I *killed* you."

Shamus waved his hand dismissively. "Obviously. But there's so much more to it than that." His grin vanished as his voice hardened. "It's because

I *put* you here."

Every moment he sat with the man he thought had been dropped into a grave long ago, Frank felt as if he were sliding deeper and deeper into a yawning, nightmarish chasm. None of what Shamus said made any sense.

And it was starting to piss him off.

"Riley," Frank said, struggling to maintain control of his tone. "What the *hell* is going on? Whose body did I see in that warehouse?"

The older man shrugged. "Some dockworker I found. Matched my size and physique."

"Who killed him?"

"HeadShot, of course. But I paid him to do it."

"Paid? You hired Portaine to commit *murder*?"

"Sure." Shamus shrugged, as if it was a normal chore carried out by regular people every day.

"But...god damn it! *Why*?"

"For the same reason I had him kill Caitlin."

Frank's throat constricted as all the air was sucked from his lungs. His eyes tunneled until he could focus only on the man across the table; the man who used to be his idol, and the idol of millions.

"Are you insane? You...you murdered your *own* daughter?"

"Of course not!" replied Shamus with an appalled expression. "What kind of a monster do ya think I am, Frank?"

"But, you just—"

"She was *your* daughter." Before Frank could react, Shamus leaned back and took a deep breath. "That's right. An illegitimate little bitch that entered this world because you...my partner...my friend...*screwed my wife!*"

Frank Offutt couldn't process what he was hearing fast enough. Caitlin was *his* daughter?

"Did you really think I wouldn't find out about you and Maria?" Shamus snarled. "I've known some time now. *My* wife, Frank. *Mine!* You had your hands on her body even though she belonged to *me*?" Then he leaned closer. "Why do you think I killed her, too?"

Jesus Christ! On adrenaline-fueled impulse, Frank reached for Shamus. But his cuffed hands, which were chained to a metal ring on the table, stopped inches from the other man's throat.

Shamus didn't even flinch. He just glared at Frank as he added, "Worse...you got her *pregnant!*"

Frank collapsed into his chair, racked by guilt over the affair with the married woman he loved so intensely, and abject hatred for the man who caused the deaths of her *and* her daughter.

No...*his* daughter.

He and Maria had only been together a few times. They loved each other. But she ended the affair because of her vows to Shamus.

But a baby? Maria would have said something.

Shamus slammed his hand on the table, pulling Frank back to the present. "Focus, Frank! Let me guess, you're thinking Maria would have told you about the baby, right? Oh, she was going to. We had a ball buster of a fight one night when she threatened to leave me. She accused me of the same shit you did when you abandoned our partnership. Maria said I was becoming too violent, that I was losing control, just because I slapped her a few times. When I refused to let her leave, she got so pissed she finally told me about your affair. She actually wanted to move to Houston to live with you."

"With...me?"

"But I told Maria there was no way she was taking my daughter. That's when she dropped the real nugget. She said Caitlin was *yours*." He took a deep breath and sighed. "That's when I hit her. I didn't mean to kill her, though. My punch just...snapped her neck. Oh, I was horrified. Devastated. But I knew I had to cover it up. So I set the house on fire and made it appear as if Weaseler killed her out of revenge. The police investigated, but they found no evidence otherwise, especially after I told them he tripped and fell to his death from a building during pursuit. Why wouldn't they believe me? I was a beloved, respected hero in those days."

Frank squeezed his eyes shut, his entire body trembling in rage. When he finally opened his eyes and found Shamus grinning at him, he exploded. He jumped at Shamus again, but the chains held him back. "I'll kill you, you mother fu—"

"I *trained* you," Shamus said furiously. "I did everything for you, and you betrayed me! First by abandoning me, and then by sleeping with the woman I cherished."

"Cherished? You murdered her, Riley!"

"That was *you*! *Your* fault! My hands, but *you* are to blame."

Frank slammed the table with his fists. Speaking between harsh, angered breaths, he asked, "Why kill Caitlin? It wasn't her fault she was my daughter. She didn't have to die."

"She was bait," Shamus said simply. "Her death brought *you* to Chicago so I could make you pay for what you did to me, especially since my first attempt to get rid of you failed."

"What attempt?"

"The explosion, Frank, the one that ended your career, but unfortunately not your life. I paid those two rednecks in Houston to kidnap that little Dunham girl knowing you'd go after them. She wasn't supposed to die. *You* were. But those idiots screwed it up and you somehow survived, like a damned cockroach."

Shamus sat back down. "So I needed to draw you here. But there was no way that prick Portaine could take Sylphe down on his own. I had to knock her unconscious and let *him* finish the job."

"Jesus," Frank muttered. "That formula you drank in the Army...it *did* drive you insane."

If Shamus heard, he didn't indicate it. "After I confronted you at the church, I put a tracking device on your car. When you headed for the warehouses, I notified HeadShot. I was there, too, hidden out of sight. I was actually surprised you managed to take him down, Frank. Good thing you passed out when you did, though. I didn't have to get my own hands dirty. You know the rest."

"You mean actually kill me yourself rather than having other people do it for you?"

"No. I didn't want you dead. I wanted you here, where you'd suffer...just like you made me suffer for so long."

"You psychotic shit! You won't—"

"—get away with it?" Shamus smiled. "I already have, boyo. There's absolutely no evidence to connect me. Not even HeadShot. I buried him in a hole so deep God Himself will never find him. And as far as the police know, Shamus Riley—and SlamRock—are dead. They think that faceless bum was me." He pointed to his mouth. "I even had Portaine yank the guy's teeth and toss in a couple of mine that I pulled. Painful, but worth it to *damn* your life to hell."

All of the energy in Frank's body flooded away as the impact of Riley's statement settled in. The bastard was right. Shamus had covered his trail perfectly. And the windowless, sound-proof room they occupied had no microphones or cameras in order to provide attorney-client privacy, so the guards had no idea what was being said. His ex-partner had secured Frank's fate with an airtight seal.

In the countless years he had fought all the scum scraped from the soles of humanity, Frank had never felt so devastated...so *defeated*. And it was by a man he used to think of as a father.

But that malicious betrayal wasn't the only thing that shattered Frank's heart and soul. It was the fact that Shamus was also right about *him*. Frank *was* partially responsible for the murder of Riley's entire family. If not for Frank's affair with Maria, she would still be alive. Caitlin would never have been born, but she also wouldn't have died such a violent death.

Shamus had murdered them, but Frank might as well have held them down for him.

God, what the hell had he done? He *deserved* to suffer.

But so did Shamus Riley.

And Frank was going to make sure he did.

"Shamus," Frank said calmly. "You're not the only one with secrets."

"Really?" Riley chuckled. "And what—?"

"I've got my power back."

"Power?"

"My psionic sense. Somehow, that slam against my head in the warehouse must have..." Frank shrugged, "rebooted it. I thought it was gone, but it must have just been suppressed. Now it's back. Don't believe it?" He leaned forward. "Try me."

For a moment, Shamus sat rock still, studying Frank's face. Then—

((*right punch*))

Frank reeled back as his ex-partner's fist just missed caving in his jaw.

The older man's eyes widened, his arm still hovering in air. Finally, he lowered it. "So what? That pathetic ability of yours won't help you—"

"It's stronger," Frank said as he tilted closer. "I can now read your thoughts, *partner*. I know *exactly* what's going on inside that twisted brain of yours."

Shamus studied him with narrow green eyes, as if trying to do some mind reading of his own. "Bullshit...."

"There's more. I've been practicing since I arrived. Not only can I read thoughts, I can also transmit them to others."

The older man looked skeptical, yet remained silent.

"And here's the kicker, you stupid old shit...I've been in mental contact with the warden from the moment you began confessing your sins."

Uncertainty and a bit of panic flashed across Shamus's face.

"He knows everything, Riley."

"He doesn't know—"

"He knows *everything*. He knows who you are. He knows you killed Maria and Caitlin. He even knows you killed Portaine and Weaseler, and had a hand in the death of little Cynthia Dunham." Frank nodded his head toward the door. "Now he's coming...and he's bringing guards. *Lots* of them."

Shamus looked unsure for a moment. He even glanced at the door. But then he smiled. "Even if that were true, boyo, it wouldn't matter. You know damn well that testimony and confessions obtained through psychic methods aren't admissible in court. Too much risk for mental tampering. None of what—"

"You don't listen to the news, do you, old man?"

"News?"

"The Mask Act. It was finally passed last year. And part of that law now allows telepathic evidence. You can look it up....*after* they lock you away, of course."

Perspiration trickled on Riley's brow. It was the first time Frank had ever seen him sweat.

"You're about to spend the rest of your life in prison, Shamus. Better yet, I hope they put the needle in you so I can visit your grave every week...and *piss* on it for what you did."

Flames seemed to erupt behind Riley's pupils. They locked eyes—mentor and ward—for what Frank knew would be the last time.

"The entire world will know what a psychotic animal you are, Riley, that you're no better than the scum you fought. No...you're *worse*. You're pathetic. You're weak. You're not even a man. You—"

((table kick))

Even with the psionic warning, Shamus erupted from his seat so quickly, Frank didn't have time to react. Riley kicked the heavy metal table so hard it flew up and slammed against Frank's chin. He felt one of his teeth dislodge as he fell back against the concrete floor, the table pinning him down.

Shamus walked to the door and wrenched the handle off. "No one's coming in here, Offutt. This is between you and me."

And then Shamus kicked Frank in the side. Flames shot through his torso as he felt his ribs crack.

Riley grabbed the cuff chains and snapped them free of the metal ring on the table. Gripping them in his left hand to hold Frank upright, he slammed his granite-like right fist into Frank's face. A white flash exploded behind Frank's eyes as pain shot through his entire body. He felt blood squirt onto his mouth and clothing from his shattered nose.

"No one is going to save you, boyo," Shamus hissed. "You owe me, and you're going to suffer!"

Then he descended upon Frank in a fiery storm of rage and screams, pounding Frank's face and head relentlessly...without mercy. Before each blow, Frank's psionic sense warned him what was about to happen. But he made no move to fend against the onslaught.

With a fatalistic acceptance, he knew was going to die. But he wanted it that way. He accepted it as punishment for his part in the murder of the only woman he ever loved...and the daughter he never knew they shared.

Frank had lied to Shamus. He didn't possess telepathic abilities. He couldn't mentally contact the warden—or anyone else. But he knew the screams would attract the guards. They would break down the door and find Shamus Riley standing over the bloody body of a man he had brutally beaten to death with his own hands.

There would be no hiding his involvement this time. He would pay for what he had done. And no level of artificially-enhanced speed and strength would save him from the deep corner of burning hell reserved just for him.

Through the numbing darkness that overwhelmed him, Frank asked Caitlin and Maria for their forgiveness. Then he let death take him, knowing retribution would be served for both Shamus—and himself.

The gods of justice would be satisfied.

Neutral Ground

Jordan Taylor

SOME MEN SAY there's an army in No Man's Land.

You can see them often—a shadow passing before the moon, a glint of bayonet steel in the glow of a Very light. You can hear them—snap of a twig, shifting earth under boots, whispers in the dark. A whole camp of soldiers wait out there, dug in, hidden in shell-holes and behind splintered trees, blending with a million corpses. Allies and Germans cast aside differences once they reach these hidden trenches. They drop their rifles, shake hands, wait the generals out. They keep stores of bacon and corned beef, jam, bread, chocolate, butter, and always a good stock of cigarettes and water—water they nick from headquarters in rum jars instead of old petrol tins, which is what we have to drink from at the front.

So the men say. An army of rebels, biding their time, watching us— back and forth between the German line to the east and the English line to the west.

But I have never seen them. Never heard a whisper on the breeze that I could not pin on the enemy line, or our own lads swearing as they dropped a duckboard on their feet. Never found a rum jar or tin of jam out there either. I've been on enough patrols, raids, and wire cutting excursions that I should have been the first to spot them.

The war has been going on a long time now. Too long. In 1914, everyone said it would be over by Christmas. By 1916, everyone wanted to know *which* Christmas. Now, three Christmases have come and gone.

A foot of churned snow, black with mud, red with blood, shrouds the ground. Some nights it gets too cold on watch to feel your hands or feet or face. You can lose track of your body in the cold: nothing but eyeballs floating in the dark at the top of the ladder.

The night was dead quiet—dead still, dead cold—when I saw a man walking upright, carrying something heavy over his shoulder, hunched forward, moving with purpose. As he walked closer and closer, my fingers clutched my rifle painfully tight and my heart smashed into my throat with paralyzing fear for him. No one walks upright through No Man's Land. You crouch, you crawl, you hide in shell-holes. You do not stride over the ground as though no bullet can hurt you and no man is your enemy.

The man stepped to the edge of the trench, thirty feet south of me, bent down, and let a body slide off his shoulder onto snow and frozen mud and sandbags. He straightened, looked at me, tipped his steel helmet—an English helmet—then walked away.

My eyes flicked to the body sprawled at the top of the trench. I looked for the man who left him. He was gone. I squinted and strained my eyes in darkness. No shape or movement.

I leapt from the ladder and ran through the traverse of trench to the spot where the man had been dropped

"Corporal?" Private Stewart said as I rushed past.

I climbed the ladder where I judged the body to be, squinting left and right over sandbags at the top. He lay two feet to my left, stretched out like any other corpse, helmet gone, mouth open, face darkly streaked. I moved another step up, leaned out, seized the man's tunic sleeves, and pulled.

After a minute of heaving, pressed back against the trench wall, throwing everything I had into those sleeves, I paused, gasping. Shivering in the cold, but with sweat on my forehead, I cursed under my breath and eased the rest of the way out of the trench, over sandbags, onto frozen mud.

"Corporal!" The snarl of Sergeant Ainscow. "What the hell do you think you're playing at?"

Flat against ice, speaking in a raspy whisper, heart pounding as I silently prayed Fritz would not choose that moment to send up a Very light, I glanced into the trench. "There's a man up here, Sergeant."

A stir below, whispers, several privates were on the spot now, watching in the dark.

"One of our men?" he asked.

"I think so. Stewart, come up here."

Private Stewart, nimble as a cat and fast as an adder, reached the top of the ladder in a second and leaned out to see the body. "Blimey," he whispered. "You don't think it's Camway?"

The murmuring grew louder below us: "Camway?" "He's dead." "How'd he get there?" "What happened?"

The sergeant hushed them with a hiss. "Richards, take up the watch. Greenwell, alert the stretcher bearers."

I crawled to the man's legs, heart in throat. "Get hold of his arms and pull," I whispered to Stewart.

He reached out. I grabbed the legs and heard a far off pop, a rush and whistle, and a brilliant, eerie, white light burst over No Man's Land. Silence and stillness fell at once. Every man, even those safe in the trench, seemed to hold his breath. Blood surged through my veins with the rush of terror. I stared into Stewart's round, gray eyes, wide with fear. We did not move, not a finger.

If you move under the midday glow of a Very light, Fritz sees you. If Fritz sees you, his snipers see you. If his snipers see you, you die.

Another minute passed before the flare faded. Stewart and I sucked in deep, desperate breaths as one, panting, rushing to push and pull the man into our trench.

Men stepped forward to help Stewart lift the body down to the trench floor of snow, ice, frozen muck, and duckboards. Greenwell ran up with Private Bryant and a stretcher as I inched down the ladder, shaking and panting. They laid the body out on it and someone struck a match. The pale face was caked in blood, which matted down ginger hair in black patches and streaks.

"It *is* Camway." Stewart breathed the words like a sigh.

Bryant pulled off his helmet and pressed his ear to the man's chest, one hand going over Camway's mouth at the same time.

"Well?" the sergeant snapped.

After a pause, Bryant said, "He's alive."

"Bleedin' 'ell," Greenwell whispered. "Been out two nights. Thought 'e was rat rations."

Sergeant Ainscow turned to him. "Bryant, Greenwell, get him to the dressing station."

They gripped wooden stretcher handles and hurried Camway down the dark communication trench leading west to the second line.

The sergeant turned to me. "What happened, Corporal?"

"I...don't know." I looked up at the trench wall and open sky. "I was on watch and I...saw him there."

"You think he crawled there on his own? And passed out?"

"I don't see how else he could have got there."

The sergeant nodded, also looking up toward sky and sandbags. "Lance Corporal Dillard says they were nearer the Hun side when Camway was hit two nights ago. They've already reported him as dead."

"Might be too soon to tell anyway."

He sighed. "You better report to Lieutenant Patterson right away.

Richards will cover your watch."

I made my way to the lieutenant's dugout with no clear idea what to say, other than what I told the sergeant—not wishing to be demoted back to private or reported as delusional.

The next day, we were pulled back into reserve trenches—four hundred yards from the front and a comfortable breather from snipers and Very lights. I went to see Camway in the Red Cross hospital, uncomfortably aware that I had never previously spared him the time of day. He was an enthusiastic youth from Canterbury who received weekly parcels of chocolates or socks or a wool scarf and homemade tarts from his mother. He volunteered for every job—raids, scouting, watch—despite being kicked in the shin or hissed at by the other lads. Camway never seemed to understand that raising one's hand went out of fashion the moment you took the King's shilling.

You never know what you'll meet in hospital. No legs? No arms? No jaw? Rotten, stinking gangrene leaving a body bloated and green with in-fection, your blood on fire and a thirst like acid in your throat?

I took a deep breath and stepped into the ward. Camway leaned back in bed with a tray in his lap and his un-bandaged left arm lifting a spoon of porridge clumsily to his mouth. His bed was last in a row, closest to the door and wall.

He looked up and smiled. "Morning, Corporal. I understand I have a lot to thank you for." His head was wrapped in white gauze. He beamed at me like I was his brother. His cheeks and nose were red, but it looked as though he had escaped without frostbite since they weren't black.

As I approached his bed, he set down the spoon and held his hand out. I met it with my left and shook it.

"You'll be my mum's hero now." He indicated a spindly chair. "They'd been just about to send out the death notice, but stopped in time."

I sat down with my shoulders stiff, as if in the presence of an officer. "I'm glad she didn't have to go through that."

Camway nodded as he ate, still smiling. "Best bit is, they tell me I got a Blighty."

"Congratulations. You'll get to see her then?"

"That I will. Wish they'd let me go into Dover, but even if it's Southampton, that's not so far."

"Great." I realized my eyes were fixed on his aluminum porridge bowl and shifted them around the room.

"Something wrong, Corporal?"

I looked at him. "What happened out there?"

Camway furrowed his brows. "Well now...I can't really remember. I remember getting hit. It was hellish cold and dark. But that's about it."

"That's all?"

Camway shrugged. "Sorry, Corporal."

I looked away down the row of beds, all full. Always full.

"James said you spotted me at the top of the trench and brought me in. I suppose I must have crawled along and been bloody lucky enough to go the right way."

"You didn't crawl in. Someone carried you."

"What?"

I glanced back at him. His spoon lay forgotten in the porridge. "I saw someone carry you in."

"A stretcher bearer?"

"No. He just walked up, set you down, walked off. It didn't...." I trailed off, rubbing my forehead. "I've never seen anything like it. We didn't have patrols out that night. No one in our company was out. I don't know who it was."

Camway's eyes were sparkling now, alight with interest. "You reckon it was one of them? One of them chaps who lives in the middle? The army in No Man's Land?"

I gave him a stern look and Camway subsided back to eating.

"You're the one saying you couldn't explain who he was. Unless he was a ghost, he's got to be someone." Camway paused, chewing the last few bites. "You reckon he's touched in the head? Shell shock? Wandered away from another battalion and going around in the open 'cause he doesn't know what's what?"

I leaned forward in the chair and rubbed my eyes. "I don't know. I thought about that. But men I've seen with it weren't usually right enough in the head to walk around so clear and calm. And how'd he know you were alive at all? He had a mind to check you were living before he carried you a hundred yards in. If he'd been a lunatic, why wouldn't he have brought in corpses?"

Camway scraped out his bowl and leaned back on the thin pillow. "Just glad he was out there, whoever he was."

That same night, I overheard men from Section Two as they heated a Maconochie hotpot on a copper brazier: "Did you hear what happened to Lieutenant Evans?"

"From D Company?"

"That's him."

"What happened?"

"Led the last raiding party and they got him. They said he was dead. An hour later, Kimble is on watch and he sees a man coming in, hunched over, carrying a body. Kimble's scared 'cause the bloke's just walking out there between him and Fritz. But it's dark and maybe Fritz's watch is dozing or some'it. Bloke walks right up to the line and lays the body down and leaves."

"What? Back into No Man's Land?"

"That's it."

"He's imagining it."

"He swears it's true. You ask him."

"You're winding us up, Marty."

"I'm telling you. You should have seen the look on Kimble's face. White as me mum's bread pudding."

A couple of the men snorted. Then, "What'd Lieutenant Evans say about it?"

Marty shrugged. "Don't know, do I? Reckon you'd have to ask him."

I longed to ask Lieutenant Evans myself, but we were in different companies. I had only seen him in passing and had no time for social calls.

We did hours of repair work that night; carrying sandbags and duckboards up the line, digging out shelled communication trenches, and filling new sandbags with clay until dawn. All the time, my mind remained on the man from No Man's Land, yet I could not bring myself to mention him to my comrades. If it got around that I'd suddenly gone superstitious, or worse, lost my nerve, it wouldn't look well for me.

We spent a fortnight in reserves, then back for another stretch in the front line. All this time, I kept hearing stories:

A private in another battalion had been pulled from drowning in the mud far north on the Ypres line. His savior vanished before the private got a clear look at him. Another was carried in all the way to the dressing station after a shelling in which half his platoon were killed. The man had laid down the bleeding soldier and walked away without a word. No one knew who he was. A medical officer was caught in another shelling, this time south of our line, and thrown into a shell-hole with two broken legs. When he woke, he was in hospital, though no one knew how he could possibly have gotten there and no one had seen another bring him in.

In one story, the stranger would be an officer. In another, a private.

Stories trickled up from French soldiers to the south. A Canadian told Richards one of their company had been saved by a stranger in Canadian uniform. Sometimes he was not a soldier at all, but a civilian. Sometimes he was a ghost. The unvarying thread of the tales was that no one ever knew for sure.

Back up the line, on a night so cold the mud under your boots would not bend, and the filthy, standing water at the bottoms of shell-holes was solid all the way to the ground, I led a raid across No Man's Land. I had done it before, but that did not keep my heart from pounding away in my throat like a live creature hammering to get out of an iron crate.

I saluted Lieutenant Patterson and led my men up the trench ladder with fog from my breath clinging about my face like a veil. The crawl across No Man's Land in the icy still of the night, with only far-off shells to dull the silence, seemed to go on for several miles. In truth, we had two hundred yards between ours and the enemy's front line trench.

We made it almost the full two hundred, close enough to hear muffled German voices, smell cigarette smoke, see a dim glow from a brazier far below in the earth. Then something exploded. A roar and wave of sound and heat and light filled my eyes, ears, mind, throwing me back like a toy boat in a wild river as heat and flying metal blasted into me.

I heard Richards give a muffled cry beside me. Ross scrabbled for his rifle but Stewart gripped his arm and dragged him back. Time to go. But I did not get a chance to order any retirement. I heard the bursting rattle of German machine guns, shouting voices. Metal and flame sprayed into our faces like a hailstorm. Pain like burning oil spread from my chest to engulf me.

Then cold. Cold and dark and still.

I opened my eyes to see dots of light over a black curtain. They swirled and twisted together, merging into shapes and patterns. I blinked. The light dots solidified into stars, high above in a still, dark sky. No clouds. No rain. Much too cold for rain. I watched my breath form heavy shrouds as I lay on my back. Breathing. Still breathing. How could that be? I listened, waiting for shells, waiting for bullets, waiting for shrapnel.

The ground beneath my body shook in a constant, steady rhythm, like a river always rushing. But the roars and rumbles, the cause of the shaking, all came from so very far away, so far. Miles to the north and south. My part of the line was dead quiet. Dead.

I waited, closed my eyes. Nothing happened. I could feel no part of my body other than my face, which seemed to have working eyes and nose and ears and mouth. I turned my head slightly to the right, saw the lip of the shell-hole I lay in. A shell-hole. That's why I was alive. I fell and no one had found me yet. Then...maybe I wasn't dying at all. My nose stung and the liquid in my eyes burned with the cold air trying to freeze it. No wonder I could not feel the rest of my body.

An outline appeared out of darkness—a black shape against the stars. I held my breath, fear bringing some sensation surging back into my frozen fingers as blood pumped faster. The man stood, apparently looking at me. I had not heard the snap of ice to signal his approach. Nor did he crouch low as any sensible soldier would.

The figure vanished. It seemed as though I were staring right at the spot when he went, but perhaps I blinked. Perhaps my eyes played tricks on me in the dark.

I allowed one slow, shallow breath, then another, my eyes still trained on the spot where the man had stood.

A tiny ball of flame burst into life five feet in front of me and a silver trench lighter illuminated the face of a man in uniform. Had I been well and with the full use of my lungs, out of this deathly cold, I am sure I would have screamed. But my body seemed unable to make the sound. My mouth opened and the breath shot from icy lungs in a gasp as though I had received a blow. My body jerked back into frozen mud, away from that flame, and my heart seemed almost to leap through my gaping mouth.

He sank to a kneeling position, holding the light out to study me. He wore no helmet, but an officer's cap and greatcoat. An English officer.

Closer to fainting than screaming, I gasped for breath as I stared into the long, lean face with the trimmed mustache and dark, concerned eyes.

"Corporal?" He spoke in a hesitant tone, telling me he had been as unsure of my identity as I was of his.

"Yes, sir." My voice was a rasp, harsh and grating as a rusted wheel. "I...don't remember how I got here. Do you know what happened, sir?"

He sat back on frozen mud as the lighter went out. "There was an attack on your party."

Of course there was an attack. I had got that far on my own. I closed my eyes, taking deep breaths, which seemed not to go at all deep. My body shook, yet I still could not feel it properly.

"I'm sorry you were hurt," he said.

I stared at him in the dark—able to see only an outline as he lifted the cap from his head and wearily ran a hand over his hair before replacing it.

Fear returned. Though I hadn't the faintest idea who he was, he didn't need to say more to tell me he was not in his right mind. The man must have shell shock. An officer would not speak to me like this otherwise.

"That's, uh, that's all right, sir," I stammered.

He looked at me. "I got Richards back."

"What? You got back? Back to our line? What the—I mean, what, sir, are you doing back out here then?"

His head tilted back and he gazed at the stars. I watched silver fog form around his face, fade, then form again.

"I'm sorry, Corporal."

If my blood wasn't chilled enough already.... "Sir, did you see Stewart and Ross? Are they all right?"

"I hope so. Richards was bleeding a great deal, but they should be able to stop that." He looked down and rubbed the bridge of his nose with thumb and forefinger. "They just can't do much, can they? That's what makes it so terrible." He laughed, a bitter, harsh sound, more like a cough. "No, that's not what makes it so terrible. Just part of the list, right? Just one long part of a bloody long list." He looked at me, as though expecting me to answer the question.

"Sir, do you think we could make it back to the line? Do you know how far we are?"

He stared at me for a moment and I wished I could see his face rather than just an outline. "I'm sorry I couldn't help Holmes. Or Kelly." He paused, looking down, then at me again. The tone became desperate, pleading, as though begging me to understand. "I can't help them all. I would if I could. You have to believe that. I'm so sorry."

His voice was strained. I thought he might sob. But he only sat very still in the dark, his face turned upward.

Then I knew. I knew who he was, yet didn't know at the same time. "There is an army out here...." I whispered the words without meaning to say them at all.

He looked at me.

"You...you...live out here. You're the one who's been...bringing them in. Or...all of you?" I glanced around, seeing only the dark shell-hole and the shadow of the man before me, but feeling as though I might see that ghostly army of No Man's Land climbing from frozen ground all around at any moment. "Are there more of you then? Is it really a whole army?" I forced my voice into some semblance of calm, though I felt sure I wasn't fooling anyone.

"What?" he asked after a pause. "No one's with me."

"You're alone out here? But surely you can't have done all those things. I've heard stories."

I watched the outline of his head nodding in the dark. "That was me, I expect. I'm the only one." He broke off and dropped his head in his hands. "*God*, why did I get myself into this." His voice had gone harsh and bitter, each word sharp and gasping as though he could not get his breath.

"You carried in Camway?"

He rocked forward, clutching his hair, cap falling to frozen ground. "I'm sorry, Algen. I'm sorry. Please, take me back. *Please.*" The last word was a whisper, a soft, desperate hiss, almost of pain.

I tried to swallow, but my tongue seemed to be fixed to the roof of my mouth as if tacked there. How he could cover so much ground so quickly, I did not know, but I understood now why he walked upright through No Man's Land: he was mad.

Minutes passed before he sat back and gazed once more at the sky. He took a deep, slow breath. "Yes. I brought in Camway. And Vaughan and Köhler and Evans and Chambers and Rameau and Huber and Fitzpatrick and Lehmann and McAdams and Cousteau and Gérard." He sighed and rubbed a hand once more over his eyes.

I watched him, the names running through my mind. "All sides? But you're...you're bringing in wounded from...everyone?"

"That's stretching the matter a bit far." He looked at me. "Not *everyone*. Just from all you stupid sods in the Allied and Central Powers' armies fighting on this damn front. Algen told me to stay on neutral ground. But he didn't have to tell me. What's the point of sides?"

"Right...well...do you think...? I'm one of those stupid sods who's wounded out here...."

I thought I saw him smile in the darkness. "I'm sorry. I wish I could help you."

"You can't?"

He shook his head.

"Who are you?"

He sighed, long and slow. "Who am I not?" He lifted the silver lighter in his right hand and flicked it on.

I blinked in the glare of flame and stared into his lean face. Straight nose and boney jaw, dark hair and eyes. Then the face changed. Not all at once, but almost in an instant. A quick shifting, compression of features. The mustache vanished. The dark hair lightened and grew out longer than

116

before. The nose bent as though from an old break. The greatcoat vanished, replaced by the uniform of a Highland soldier complete with kilt and soft Tam o'Shanter cap draping over the right temple.

I had never hallucinated before. But I heard others speak of it enough times to understand what was happening. It would be the cold. The shock of what had just happened. Perhaps I had lost a bit of blood, though I could not feel any wounds in my numb body.

The man glanced down at his own chest and legs with pale eyes, perhaps blue though it was hard to tell in the small, flickering light. "Bonny outfit this," he said with interest. "Wee bit chilly though."

The face shifted again. The khaki tunic was replaced by a long, heavy, gray coat. The kilt became thick, black trousers stuffed into tall, black boots. The Tam o'Shanter morphed into a Stahlhelm.

He smiled at me, showing even teeth in the smooth, handsome face of a young man Camway's age. "*Ist das besser?*"

I stared at him, wondering how my hallucinating brain could produce German when I did not speak it.

The lighter went out. In near darkness, I watched as he pulled the steel helmet from his head. "Nice design to these," he said in English, though with a German accent. "Much better than those flying saucers you Tommies wear." He looked at me. "Are you scared?"

"No."

"You don't believe this is happening, do you?"

"No."

He replaced the helmet on his head, then drew up his knees and rested his chin on them, wrapping his arms around his legs.

"Who are you?"

"Oh, I see you don't think that's been settled?"

"No."

I saw the whites of his eyes glint in starlight as he rolled them upward to study the heavens. "I can be whoever and wherever I want to be. I'm good with danger—like feeling when someone's watching me, you know? If I feel a sniper's got me spotted, I can shift a hundred yards away. Can't carry anyone with me when I shift, but you learn to drop soldiers and scram out of places pretty fast. That's why Algen sent me. He said I could help if I didn't do anything too stupid. Well...that's not the only reason he sent me."

He sighed and his eyes came down to settle on me. "I...was upset. Algen has two new students and I...well...was showing off a bit, I guess.

But that doesn't matter," he added the last in a rush. "We're all supposed to work together back home. He doesn't think I respect the others. He wanted to teach me a lesson. He did. Trouble is, I can't get home. I was supposed to have already been brought back. But...here I am."

I smiled, doubtless in a patronizing manner, but what could a hallucination see in the dark anyway? "Why don't you just fly home?"

He laughed, a soft, light sound that startled me. It sounded so...human. So real. "I can't fly. But it wouldn't help anyway. I told you: I can be wherever I want to be." He vanished. "See?"

I jumped and gasped. He was sitting right beside me, his face not two feet from mine, smiling at me.

"How do you think I knew who you were?" Again, he vanished.

I gave only a small start this time before turning my head to see he was now on my left.

"I haven't been living all this time out here in the middle. I've been in and out of the trenches with you fellows. But that's not the trouble, like I said. Yes, I can appear as anyone I wish, and be anywhere I wish. But I cannot be any *when* I wish."

"When?"

"This is not my time."

I said nothing. There was something wrong here. If this man was a hallucination, how had he saved the lives of all those soldiers? That had not come from my brain.

"Algen sent me. He's the only one with the power to manipulate time, and he almost never does. It's a dangerous thing to play around with. Something's gone wrong, or he'd have me back by now."

"Oh."

"Algen's our mentor. He finds us and teaches us how to harness our gifts. I do know one person who can fly." He smiled at me. "We do all sorts of things. I'm not supposed to tell anyone who I am of course, but...." He trailed off, his eyes on my chest. "I'm sorry. I wish I could help you. That's why I'm here. I mean, I guess that's why I'm here. Algen didn't say. Only, at home, in my time, which is a long way in the future compared to your time, that's what he trains us to do. We have our own wars where I come from." He closed his eyes and his chin dropped to his chest. "But not like this. I've never seen anything like this. So many miles of blood."

We sat in silence for a long time. At last, I said, in little more than a whisper. "Take me back."

He looked at me.

"Please. Take me back to the line. I can't feel anything. If I try, they'll see me."

"I'm sorry."

Anger flared through my chest, almost warming for a moment. "Why the hell do you keep saying that?"

He gazed at me for a long time, then lifted the lighter and flicked it on with a click and sudden blaze of heat. He held it out, low, over my tunic. I looked down. My chest was a black hole of scorched flesh and clotted blood matting down shreds only of tunic and gray shirt. The webbing that always hung across my shoulders seemed to have been blown clean away. Farther down, past a frayed edge of khaki cloth, both legs were so shattered and blackened, they scarcely looked like human legs at all. But the blood flowed out slowly, very slowly in the cold, despite the many places it had to flow from, giving me extra minutes to live.

I looked up into his sad, brown eyes, blinking slowly at me under the Stahlhelm. "That's why I'm sorry," he whispered.

"I see." My mouth felt so dry it seemed more than blood flowed away from me.

The lighter went out. He sat back beside me.

"Well," I started, but paused as the faces of my family rushed through my mind—my mother and father, waiting for the next letter, Edith and Mary, helping in the store with all the lads gone. I hoped they never found out how it happened. I hoped they thought I was surrounded by friends and it was all very quick.

"Well," I tried again. "I hope you get home."

"Me too."

"I never thought I'd spend my last moments with a phantom German in the bottom of a frozen shell-hole."

He rubbed his chin. "You want to see what I really look like? I'm not supposed to change into the real me either, but...." He shrugged.

I watched as he lit the trench lighter once more and held it out so I could see him. He sat very still, gazing at his knees, then looked sharply at me, as though seized by a sudden idea.

"Is there anything I could do for you?" he asked. "I mean, there's nothing they could do"—he jerked his head to the west—"even if I got you to them. But if there's anything else, I'll do it."

"Why?"

"Because I hate that this is happening to you."

I looked into his eyes in the guttering glow of the flame. Tears glinted there that did not fall.

"All of you," he added in a whisper.

"Are you real?"

"Yes."

I swallowed. "Can you go anywhere?"

"Yes."

"Go to my family. Tell me if they're well. What they're doing."

"Where will I find them?"

"Number five, East Doyle Road, Woking, Surrey."

He nodded, tried a brief smile. "Back in a bit."

The lighter went out and the man vanished. I sat still against the wall of the shell-hole, listening to faraway shelling, feeling nothing in my body, and too much in my mind. I looked up at the stars, which seemed to be merging together, as they had when I first opened my eyes down in this grave, and wished I could be seeing the faces of my family instead.

The stars were no more than streaks and smears of light in the darkness now. I could not even feel my eyelids blink, though I knew they did it from tiny moments of blackness.

Something beside me made a noise of cracking ice. A lighter blazed into life. A young man with cheeks flushed by the cold and sparkling gray eyes looked down at me. He wore the khaki tunic and round helmet of thousands of other British privates.

"A woman sitting in an upholstered chair by the fire," he said. "Knitting a long wool scarf, very nice for a night like this. A man smoking a pipe as he reads war news from the *Times*. Two girls, nearly grown, playing with a gramophone, tapping their toes and singing along. The man smiles at them now and then over the paper."

My eyes burned, but if a tear fell from them I could not feel it.

"I wish I could do more for you, Corporal." His flushed face was anxious, strained and worried as he gazed into my eyes. "I'm sorry."

I closed my eyes, smiled. "No need to be sorry." I opened them. "You said you'd show me what you really look like. Is this it?"

He chuckled. The face shifted and changed. The helmet disappeared. The hair shot outward from the head until it fell past the shoulders in a silky curtain on each side of the delicate face, with a small mouth, pointed nose, and large, green eyes. The uniform was replaced by a violet sweater and tight, dark blue trousers made of some heavy material like canvas.

She reached out to touch my face. I saw the slender arm and long fingers, but could not feel them touch my skin. "I wish Algen sent a healer instead of me. I'm useless out here."

I stared into her face, absorbing the voice slowly, as though hearing it from far away. "You're American."

"Yes. But Algen finds us all over the world."

"You're...." My eyes flicked up and down her body in the dim light.

"Yes, that too." She smiled sadly at me. "Your family will be all right."

I nodded slowly.

She withdrew her hand, sat back on her heels, eyes on the ice of the shell-hole bottom.

"You weren't useless," I murmured. "What about Camway? And Lieutenant Evans? All the others?" She looked up at me and I closed my eyes. "And me."

As if from a great distance, I heard the rushing sound of wind slice through the shell-hole. I opened my eyes to see the young woman standing before me, illuminated with some strange glow beyond the feeble lighter. The light seemed to come from her own body. Her face was transfixed by joy, smiling dazzlingly as she looked down at me.

"Goodbye, Corporal. It will all be over sooner than you think. Wars don't last forever."

She was fading before my eyes. Or was it me who was fading? Drifting farther and farther away, heart so slow, it seemed to beat only at random moments. *Long way in the future. In the future.* The words hammered in my ears as though for the first time.

"Wait!" My eyes snapped open. "Who wins?"

Her eyes grew sad again and she shook her head. "No one wins in war. Least of all this one."

"Do we win?"

She smiled a little smile as she faded away to shadows. "Neutral ground, remember?"

"Please, please, just answer me."

Her last word sounded like the breath of a sleeping child, soft and endless: "Yes."

I closed my eyes. The light was gone—all sound and sight and smell. But I smiled and whispered, "Thank you."

Breaking The Circle

Derek Tyler Attico

A HELPLESS SPECTATOR, I watch as with a flick of the wrist the Beast sends a city bus airborne, arching through the air faster than anything that large without wings is meant to go. It hurtles towards the hero of New York, towards the Vitruvian, Christopher Kincaid, my husband.

Everything around me seems to slow down; I catch a glimpse of some of the people inside. An old woman, a businessman, kids pressed up against the windows like spectators on some macabre amusement park ride—their faces drenched in fear, their screams imprisoned within the plexi-glass windows they once used to look out onto the world.

I see Chris, the Vitruvian, his face reflecting their desperation as the bus rushes towards him. But he doesn't even flinch as the fifteen-ton monstrosity bears down on him. Like a priest welcoming sinners he extends his arms to embrace the makeshift missile and I watch as flesh and bone rush into the metal and glass of the vehicle, taking hold, taking command.

I feel the raw power as the bus slams into him, but he's holding it as effortlessly as I would a chair; only his cape stirs as if caught in a breeze.

To everyone watching it's a superhuman feat, but I know it's the inertial dampeners in his fingertips. The crowd goes wild with cheers and applause punctuating the moment, and that's when it happens. In a blur of motion an SUV slams into the bus and instantly the trio are consumed in a vortex of flame, debris and chaos.

Then I hear a sickly wet gurgling sound, drowning out everything else. Eyes aflame with some untold force that refuses to be contained within its monstrous shell, its maw open wide, tendrils of raw energy cascading off of what must be dozens of fangs; the Fenris Beast.

It's beating its fur-covered chest in triumph. That's when I realize, the sound it's making...it's laughing.

Like a perverse tennis death match the crowd turns back to see that the explosion has knocked the Vitruvian into a hole in the wall that ten seconds ago was the Coffee House behind him. For a moment everything goes quiet except for the flames licking at the side of the Chrysler Building and the shrieking car alarms along Lexington Avenue. The smoke coming out of the hole fills the air with a putrid combination of coffee and burning flesh.

The Vitruvian steps out of what used to be the corner of 43rd and Lex. There's nothing left of the SUV, bus or the decimated coffee shop except for the blood on his uniform of the people he just tried to save. My husband glares at the Fenris Beast and I find myself sharing in his pain for the lives the monster has taken. But I know his glare is more than just anger: behind his pupils solar collectors are amassing the power of a sun and the fury of one man.

Without any other warning, the demon bursts into flames. I expect it to cry out in agony, but in two steps it's across the street, its energy tipped prehensile tail wrapping around the Vitruvian's throat.

The creature is so massive next to my hero, the Vitruvian's brown face seems to be a diminishing blot against an avalanche of white fur. I can't ignore the contrast not only of color, but also of despair trying to eclipse hope. But the protector of New York doesn't miss a beat in this overture of good versus evil. With every blow, windows capitulate to the shockwaves created by the Vitruvian's fists of steel.

His eyes go nova and burn through the serpent's tail. This time the creature howls as it bleeds raw energy. Retaliation comes a millisecond later as its talons rake across the hero's chest in an arc of crimson and for the first time we all see the unimaginable: the Vitruvian, bleeding.

I know if Chris falls New York is doomed.

The sight of blood has unhinged the demon. Pressing the attack it sinks its fangs deep into the Vitruvian's shoulder as it searches for what has eluded it until now—his cries of agony.

My husband's face says it all. He's faltering, weakening; the beast bares its fangs in a snarl that I swear is a smile.

As retaliation, instead of trying to rip its head off, Chris places his hand behind the beast's neck tenderly, gently, and almost in a lover's embrace leans in and says something to the monster. Then, in a motion nearly faster than the eye can follow, he body slams the Fenris Beast through concrete and steel, through power-lines and subway tunnels into the bowls of the city.

I try to scream, but can't. I'm falling into a cacophony of horror—without a foundation the Chrysler Building is imploding. In a panic I reach out for something, anything that will save me. But it's no use. I'm a speck caught up in a maelstrom of falling glass and steel. As the darkness rushes in to claim me, I don't hear the sirens or the cries for help; I don't feel the heat from the fires raging out of control or taste the blood in my mouth. The only thing I can focus on, the only thing in my head or on my heart is that I'll never get the chance to tell my husband about the precious life inside me.

The lighthouse was like none other in existence. Instead of sitting on a hazardous coastline, an ever vigilant sentinel ushering ships to safety, this one resided two hundred feet underground. The light from its two-story wall length lens peered not through a sea of darkness, but into the deeper oceans of time.

Yet the temporal lens-wall wasn't just for viewing; with the right spatial geometry, access to the past was possible across the space-time continuum. The power needed to achieve this god-like feat didn't come from a string of super computers or a fission reactor, but from a chair whose sole source of power was a man.

Forefather could feel the energy coursing through him; he gripped the armrests desperate to hold onto this moment he'd captured—and his sanity. Whispering was almost too much for him to bear as he fought to keep his concentration. "Report."

The young woman at the console behind him didn't have time to look up at the lens-wall or react to the mix of strain and desperation in Forefather's voice. "Maser pulse canon missed both targets, damaged superstructure behind them. Temporal lensing stable, fifteen arcseconds to weapon realignment."

The gravity of Reverse Engineer Pope's words reached through the ocean of agony Forefather was drowning in. He'd never held the past open this long before. "I can't hold it."

The woman glanced at the console scanning Forefather. The epidural hematoma forming in his brain agreed with him. "Hold on, Forefather, we're almost there. Realignment in ten arcseconds!"

Through a haze of near madness, Forefather watched the images on the lens-wall without blinking; he knew he couldn't afford the luxury and the rings he'd strapped over his eyes made sure he wouldn't. He watched the Vitruvian and Fenris Beast play out their dance macabre. Now if he could just hold on, he could end their miserable existence from all time once and for all.

Slowly, he felt the tickle of something wet along his ear. He knew it was what he was already tasting in his mouth: blood. Suddenly the images on the lens began to dim, and then, without warning, the lens was clear, the images gone. A long silence passed. When Forefather finally spoke it was more to himself than anyone else. "I couldn't hold it."

How long had the two of them been at this since they lost the rest of the team? Weeks? Months? Engineer Pope knew that to leave this facility meant certain death. But more importantly, she knew she was his last tether to humanity and quite possibly sanity.

"You can't keep this up, Forefather. Opening the past is too much, even for you. This machine you created is killing you. According to my analysis you can do this three, maybe four more times before your brain suffers a massive cerebral haemorrhage. And we still haven't achieved our objective; we just hit the Chrysler Building—over eleven thousand people are dead."

The Engineer was right. Forefather did feel like he was dying. But it wasn't the machine that was killing him; it was the choices that he'd made. "I'm not interested in eleven thousand deaths, I just need to kill two." The look on the Engineer's face told him she still had a soul. But for him, a soul, like blinking, was another luxury he couldn't afford. "Although, you may have a point. I believe a change in tactics is warranted. Take the package out of stasis and prepare it for delivery."

The young woman left the enclosed confines of the console to face her mentor. "Unleashing the package on New York may achieve our objective, sir, but you'd be condemning a city, perhaps the entire United States, to a life of complete slavery."

Forefather thought about the engineer's words as he juxtaposed them against the reality of the world he now lived in, forged from the choices he'd made. Under a pack of gray hair his weary unblinking cobalt eyes captured her in his gaze. "I can live with that."

Everything is a haze. My living room is in near darkness. Light from the television paints shadow demons on the walls around me, laughing at me, taunting me. The reporter says it's been eight days since the world has been turned upside down, but I'm not sure how that's possible. I don't understand what happened. I don't even remember how I made it home.

I can't stay away from the TV, hoping the footage of what the media is collectively calling the "Battle for Manhattan" will give me the answers I don't have. I'm a slave to every special report, every piece of breaking news, but it's become a feeding frenzy of reports and interviews as the press turn panic and fear into points and profits.

I just want to know where my husband is.

He's alive, he has to be.

There's a daily television show called *HERO-WATCH* where the pundits spew guesses stacked on top of conjecture. Some of them are actually suggesting Chris staged all this to show the world just how badly it needs the Vitruvian.

When I first met Doctor Christopher Kincaid he was doing what doctors do: healing people, helping them, putting others before himself. But his life changed forever when he learned a group of scientists from the future called the Reverse Engineers were experimenting on his patients. To stop the Engineers, he did the unimaginable: he injected himself with their own nanotechnology. The nanoscopic machines endowed him with incredible superhuman powers that enabled him to ultimately defeat them.

The first time he donned his black and gold uniform and presented himself to the world as the Vitruvian, a reporter asked him why he chose that name. He just flashed that charming smile of his and said "Superman was already taken."

It had actually been my idea to embrace the name of the drawing created hundreds of years ago by Leonardo Da Vinci. I felt he should wear a version of the image on his chest because it represented the *ideal man.* I knew that was how everyone would see him: as perfect—a super man right out of the comic books dedicated to making their lives better; their world brighter.

Not a *super* hero, but a selfless one. That's Chris; it's one of the reasons why I fell in love with him.

He's not dead; he got away at the last second.

That's what I'm praying for. I keep watching the footage and hoping maybe I'll see something I didn't before, something I missed, like the familiar black and gold blur of Chris's costume speeding away at the last instant. Something…anything. But it ends the same every time. He's gone.

For the first time in ten years I'm truly alone.

It took the excavation teams four days to reach the bedrock epicentre of the crater. But when they finally reached it, they didn't find anything—or anyone.

That's because any second he's going to come through the door.

As much as I want to believe that, I know it's not true. The city's in trouble. Even if Chris couldn't be with me, he'd be here for New York.

The Mayor has declared a state of emergency. Riots, civil unrest and crime are on the rise; the delicate tapestry woven out of the safety and security of the Vitruvian's presence is unravelling.

Villains and vigilantes are turning up faster than they can be put down. Every two-bit thug with enough power to call himself a super-villain is making a play for the city. The cyber-armor National Guard is taking care of most of them, but yesterday Lord Malevolence showed up. Six years ago, Chris fought the supernatural villain, but Malevolence vanished in a flash of light before he could be apprehended. Now he's back terrorizing the city.

The Freedom League showed up almost immediately to confront him. Those kids idolize the Vitruvian; always said he was the main reason they came together.

Malevolence killed them all in half an hour.

Ms. Majestic stood up the longest; a full eleven minutes before that fiend used a spell to rip through her armor like it was something a kid would buy in a toy store. The cameras made sure to get a close-up as he held up her spine in triumph like it was a goddamn sceptre.

The Parliamentarian is said to be on her way, but it's rumoured that she's having problems of her own with the London Six. It must be bad, because I didn't think anything would stop her from being here.

The reality is there just aren't that many super-powered people in the world. And most of them aren't using their powers to help people. Super heroes are rare.

The government is vowing to deal with Malevolence, but no one really believes they can. New York is becoming a city falling into darkness; a city without hope. Without any real opposition Malevolence is declaring himself Supreme Ruler of New York. The megalomaniac is even claiming that the Fenris Beast is something he conjured up, that he's responsible for killing the Vitruvian, and he's going to prove it to the entire world tonight where it all happened.

It's not true.

I don't believe it. I don't. But I have to go. I need to see for myself. I need to be sure.

Five blocks from where the Vitruvian vanished, the air takes a bitter turn. It chokes me as I breathe in ash and smoke from the still smouldering implosion site. Pictures of the missing have been wallpapered over shops, bus stops; anything with a flat surface. Even before I turn the corner I know what every New Yorker, what the world knows: the Chrysler Building, Grand Central Terminal, everything that was at 42nd street and Lexington Avenue simply no longer exists.

The military barricade is two blocks from the implosion and the crowd is still larger than I expected. Despite the rantings of a madman, they've shown up. I'm not sure if its morbid curiosity or New York stubbornness. Maybe they feel like I do: if the Vitruvian is going to make his appearance and rescue us from this nightmare—it's going to be here.

The tanks and cyber-armored soldiers around the perimeter of the hole are impressive. The show of strength actually starts to make me feel a little better. But then I see what the crowd, the soldiers, the media, what everyone is staring at—a sphere hovering over the mouth of the implosion site.

And the two forms inside are unmistakable. Lord Malevolence and the Fenris Beast.

Malevolence doesn't even seem to care that every gun for a mile around is trained on him. He's too busy revelling in the moment. There's also a new addition to his cowl and tunic, a cape.

It's the Vitruvian's cape. Chris's cape.

The bastard is sporting it like a trophy. I use to love how majestic it made Chris look. But now, here, twisted like this, the perversity of it sickens me.

That's when I get a better view of the horrid thing that fought my husband to a standstill. Domesticated like a show dog, the Fenris Beast is wearing some kind of glowing collar with a lead connecting it to its self-proclaimed master.

This can't be happening. Could this lunatic have done what so many have failed to do: murder my husband? And did Malevolence create that thing to do it?

"God, Chris, please be here. We need you...*I* need you."

I start to sift through the crowd praying for a glimpse of the man my heart desires, when all of a sudden Malevolence turns around and speaks directly to me.

"Finally. Hello, Kendra Kincaid."

The air around me becomes stale, putrid like it's coming from someplace full of death and decay. Then people start to scream. I see ebony tentacles created by Malevolence coming down the street reaching past—no, *through* the tanks and the people. They eviscerate both man and machine indiscriminately.

My heart starts pounding in my chest, panic grips my lungs. I turn to run but there's just too many people, too much confusion. Over the screams I hear the order given to open fire. The tanks come alive with thunder, but almost immediately the tentacles envelop them into silence. Blood and oil spill out of their broken shells.

A tentacle brushes against my skin—it feels like I'm being bathed in ice. A half second later it explodes in an assault of energy from a weapon being held by an armoured National Guardsman. "Get the hell out of here!" he screams, the speakers in his suit seeming to amplify his fear. Like a man possessed he starts blasting a path for a few others and me. I know I should move like he said, run as far and fast as I can, but everything starts to look different, feel different like I'm viewing the world through a collage of images from some far away place: A woman dragging her severed arm behind her…shells from the tanks exploding harmlessly off of the magical sphere…a wave of soldiers rushing past me towards Malevolence….

The sounds of creaking metal pulls me back into the now. My eyes try to find where it's coming from and then I realize it's coming from all of the soldiers. Their armor is shrinking—but the men inside aren't. Fortunately the squeezed-out pulp they become dies quickly.

Lord Malevolence's laughter erupts from everywhere. "Where is your hero now, New York!"

I trip on a boot and the tentacles wrap around me, envelop me. My muscles stiffen as I feel Malevolence pulling me towards him. A thought later and I'm at his feet. I try to take a breath but it's like trying to breathe through sand.

He turns my head with his boot so we're face to face. "Not as pretty as I expected for the consort of a titan like the Vitruvian," he says. "He must actually have loved you."

The Fenris Beast is crouched over me in complete silence; more puppet than predator. Eyes that were aflame with hunger are now devoid of any life.

I struggle against the arcane bonds but it's hopeless. The obsidian bands are so cold; they're doing something to me. My rattling teeth feel as if they're going to rip right out of my skull. From somewhere deep inside me I know—without understanding—that my soul is being slowly bled out of me.

At that moment I want to do what the Vitruvian vowed never to do. I want to kill Lord Malevolence. I want to scratch his eyes out and watch him suffer for what he's doing to me, to New York, to the memory of my husband. I scream at him but there's so little air left, so little life left, what I say is barely beyond a whisper. "Why?"

He looks down at me; his face submerged in the cowl is slightly illuminated by the glowing runes carved into skin devoid of colour. I can almost taste the contempt in the albino's smile.

"I'll tell you a secret, if you promise not to tell anyone," he says. The magician looks at the demon to his side for a long moment then out onto the chaos and screams and gunfire beyond the magical shield surrounding us. "I didn't think he was dead, not even when I...retired the Freedom League, I just figured he was licking his wounds somewhere." The madman kneels next to me like you would a wounded animal. "But before I take credit for the murder of the millennium, I had to be sure, right?"

The wind blows against us and Chris's cape covers my hand. I manage to grab hold with my thumb and forefinger, but I can't feel it, can't feel anything except the misery in my heart.

"I knew once I set the stage I could use a simple reveal spell to show me the one who loves the Vitruvian," he says. "Not some fan or sicko groupie, but someone he knew and loved intimately. And once I had that person, it would bring the Boy Scout running, even if he was near death."

In a gentle motion Malevolence reaches out and moves away some of my hair that the tentacles pushed into my face. The hatred in his eyes is overwhelming, but what catches my attention is the speck of something far above him in the night sky streaking towards us.

"So my dear, this...*all* of this...was for you." Twin pools of hatred gaze over me in disgust. "It was actually easier to spot you than I thought it'd be. The stink of your love for him is all over you."

High above the city, I watch the speck silently make a turn, lining itself up behind Lord Malevolence.

I can feel the darkness now—pushing in on the edges of my life, dimming everything. I stop struggling against the tentacles.

Malevolence must see it in my eyes because his rotted teeth curl up in an inhuman smile as his charcoal tongue licks pale lips. "Yes, that's it. You feel your death drawing nigh don't you? Your man isn't coming to rescue you. He's dead and you're about to join him. Tell me, how does it feel to die an agonizing, horrible death at the hands of someone you despise?"

The speck is moving faster now, almost here. I try to focus on it, see what, who it is, but I'm slipping too quickly into the void. And then, from somewhere close, yet far off, I hear a voice...a powerful voice. But it isn't speaking to me. It's talking to Malevolence.

And it's answering his question. "You're about to find out."

As I swallow my last gasp of life and the darkness claims me, my bones begin to snap, finally submitting to the twisting and turning of the tentacles. But I can't help smiling. Because Lord Malevolence is screaming.

Forefather slumped back in his chair as the images on the temporal lens-wall faded from view, grains of sand lost in the maelstrom of time. Engineer Pope shut the machine down for what she prayed was the last time. Many believed the machine was a chance for life; she understood its necessity but knew its imperative had always been death.

"The package has been delivered," she said.

Forefather waited a full three seconds before voicing his disgust. "The package failed."

His Temporal protégé keyed up the logs from the machine as she spoke. "Sir, are you certain—"

Impatient with her line of thought, Forefather interrupted. "If Malevolence had killed Vitruvian and the Fenris Beast as I programmed into his subconscious, the last twenty seven years would've unfolded differently." The scientist unstrapped the steel rings from his eyes as he rose from the control chair. "Abduction, nanites, temporal intervention, nothing is working."

Pope finally spoke the words that had been on her mind for an eternity. "The events have already happened; perhaps they can't be stopped from happening."

Forefather turned his back to Pope and stared at the dark lens-wall. "You're suggesting this is some sort of predestination paradox. I won't accept that...I can't."

As the room began to fall into silence the lights abruptly dimmed to emergency levels.

Forefather calmly turned around. "Report."

The young woman's hands raced across the controls, no longer able to hide the stress and fear that was welling within her. "The Fenris Humans...they've found us!"

After everything, it had come down to just the two of them, and now it was clear to Forefather that Engineer Pope was unraveling from it all. For the last seven years he'd worked beside her, her compassion and intelligence had touched him in ways he'd never reveal. How ironic, he thought, a man that can manipulate time couldn't afford any for a luxury like love.

She was the last NASA engineer, the last of his team, and quite possibly the only other non-infected human being on the East Coast. Although he refused to show her love, he realized he needed to show her compassion.

"It's going to be okay, Dianna. We're two hundred feet under the ruins of the Kennedy Space Center. It's probably just another patrol. Run a passive scan."

The gentle tone in Forefather's voice surprised Dianna Pope. As she carried out his order, she felt his words giving her strength...until she read the display. "Oh my God. Scan shows over eight hundred fifty thousand Fenris Humans converging on the Space Center!"

Forefather kept his eyes locked on Pope as he moved quickly to the control chair. "Feed the surveillance grid to the lens-wall. I want to see what's going on up there."

As the lens-wall came to life, hordes of anti-humans filled the screen.

The Fenris Humans were neither creature nor man, but a misshapen ever-changing hybrid of man and monster. One of the cameras focused on a little girl no older than six. One moment her face was full of fangs, the next it was normal. But then her hands became talons. Yet, as the changes continued, her eyes were a constant blood red, the color of the virus that had changed her—and the other infected humans.

Forefather watched as the enemy he'd fought his entire life approached his doorstep. "They must've discovered the microwave amplitude frequency of the Maser. It's the only explanation."

"They're in the old launch silos coming down towards us." It was clear Pope was scared but her voice was steady, no longer shaken. "Should I incinerate the silos, Forefather?"

After a long pause, the time traveler strapped the steel rings back onto his eyes. "No, no. We've lost the war here; it's time to change the battlefield. Set the Maser to overload. Prepare for temporal lensing."

A sliver of sound, a glimmer of light, air rushing into my lungs...and unbelievable pain. That's when I put the pieces together and realize—I'm still alive.

I try to raise my hand to filter out the morning sun, but the cast covering it and the three-alarm fire inside my shoulder protest. A woman in army fatigues with a stethoscope around her neck stares at me. The rank on her sleeve says Lieutenant.

"Take it easy, ma'am," she says. "You've had a traumatic experience."

You have no idea.

"Where am I?" I ask.

The doctor flips through a medical chart as she speaks. "We've evacuated the survivors to the recovery center at Bryant Park."

Survivors. She says the word with regret, but I can still smell the death, still see that rotted smile, feel the tendrils of evil wringing the life out of me. Survivor feels like an exclamation of life. "What happened?"

The young soldier becomes all business and I presume I'm not the first to ask this question. "Intelligence is still coming in, ma'am, but we think a B-2, a stealth bomber, hit the area. Our best guess is when that happened it didn't destroy Lord Malevolence's shield, but it must've broken his control over the Fenris creature. Reports came in that it could be seen through the flames tearing him to shreds. Then we lost track of it."

The predator became the prey; Malevolence must've been so surprised.

"Are you certain it was one of your aircraft? Did anyone see...?" I look away from the soldier, knowing my eyes are asking much more.

"The Vitruvian?" she asks. "Odd. A few others thought they saw him, too. But no, ma'am, there's been no sign of him." The young doctor takes a long look at the rows of beds filled by soldiers and civilians alike. "Perhaps it was wishful thinking. Besides, if he were alive, there's no way he'd let all this happen."

Dead. Everyone believes he's dead.

"I...I guess you're right." I try to sit up, but my chest feels like a semi has parked on top of it.

The trained professional catches my stare and answers the question with an uncommon smile. "Broken arm and wrist, several fractured ribs. But you came in a lot worse."

I tilt my head, which thankfully my body doesn't have a problem with. "I don't understand, worse?"

"You were in cardiac arrest. There was a lot of confusion, but a good Samaritan kept giving you CPR until I got to you. He even stayed with you through the night."

My head starts to spin, and not from the pain. The words reach out and grab my heart tighter than anything Lord Malevolence could ever conjure up. My eyes scope the makeshift ward, searching frantically for an answer, for hope, for Chris. "The Samaritan, is he here now?"

The doctor stands as a moan from across the ward grabs her attention. "No, he left about an hour ago"

I fight to keep the desperation out of my voice. "Tell me...what did he look like?"

She's five beds away, doing more walking than talking when she answers the question. "Umm, I'm not really sure, he was African-American, tall. Oh, and he wore glasses."

My God...it *was* Chris. I feel like I'm on a carousel of confusion; eight days of nothing and then he shows to save my life only to disappear again.

A wave of helplessness threatens to overwhelm me—and that's when I see part of it. Scribbled with a marker on the bottom of my cast, the symbol that the whole world knows: the emblem of the Vitruvian.

I grit my teeth and lift my arm to read the message next to it: *Central Park 1:00 AM –C.K.*

Standing in Central Park, I look up and see the angel atop the Bethesda Fountain staring down on me. I remember the bronze seraph the way she looked in the sunlight on our wedding day, full of happiness and hope and love.

"The Angel of the waters is a healer," my hero had whispered to me as he held me tight. "She'll bring us luck."

That was a lifetime ago. Tonight, her face is cast in shadow by the moonlight. I don't know if the pity I see there has always been, or if it's just a reflection of my own emotion. The fountain is devoid of the water this stoic healer once stood guardian over. Now she stands alone amidst an empty shell of what was.

Like your marriage.

I'm trying to understand Chris's silence, his cryptic message, his choice of this place, when thunder interrupts my thoughts. As I look up a falling star changes its trajectory and rushes towards me, its heat from re-entry illuminating the night sky.

The Vitruvian has arrived.

He lands on the far side of the fountain so softly I find myself looking to see if his feet touched the ground.

Why did he land so far away? What's wrong with him?

"Hello Kendra." His voice isn't full of the sweet tenderness that I'm use to from the man that shares my bed. There's a distance in it that's oddly familiar to me.

And that's when it hits me. It's not my husband, Christopher Kincaid, speaking to me...it's the Vitruvian.

"Chris? I can't believe it. You're really here. What's going on? I—I thought you were dead. We all thought you were dead."

I take a step towards him and he takes a step back, clenching his fists as he does so.

"That's far enough, Kendra, stay where you are."

In the dimness, Chris's eyes take on an azure glow. Tiny needles begin to cascade over my body and I realize my husband is scanning me. I force a smile. "Baby, what's going on, where've you been?"

"I've been…close, keeping an eye on you while I regenerated."

All this time you thought he was dead and he's been watching you. Is that love?

"You've been watching me? So yesterday that was really you?"

I want him to silence the screams of doubt. I want my husband to make sense of all this, to take me in his arms and tell me how much he's missed me and that he loves me more than anything in the world. Instead, he approaches me, slowly, like he's being cautious of some rabid animal.

He steps into the light of a park lamp. Clearly, he's still hurt, but it's not the cuts and bruises that scare me. I've seen them before. Being the wife of the Vitruvian I've even gotten use to them. I know that right now nanites are repairing his body on a cellular level. What shakes me to my core is that, even with of all the unimaginable battles he's fought, I see something on his face I've never seen before.

Defeat.

"I didn't make it in time, but yes I was there yesterday," he says. "I took you to the recovery center and stayed with you."

And then left again when you needed him most.

"Why'd you leave me?"

He closes the distance between us in silence. When he finally speaks, he looks away and his voice is just above a whisper.

"I didn't want to, but it was better that we meet here, away from people, where we can…talk."

Talk about what?

"Chris, you're scaring me. Please stop this!" His eyes slowly come up to mine and it's clear that my husband wants to strike me with every fiber of his being.

"Stop this? That's something I should have done years ago. Now look where we are. New York is in ruins, Kendra. Over eleven thousand people are dead. The Freedom League's been murdered all because I didn't stop this when I should have…all because of what *you* are."

The weight of the world is too much for him. He's cracking. Now he's blaming you for the wrongs he cant right…for all those lives. He's saying you're evil.

"Me? Chris, I'm not responsible for what's been happening."

"Aren't you? Tell me, Kendra, did I stop the Reverse Engineers?"

This is totally absurd. Why is he asking me something I lived through with him?

Isn't it obvious? He's testing you.

"No," I tell him. "One of the patients that was experimented on had already killed all the Engineers."

As soon as the words come out of my mouth, the look in his eyes tells me everything. I failed the test.

"Not exactly. I spent seven years hunting down the patients and bringing them to justice. All except one, the most powerful of them all, the one who killed the Engineers. But it wasn't a patient who killed them, it was a doctor. It was you. You are *Doctor* Kendra Kincaid. "

My body starts to shake. Tears that have been held back with walls of hope and love flow freely; not because of some arcane spell by a madman, but because of the poison in the words from the man I love.

"I was your patient," Chris continues. "The nanites the Reverse Engineers used on me corrected my insanity. But when you injected yourself so that you could also confront the Engineers, your healthy mind suffered a psychotic break. Your mind created a separate personality to cope with the trauma, and somehow your nanites only interact with the personality you created...the Fenris Beast."

"Chris...What the hell are you saying? That I'm a monster? That I killed all those people?"

There's someone in my head and it's not me.

"You're wrong! I've never been anything but your wife. Lord Malevolence created that creature, not me!"

"Malevolence was a con man and conjurer, Kendra, nothing more. That Fenris Beast with him was no more real than the copy of my cape he wore."

Listen to the way he sounds, like he's talking to a child, not his wife

"Bullshit, Chris. I think I'd know if I was a monster, or a doctor for that matter. People talk to themselves every day. It doesn't mean there's an evil creature inside them."

Chris shifted uncomfortably as if my every word was hurting him. "Really? Can you remember where you were when I fought Fenris? Even though you become the Beast, you always remember events as if you've viewed them. My scans show you're fully healed less than a day after Malevolence's attack. It's because of the nanites. They heal Fenris...they heal you. The mind can be a wondrous and frightening place, Kendra. In the face of need it can turn hell into heaven or heaven into hell."

We stand there in silence. I watch the struggle as if finding just the right words will bring clarity to the madness of what he's telling me.

"When I first realized what you are," Chris says, "I knew I should kill you. But when I was nearly lost in the depths of madness, you kept me tethered to reality. The nanites made me sane, Kendra, but you made me whole. I knew then the only real choice I had was to marry you."

For the first time since this nightmare started my husband reaches out and touches my face. I want to feel his lips on mine, the warmth of his body, the beating of his heart. But as I look into his eyes, I don't know if I see love or pity.

"I've heard enough. I don't know what's happened to you, but I can't listen to this insanity."

Before I've fully turned away, Chris is already on the other side of me, blocking my exit.

"I can't let you go."

I look at his hand on my arm instead of into his eyes. "What are you saying, Chris?"

"All the things I can do, all these powers, and I can't save you. I can't let love blind me to what needs to be done. Too many lives are at stake."

At the speed of thought the hand of my hero is around my throat...tightening...ushering in the darkness that nearly claimed me at the hands of a villain. "Chris, you're hurting me."

My *husband* doesn't answer. But the Vitruvian tightens his grip and I can feel my life slipping between his fingers. The protector of New York turns away from me as the sobs of my husband echo through the night.

Now do you see? Do you understand? Is this love? Does love kill?

I know that our love created life, but before you can love you must first believe. A far-off memory touches me of believing in a man that didn't believe in himself. And out of that loving him, not a Doctor like the voice in my head has always told me; but a patient; named Christopher Kinkaid. "Please...please Chris...don't...I...I'm pregnant."

Our eyes meet and the darkness of doubt and pain slip away in the light of love. The Vitruvian lets go of my throat because my husband holds onto my heart.

"Kendra, I'm so sorry."

I try to hold onto the memory, onto the woman and life of that memory, but a different kind of darkness reaches in from everywhere and nowhere as I realize it's all true. What Chris told me is true.

You can't have that.

And I slip away into the forest of the Fenris Beast.

I'm looking into my wife's eyes when I see something I haven't seen there in over ten years, recognition. I don't know how, but Doctor Kendra Kincaid, my wife is back. The smile on my face is one of pure joy.

And then a fist hits me at lightning speed.

It's five seconds before I realize I'm ten yards away lying in the ruins of the Bethesda Fountain on top of the shattered remains of the bronze Angel; the healer. I look up at the woman who's standing over me; the recognition in her eyes from a few moments ago is gone, replaced by something different...something frightening.

"Kendra?"

"I'm sorry, Doctor Kincaid isn't here right now, but you can leave a message. I'll make sure she gets it." The drooling grin belongs to the Beast. We were so close. "Damn it, Fenris! I want my wife back!"

The laugh from the thing wearing the shell of Kendra is sensuous and dark. "First you want to kill her, now you want her back. For a superhero, Vitruvian, you really are indecisive."

As I get to my feet I order my nanites to quadruple my molecular density. The concrete cracks under my weight, but I feel as light as a feather.

"I almost did the unimaginable, Fenris, because of what you've done to my wife, to this city, to me. But looking into her eyes I realized where there's love, there's life. And where there's life, there's hope. I'm getting my wife and child back, demon. Tonight! And I'm going to put you in a hole so deep, so dark you'll never come out again."

I've seen it dozens of times before, yet I'm transfixed in the moment of her metamorphosis. Kendra Kincaid cries out as the last vestige of humanity is ripped away. Nanites obey their schizophrenic mistress, twisting the mind, transforming the body and finally corrupting the soul. Like an ophidian shedding its skin, the Fenris Beast tears out of its smouldering blood-drenched prison of shredded flesh.

"Very intimidating, hero. I'll remember you said that when I'm listening to your wife's screams as I'm sucking the marrow from your bones."

I feel a tightness in my knuckles as I bring their quantum accelerators up to maximum velocity. Hold on baby, I'm coming for you. Then, to the Beast, I cry, "*Bring it, bitch!*"

Forefather watched from the shadows under the Bethesda Bridge as the struggle between good and evil played out its inevitable conclusion, again.

Engineer Pope stood beside him, her attention not on the titans but her handheld device. "According to my analysis our recent manipulations of the timeline has caused an eighty-nine percent chance that the battle that leads them to the Indian Point nuclear facility won't be in ten years as it once occurred, but tonight."

The Engineer who had stood at this man's side and watched cities burn and loved ones die, expected her words to evoke some response from

Forefather, a response other than silence. As she looked up at her mentor, the tears slipping down his face frightened her more than the battle being waged a few dozen yards away. "Sir?"

Connor Kincaid had spent a lifetime as Forefather, Earth's last hero and only salvation. To fulfill his mission and save the world, he had abandoned the luxury of emotion and never looked back. But now, as he watched his parents in mortal combat, not through a lens, but right in front of him, he couldn't help but feel...everything.

"I thought I could save them from this, you know. I told myself it was my destiny to go back and give them the nanite antibodies to prevent the Fenris Virus. I would save them. I'd save everyone. But all I really did was fulfill time's paradox. I cured my father's madness, but created my mother's insanity. I created the Vitruvian and Fenris Beast, and because of that, ninety percent of the world has become infected with a nanovirus that turns the world into creatures. And to cover my mistake, I've been doing everything I can to eliminate my parents. *I'm* the true threat, not them."

Connor silently watched his parents rip apart what was left of Bethesda Terrace. According to history, it wouldn't be long before the fight spilled out onto the streets of New York—again.

"We should let them destroy the nuclear plant tonight," he says. "She will kill him, and in his death throes, he will cause a nuclear meltdown to stop her. I won't be born, thus I can't abduct them to conduct our tests to prevent the virus. Effect will no longer precipitate cause. The circle will be broken. Some will perish tonight, but the world will be saved."

Dianna looked up at Connor. "And what if the radiation warps the Fenris nanites into a virus as it did before? Ninety percent of the world will once again become infected, but now there will be no Connor Kincaid with inherent nanites that act as antibodies for the NASA reverse engineers to study; no Forefather to push back against the tide of infected Fenris Humans."

The young woman abruptly looked away from her mentor. As she did, her auburn hair swept over her face masking the emotion of the words she whispered. "No one for me to love."

Connor had never known what it felt like to go on a date or have a first kiss. But as he stood next to Dianna in silence, he realized he now knew what it felt like to love and finally to be loved.

The Fenris creature howled from a particularly nasty blow delivered by the Vitruvian, pulling Forefather back into the moment. "Of course you're right. We have to ensure the virus never happens. But this...hell has become a Gordian knot that I cannot unravel. No matter what I attempt, conflict is what feeds the Fenris Beast and resolving conflict is what feeds the Vitruvian. Every outcome...results...in...conflict."

For the first time in his adult life, Connor smiled. Despite the battle that raged on not far away, and despite the impending doom, Dianna Pope found herself returning the smile. "You have a solution?"

Forefather moved close to the Engineer. The aura of raw power emanating from his body was intoxicating, near overwhelming. When he kissed her, it was as if the air in her lungs had been sucked away. At the same time, she felt as if she'd been infused with but a fraction of his power. She felt more alive then ever in her entire life.

As Forefather stepped away from her, wisps of energy began to emanate from his eyes. "I'm going to cut the knot. If I'm successful, the circle will be broken. I love you. Goodbye."

Her mouth open to frame a million questions, Pope realized it was too late, Connor was gone. Almost instinctively she turned to where his parents were fighting, but they had disappeared as well.

And then, before she realized it, so had she.

With a flick of the wrist the city bus is airborne arching through the air faster than anything that large without wings is meant to. A lone figure watches silently as the fifteen-ton monstrosity bears down on him with the velocity of a guided missile, his face reflecting the desperation of the people trapped inside.

Without warning, powerful talons rip into the side of the bus, stopping its arc of death. The Fenris Beast looks at the Vitruvian, perplexed. "We don't have time for theatrics, hero. Forefather has come out of nowhere—again. We've got to put him down hard this time!"

The Vitruvian briefly studies the creature that's his rough-around-the-edges ally, and, unbeknownst to the world, his wife. As powerful as *he* is, she could probably take him. But he'd never tell her.

Forefather is the most powerful villain they have ever fought. But as long as they face him together, Christopher knows he and his wife can defeat him.

And they'll have to do it quick. Because babysitters charge extra on the weekends.

The Dodge

K. Stoddard Hayes

FOR LONG SECONDS after the gunfire stopped, powder smoke curled thick around me, stinging my eyes to tears and burning in my nostrils. I kept my mouth shut so I wouldn't cough, because coughing during blind gunplay is the dumbest way I know to get yourself shot. I couldn't see half a meter in front of me—hell, none of us could, either side of the street, not after firing a couple hundred rounds. Back on Earth they had switched to smokeless powder three hundred years ago. But here on New Colorado, we still used black powder because the planet provided its ingredients in abundance—one of the few things besides sunlight that our colonial forebears had found in abundance here.

So I stood in the street in a cloud of gunsmoke, under a sky burned from its normal jade to the tint of weathered copper by the summer sun. And I listened hard in the sudden calm to hear if everyone was where they had been when the shooting started moments ago. I knew that at least one of my two deputies, my sister Demeter, wouldn't have moved from the door of the jail, a few paces to my left. Her task had been to stay there and cover the side door of the Green Sky Saloon across the street, and she never abandoned a task.

In a moment, I knew that the other deputy, my little brother Ulysses, was still just to my right in what remained of the tailor's big window, because I could hear him humming to himself as he reloaded. I could also hear broken glass crunching under his feet, and Mary, the tailor, swearing like a whore under her breath as she crouched behind her counter. I couldn't blame her. She'd had that thermal glass installed only a week ago.

Across the street, about ten meters in front of me, I heard a whimper and a little scuffling of dirt. That would be the wounded outlaw lying in the street, the one who'd been shooting from the balcony of the saloon until Dem picked him off through a break in the smoke. And it sounded

142

like the other six members of Valentine Kelley's gang of desperadoes were still inside the saloon, taking cover below the shattered front windows. Through the whoosh of the big solar-powered fans cooling the saloon, I could hear the tiny tick-tick of someone's trigger clicking on an empty chamber; the crunch of someone breaking a shotgun to reload; and some sandbrain coughing up a storm in the smoke. That one would have a short life as a gunman for sure, giving away his position like that. Lucky for him, he was going to be in jail in five minutes instead.

"Jase," Dem said to me in a stage whisper. "Smoke's starting to go."

So it was, rising and billowing in a breath of updraft. I had only a few more seconds of cover in which to start our usual frontal assault.

"Let me do it," Ulie whispered.

I felt my jaw clench. *Gods, not now!* He'd been arguing for weeks that he should have a turn going in first instead of providing cover for me. I knew he thought charging the bad guys would prove him as brave as his renowned big brother. But he was still too green to be told the real reason that job always fell to me.

"Let me, Jase!"

"Jason!" Dem prodded urgently, too far away to hear Ulie's whispers.

"Too late to change now," I whispered to Ulie. I laid my empty rifle down at my feet, pulled out my two pistols, and whistled my "ready" signal: a line of *Buffalo Gals, Won't You Come Out Tonight.*

Right on cue, Dem yelled into the saloon, "Give it up, Kelley! We got you all covered. You're going nowhere but jail."

"Come and git us, Wilder!" someone yelled back. Someone else fired a revolver, probably shooting blind toward Dem's voice.

I waited at least three more seconds for Ulie to start his covering fire. That may not sound very long, but it feels like forever when you're not sure whether your little brother is going to stay put and shoot like he's supposed to, or try risking his skin by charging into gunfire.

At last his rifle went off, and I unclenched my teeth, counting the shots silently. *One—two—three*—I gathered myself—*four–five*—! On *six*, I charged across the street.

"They're comin' in!" one of the outlaws yelled. A fusillade of gunfire erupted in front of me.

I felt the bullets pass, felt them yank and tatter my long canvas duster end to end like a flag in a sandstorm. Then I was through the doorway and two strides beyond the shooters, spinning around to face them. Before any of them could turn around from the windows and draw a bead on me,

I had both barrels leveled, one to each side of the doorway, covering all of them.

"Hold it!" I barked.

All four of them froze, eyes staring white above the bandanas pulled over their faces, hands slowly pointing their guns in the air.

Four? There had been seven when the fight started, counting the wounded one in the street. What in the name of ruination—?

Another look told me at once that the Kelleys were gone. These four had faces and hands as brown as mine, while Valentine Kelley and her brother had much lighter skin, an unusual trait in our world's strong sunlight and thin atmosphere.

"Where's Kelley and Ben?" I demanded, and got nothing but shifty eyes in answer. Shifty eyes looking toward the back window.

Slipped away, damn it!

Dem came running in, with Ulie only a step behind her.

"Kelley's gone, and Ben with her," I snapped. "Lock up this trash and follow me. They'll be headed for the Rim." I shouted the last over my shoulder as I made for the door.

"You're too late, Sheriff!" one of the gang jeered at me. "You'll never catch 'em now!"

As I sprinted across the street, I heard Dem start in on Ulie: "What took you so long to fire out there? You ought to know by now...."

They'd been bickering over Ulie's fitness—or lack of it—since he turned 18 last year and took up with us at the peacekeeping trade. When we were children they had bickered over whether Ulie was old enough to join Dem and me in whatever sand-blind scheme we had in mind. Some things never changed.

Let them sort it out. By the time I reached the back of the jail and the horses we always kept saddled there, I had put my sibs out of my mind and started figuring. The Kelleys might have as much as a ten-minute lead on me. They probably slipped out the back the moment the shooting started, so we wouldn't hear their horses through the gunfire. Hell, Valentine probably staged the gunfight just to cover their escape. That would account for the trouble jumping up out of nothing in the middle of a quiet afternoon. She must have figured out that we'd be getting a warrant for Ben in the afternoon mail. Valentine Kelley would sacrifice her whole gang to keep her monstrous little brother Ben from the hands of the law. And the gang was scared enough of her to let her do it.

Ten minutes. Maybe eight kilometers at a run on the Down Canyon road, the quickest way to the Rim trail. They'd be long out of sight, but in this weather, their dust trail would hang in the air behind them for a good while. And their horses would be slowing down considerably by now. Gene splicing had allowed horses, like people, to breathe the leaner air of New Colorado, but it hadn't yet made any super horses.

I swung into Roswell's saddle and lifted him into an easy lope heading out of town. No need to drive him to a flat run; he could overtake them easily with his thoroughbred speed and hill pony stamina. I'd catch them on the Rim trail, about when they started climbing. If I planned it right, I might even bring in both Kelleys without any help. Keeping Dem, and especially Ulie, away from any more gunfire would suit me just fine. Protecting them wasn't just my job as their boss, it was what my parents expected of their eldest child.

Peacekeeping had been a Wilder family tradition since before any of us was born. Our parents had met in Landing when Pa was a deputy sheriff and Ma was a schoolteacher fresh off a colony ship. Pa's peacekeeping work took him from job to job all over the Big Canyon, and Ma had stuck with him from Landing to Gandhi to Wind River before she got tired of wandering after him. They bought a little farm in Wind River and there she stayed to bring us up. I had learned peacekeeping from Pa when I was grown, but it was Ma who had drilled me, from the day Dem was born, on the importance of looking out for my sibs. So I had no intention of letting either of them take unnecessary risks today. Not even to bring Ben Kelley to justice for murdering two unarmed Indians who had objected when he tried to use their young daughters as whores.

About five kilometers out of town, I tasted a whiff of dust on the air, and knew I was catching up to the Kelleys. Coming over a rise, I saw their dust trail, a little mist of yellow hanging over the purply green brush just down the slope. A kilometer ahead along the Down Canyon road stood the lonely monolith of Broken Stack, a chimney of ocher limestone left behind by the rivers that had carved out this part of the Canyon. The road up to the Rim bent off to the right at the Stack, and sure enough, the dust trail bent right, too.

I looked back. No sign yet of Dem and Ulie. All the better if I could catch the Kelleys on my own. Then Ulie would have no opportunity to date Ben Kelley's marksmanship just to prove himself my equal.

My equal! He was showing ten times my bravery every time he ran toward the sound of gunfire. I would be glad when he grew reliable enough for me to explain just why *I* had no reason to be afraid of bullets.

I put Rosie into an easy run and we cantered past the Stack and turned toward the Rim.

From anywhere in the middle of Big Canyon, the walls are no more than backdrop to the vast sprawl of the canyon floor, just color and shadow in the distance, tapering to the remote horizon. But now I was riding straight toward the North Wall, and it towered in front of me, filling my view. Its base was three hundred meters of compacted talus slope dotted with brush. Above that, another thousand meters of terraced cliff, in every color from chalk to sepia, rose to where the Rim met the jade sky.

On the lower slope, a bare two kilometers away, I could just make out fresh dust stirring. The Kelleys had reached the Rim trail, but they'd never make the Rim top with me so close behind them.

Rosie and I were passing the first outlying boulders scattered at the foot of the talus, when I noticed that the stirred-up dust ended just above the talus line, where the trail bent around a limestone outcrop. The Kelleys weren't climbing the Rim trail any more. They must have seen me coming and taken cover behind the outcrop. That would have been a stupidly obvious ambush for most folks, but it was perfect for Ben Kelley, a dead shot with most rifles, and reckoned to be near infallible with his own sniper rifle. He was notorious for shooting from extreme range, and preferably at an unsuspecting target.

All this passed through my mind in an eye blink, then I spun Rosie to get behind the nearest big boulder. Ben must have seen Rosie's head turn, and he fired before we could reach cover. From long habit, I was already prepared to *dodge,* so the bullet zipped harmlessly through my left shoulder almost before the pan of the shot reached my ears.

Next second I rolled to the ground, holding Rosie's reins to pull him with me to cover behind the large boulder. I'd need him if it came to a pursuit up on the Rim.

Out of habit, I patted down the singed holes in my duster either side of my shoulder, to make sure the heat of the passing bullet hadn't ignited the fabric. I had a two-inch burn weal on my ribcage from being careless enough to let a bullet hole in my jersey catch fire a couple years back.

The stillness after the shot stretched out for a couple of minutes, during which I coaxed Rosie to stand close alongside the boulder.

Then Valentine Kelley shouted, "Sheriff! We know Ben hit you! Give us your word not to follow us, and we'll let you ride back to town."

"Give it up, Kelley!" I shouted back. "No one's coming to help you. We've got all your gang in custody."

"They weren't coming with us anyway," she shouted.

I realized then that she had offered the gang a choice between holding us off in the saloon, and trying to cross the Rim with her and Ben. Those bravos must be smarter than I figured if they'd chosen jail over three days in the desert and Kelley's mad dog brother.

"What's it going to be, Wilder?"

"You're not getting away that easy, Kelley! There's two dead men to account for."

"Indian trash!" Ben yelled. "I ain't going south for the likes of them, but I'll sure send you after 'em!"

"Shut up, Ben! I'll deal with Wilder." Valentine spoke sharply, not yelling, and surely not intending me to hear, but some trick of the canyon carried her voice to me. She shouted out again, "Two corpses aren't worth your life, are they? You'll bleed out if you don't go back for help."

"Sorry to disappoint you, but I'm feeling just fine. I'm coming for your brother and I'm taking him in for murder."

"Just try it, Wilder!" Ben yelled. Another shot sang out, and the bullet smacked off the top of the boulder, showering Rosie and me with rock chips. Rosie snorted, but otherwise stood calm.

Sure didn't take much to make Ben lose his temper.

Another silence fell. I fished my dentist's mirror from my vest pocket and extended it past the side of the boulder to look over the ground between me and them. After a moment, I heard them speaking again, too quietly for me to distinguish the words at first, but loud enough for me to know they were arguing. I heard Valentine say something about sundown, and Ben say something about "just stalling," and "...shot him good."

"He doesn't sound like he's hurt," Valentine answered.

"Damn you, Val, I know when I've shot someone!" Ben's voice was plenty loud now. "And if he ain't shot, he really is the luckiest son of a bitch in the Canyon."

I tucked the mirror into my hatband just long enough to poke my rifle into the open and fire one shot in their direction.

"Shit!" Ben yelled. I must have come close.

"I told you," said Valentine, and silence fell again.

Yeah, I'm the luckiest son of a bitch in the Canyon. Some kind of luck, being a genetic hiccup.

I discovered that I had this peculiar talent when I wasn't much higher than the middle rail of our corral fence. I'd been practicing throwing my new jackknife into a tree trunk when it fell into a powder bush. Without thinking, I reached into the bush, just too late to notice the black assassin coiled in the shade beneath it.

Even as I went to yank my hand away, I knew the snake would be faster. When it struck, time seemed to slow to a crawl. I saw its head strike—and go *through* the base of my thumb and slap on the dirt as if my hand wasn't there. My other hand brought up a broken branch and scooped the snake up and away into another clump of brush. Then I just sat there, choking on tears of shock and terror, and staring at my perfect, unbitten right hand.

I had spent a week just thinking things over and reliving that moment again and again. Then I had started testing what I could do, carefully at first, then more recklessly, as I discovered I could—well, somehow just *dodge*. Not just with my hand, but with my arm, or my head, or a foot, or my whole body. And more than that, the Dodge worked both ways. It wasn't just that I could let solid things pass through any part of me, like a snake's fang or a knife blade or even a bullet. I could pass through them, too. I could reach through a door to turn the lock, walk through a fence or a wall, even pass unscathed through fire or scalding liquid.

The only thing I couldn't do was extend the Dodge to anything I held or touched. I found that out early, when I tried reaching through the icebox door to steal one of Ma's johnnycakes. Not a crumb came out on my hands, but Ma still divined who had created the mess inside the icebox, and made me scrub out the whole thing.

Even after I accepted what I could do, I kept it secret until I was nearly grown. We'd sometimes heard stories about people who could do odd things, but the stories always ended badly, with the oddball either horribly dead, or shut away in a secret lab being studied by nefarious white suits. The idea that someone might take me from my family and shut me up somewhere terrified me. And by the time I was old enough to understand they were just kid stories, my habit of secrecy was too strong to give up.

Even now, it was keeping me from closing in on the Kelleys. My mirror showed me precious little cover between my boulder and the spot where I thought they were hiding. The nearest big boulders were too far apart, and the brush was too sparse to screen me from Ben's high power gun sight. Of course, I could have covered the ground between us unscathed, but I never thought of trying it. Ben would start shooting, and then— well, I wasn't going to throw away fifteen years of secrecy while I still had other options. So the Kelleys had me pinned, sure enough, though not for the reason they believed.

Still, if Ben's bullets could reach my boulder, the Kelleys were probably within range of my rifle, too. If I could spot their cover, maybe I could keep them just as pinned.

"Kelley! I've got an offer for you," I called. "Weather bulletin says there's another sandstorm heading our way topside. You'll never get across the Rim top to Green before it hits, so why don't you save yourselves a skin blasting and come back down here?"

"We've traveled in the sand before," Valentine shouted back.

"I know you have, getting Ben away from Cotton Flats two years back." I angled my mirror toward the outcrop. "Must have been an epic ride, two hundred kilometers through that storm, just to save a murderer from his due."

"That was self-defense!" yelled Ben.

"Self-defense, against a seventy-year-old bank teller? And what about last week, Ben? A couple of unarmed Indians? How's that self-defense? And you, Kelley, how much longer you want to keep pretending little Ben isn't a killer? Who else does he have to kill to convince you? More old folks? Children? Puppy dogs?"

Gunfire burst out of the shadows of the cliff, smacking my boulder over and over. And my handy little mirror showed me exactly which crevice the smoke bursts came from.

I knew that temper of Ben's would work to my benefit.

I was just getting ready to try a ranging shot when Ben's firing pattern changed. The hits on the boulder stopped, and I couldn't even hear the bullets pass. He had to be aiming far wide of me.

At what?

Then Rosie whinnied the clear, loud neigh of a horse calling to a stablemate, and another horse answered from behind me.

Ulie. Even before I glimpsed the ruddy brown of his mare's coat through the brush, and that high-crowned chapeau he insisted on wearing, I knew it had to be him. And he was alone, because he was riding straight up the trail toward us. Dem would have heard the gunfire three kilometers away and turned off the road to come at us from the side, out of sight. And any other traveler would have just kept clear.

Now what in the name of ruination had the boy done to talk Dem into letting him come out here? Too late to stop him now as he came riding blithely forward. In a minute, he'd be in range of Ben's rifle. I aimed my rifle at the crevice where the Kelleys were hiding and laid down a barrage of covering fire, praying that Ulie would make it to my boulder before I had to reload.

Just as my trigger clicked on the empty magazine, I heard a rumble of hoofs, a thud, and Ulie was beside me, thumping my shoulder in delight.

"Hey, brother Jase! You ready to bring 'em in?"

I pulled in the rifle and reached into a pocket for a fresh magazine, giving all my attention to reloading before I even looked up at him.

He got the message. "You're riled again, aren't you? Aww, come on! You and Dem both think I can't do anything right."

I stood up and fixed him with the glare I'd learned from Ma. "And we have reason! What were you thinking, riding in the open like that with Ben Kelley around?"

He ducked his head for a second, then looked back at me, mustering a little bravado. "I thought you'd need some help."

"And what in the name of Hades are you doing here anyway? You

150

should be guarding the prisoners."

He glared at me defiantly, his dark eyes just like Pa's in his brown face. "Figured it was my turn to join the posse for a change."

"You snuck off without telling Dem, didn't you? Of all the times to pull a stupid stunt!"

"It's your fault, the both of you!" His voice beat over mine. "You never give me a chance! How'm I going to learn anything if all I do is mind the jail while you two go out and—"

"Keep your voice down!" I hissed. "They can hear us from the Wall. Now listen," I dropped my voice almost to a whisper, "they're holed up behind that limestone outcrop where the trail starts to switchback. We have to close the distance before dark so we can keep them from slipping away. You think you can keep their heads down while Rosie and I make a dash for that big boulder over there?" I pointed to a shed-sized chunk of limestone two hundred meters closer to the Wall.

Ulie nodded and pulled his rifle from its holster. Luckily, he had brought the MacPherson, with its long, accurate bore and heavy caliber. And if Ben got off one or two shots at me in spite of Ulie's fire, he wouldn't be able to see for sure whether he had actually hit a rider moving at a flat run, so my secret would still be safe.

But Ulie surprised me by shooting well enough to keep Ben from getting off even a single shot in the twelve seconds it took Rosie and me to make the sprint. I shook my head over my doubts as I dismounted and got ready to cover him. Maybe he was right that Dem and I were holding him back too much.

He wore down my doubts still more in the next hour as we moved from cover to cover, scanning the cliffs each time before we moved, to make sure the Kelleys hadn't moved to block us. He was quick, careful, and didn't need me to correct him even once.

Finally, we reached the place on the trail that I had been aiming for. It was a ledge that ran back off the main trail for about twenty meters and ended in a little bay notched into the cliff by a long-dry waterfall. The bay was big enough and its walls high enough, to give us and the horses cover from anyone shooting from the next higher switchback of the trail. Close to where the ledge left the trail was a place where a man could scramble up to lie above the ledge and watch the whole stretch of trail for half a kilometer on either side of the Kelleys' temporary hideout.

"This looks good," said Ulie, before I could speak. "We can cover the trail above them all night if need be, and they won't be able to take pot shots at us unless they climb right down here. Which I doubt they'll want to try in the dark."

"I agree," I said, impressed at how quickly he had caught on to my choice. "I'll keep an eye on them while you see to the horses, then you can take a turn. Keep 'em saddled."

Ulie nodded. We both knew that if it came to a sudden pursuit in the middle of the night, we'd have no time for putting on tack.

"Bright auroras tonight, so we'll have decent light for watching," I added. Few people on New Colorado bothered with solar storm reports since we'd given up the everyday use of most electronic devices. I still kept track just because I liked knowing when the night sky would light up with rainbow curtains of fire. And sometimes my little hobby came in handy, like now. Ulie nodded again, and turned to water his mare.

"I brought all the canteens." Proudly he showed me the four full canteens that we always kept with our tack, just for days like this.

"Pretty stupid if you didn't," I said, deflating him. I couldn't afford to have him get even a little bit cocky on this ride.

As for the water, those four bottles plus the one I carried gave us fifteen liters. Not a lot for two horses and two men who might have to travel the Rim top in summer. We'd have to go easy.

I turned to walk back toward the trail, when Ulie whistled behind me.

"Hay-deez, Jase, look at that coat!"

I glanced down. Between the gunfight in town and Ben's marksmanship on the trail, the tails of my new duster weren't much more than rags.

"I just paid for this coat!" I said, swearing a little. "You think Mary Tailor will still make me a new one, now that we got her new window smashed up?"

But Ulie wasn't to be distracted. "You sure you aren't shot somewhere? Best let me have a look. Come on, off with it!"

He pulled off the coat and looked me all over for signs of blood. When he failed to find any, he held up my coat, spread the tails to the fading daylight and started counting bullet holes. He counted up to seventeen before he found the matched pair Ben had put in the left shoulder, front and back, five inches below the seam. Then he let out an oath that would have made our Ma reach for her ruler.

"What the howling horntail ass is this?" He held up the duster with his finger through both holes, and stared at me like a ghost.

I kept my face calm as one of Ma's classical statues. Ulie was a fearless backup man, and he was learning to think strategically in a situation, but he couldn't keep a secret to save his life—or mine.

"You think that happened today, you bufflehead?" I said. "This coat was hanging over the door of the jail the other day, when those trail hands from Orinoco shot up the town."

"I don't remember that," Ulie pulled out his finger and brought the fabric close to his face. "Looks new to me. Smells new, too."

"Sure, Ulie, it's a fresh bullet hole right over my chest. That's why I'm standing here waiting for you to hurry the hell up and give me my coat so I can go watch the trail."

"All right, hold your piss!" He turned the coat once more in his hands, then tossed it back to me. "But I never saw anyone with luck like yours, not even Pa. Near twenty bullet holes and not one even skinned you. I wish you'd tell me how you do that, day in and day out."

"You should know. You've never been hit either," I pointed out. *Mainly because Dem and I have done our best to keep you away from bullets.* But of course I wouldn't say that, and I needed his attention elsewhere for several good reasons. "Now get those horses watered and fed, and call me when our supper's ready. I'll be out by the trail."

After supper I had Ulie take the first watch, figuring that Valentine was more likely to make a move later in the night, when she'd expect our vigilance to soften. I also hoped that long before morning, Dem would find someone in town to stand as deputy so she could join us.

Until then, all I could do was try to sleep. If I looked to my left between the enclosing walls of the bay, I could see a spark of light from some isolated farmhouse out on the Canyon floor, and in the distance, the glow of Gandhi, the nearest big town. The only other light was the stars, flaming across the sky like a million glittering fireflies. Of course there are no fireflies on New Colorado, nor anything like them. I knew about them from Pa telling me bedtime stories about his pa catching fireflies back on Earth.

Pa was the reason I had never told Ulie about the Dodge. When I was eighteen I had decided it was time to test my gift for real, so I walked into the middle of a saloon gunfight. I was the only one to emerge unscathed. I don't think I would have tried it if I had known that Pa would come home the very next day on one of his rare visits. We had all learned at an early age that nothing brought Pa's temper down on us faster than our upsetting Ma with some unusually stupid or dangerous stunt.

Sure enough, the minute Pa walked in the door and put down his saddlebags, Ma lit into him. She went on and on in her strictest schoolteacher manner, about how I was likely to get myself killed trying to be like him, and he'd better teach me how to be smart and careful if he wanted to be a grandfather.

All the while she was holding forth, Pa just kept nodding and occasionally interjecting that he sure would talk to me. He never once blistered me with his customary "Why'd you rile your Ma?" glare, and that both worried and perplexed me. It was almost as if he wasn't angry with me at all.

That afternoon he followed me out to the home grove, where I was cutting up a fallen tree for firewood. I didn't see him coming until he was close beside me. Before I could brace myself for the expected talking-to, he said, "I wondered if one of you would inherit the Dodge."

I just stared at him, letting the saw hang idle in my hand.

"I guess you're the only one," he went on when I still didn't speak. "I don't see your sister or your little brother trying to walk through bullets, and I know you ain't stupid enough to risk your skin the way I do, unless you got good reason to know it's no risk."

I sat down heavily on the tree trunk. "You—you can do it, too?"

In answer, Pa reached out as if to grasp the saw blade, but instead passed his hand right through it. "I discovered it when I was a mite younger than Ulie."

Then he sat down beside me and told me what he knew about how to use the Dodge, what it could do and what it couldn't—information I had mostly discovered for myself along the way. But I still had questions.

"Pa, where's it come from?"

"I dunno, Jase. My pa didn't live long enough to tell me if it came from him, since he was first generation,"—he meant the first in his family to come from Earth and have the gene splicing—"but there's always been stories about the splice doing more to some people than fixing our lungs and our eyes so we can live on this world."

So I had been right about being an oddball. But if I was one, so was Pa, and nothing bad had ever happened to him. Rather the reverse—he had gained a reputation throughout the Canyon for plain dumb luck when it came to walking away from trouble that would kill anyone else.

"What else can I do with it besides dodge bullets?"

Pa let out one of his rare deep chuckles. "People in Sweetwater still think I'm the luckiest drunk alive because I didn't get crushed by a roof cave-in."

"A roof fell on you?"

"Yep, during a windstorm. I wasn't drunk, not even a little bit, but I had to pretend to be, to explain how I survived." Then he stopped smiling and pinned both eyes on me. "Don't you ever tell anyone you can do this. Not ever! Not your sibs, not your best friend, not the woman you love. 'Cause all it will take is one wrong word from someone to let slip the fact that you ain't quite playing fair. I don't have to tell you, there's plenty that would go gunning for you special, for no better reason than they'd want the credit for killing someone unkillable."

I swung up the saw and passed it right through my other arm. "But I *am* unkillable."

"You ain't!" He grabbed my wrist and wrestled me up nose to nose with him. I tried to dodge through his grip—and couldn't.

He gave a short laugh like the snap of a hammer. "I've got the gift, too. And that means you can't dodge me, boy, any more than I could dodge you. Now you listen to me, if you want to live a long life. Can you see behind you? Can you stay awake forever?"

I shook my head.

"Never forget that! You can't dodge what you don't see—the bullet that's aimed at you from behind, the rock falling from above, the knife in your sleep. If people ever learn you're a specially prime target, you can't possibly dodge everything they'll throw at you."

He let my wrist go at last. I sat there rubbing it, smarting inside and out. The silence stretched another long minute before he spoke again.

"Son, maybe you think getting yourself killed ought to be your problem, and maybe it is. But from now on, I'm giving you another problem: if you ever let your secret out, you'll get Dem and Ulie killed trying to look out for you."

I hadn't thought of that. My sibs would go to protect me, no matter what. Just as I looked out for them, they had always stood up for me against all comers, from the time they were tiny.

"Yessir," I said, abashed.

He spoke more gently. "Just keep it secret, son, and you'll be fine. You got a good head on you, when you remember to use it."

The next day, Pa stunned the family and me by announcing it was time I began my apprenticeship with him. That was the beginning of my career as a lawman. I worked side by side with Pa for nearly five years, learning everything I could about keeping the peace and keeping our secret. Then one day in Saltpeter he walked out of a lunchroom during a sandstorm, and into the path of a runaway ore wagon. He never saw it coming.

After that, I had stayed near home for a bit—not that Ma ever seemed to need me to look after her, any more than she had needed Pa. Mostly, I was waiting for Dem to get enough years on her to become my deputy, the way I had been Pa's. She proved a good, steady second, but even so, I never told her about the Dodge until she saw me get shot from ambush one day.

As for Ulie, I still had doubts if he'd ever be steady enough to trust. He was overeager to prove himself, and that made him likely to rush into situations, like his impetuous arrival this afternoon. And while Dem could go a whole day without saying a word, Ulie positively loved to talk to anyone who would listen. Let him get a drink or two in him and a pretty girl to impress, and for all I knew he'd brag my secret to the whole Canyon.

I dozed off wondering about him, and was dreaming of Pa when a sharp, echoing boom woke me. Overhead, the sky was afire with shimmering curtains of green and purple and white. I rolled off my blanket and grabbed my rifle as Ulie shouted, "Oh, no you don't!" and fired again.

This time the boom was followed by a metallic ping ricocheting off the cliffs. As I ran back along the ledge toward Ulie, Ben let out a yell from above us. I heard their horses snorting and scrambling, their hoofs unleashing a rattling avalanche of gravel and dust down the cliff. A brighter flare of the aurora showed me their shadowy figures hurrying back from the open trail above us to regain the shelter of the limestone stack.

"That's right! You just scurry right back to your little hidey hole!" Ulie called, laughing. "Next time, I won't aim so high! You see that, Jase?" he added as I reached him. "Those varmints almost snuck right by us."

"You hit something with that second shot," I said.

"Pretty good shooting in the dark, wasn't it?"

"No, you sandbrain, we don't want Ben Kelley dead unless it's the only way to bring him in."

"A bullet's cheaper than a trial," Ulie argued.

This was an old debate in the less settled parts of the Canyon. I wasn't about to start it up with him now.

"You go get some sack time, I'll keep watch," I said. "And don't argue! We both need enough sleep to stay alert. I'll call you in a couple hours."

Ulie headed back to the campsite, and I settled down for my watch, sitting cross-legged on a narrow rock shelf at shoulder height above the ledge, with my rifle cradled in my arms. If I started to doze, I'd lose my balance and roll down onto the ledge, which was plenty wide enough to catch me before I hit the steep, crumbling slope of limestone below us.

It was a little past midnight, and all sound from the Kelleys had ceased.

Even with the brightest aurora, I couldn't see into their hideout in the deep shadows of the cliff. But any sound they made would reach my ears in the stillness of the night. So I sat looking out over the Canyon and up at the stars and the auroras, and listened with all my hearing.

It must have been almost two hours later that I heard, out of a deep silence, a soft, sudden crunch—the sound of a boot slipping on a loose stone. Not meters away up the slope, but startlingly close. I dove off the shelf and pressed close to the wall of the ledge, peering through the dimness toward the trail, my rifle ready to fire, my body ready to dodge.

I saw and heard nothing for as long as it took my heart to stop hammering. At last, I said, "I know you're there, Kelley. I won't shoot if you come out with your hands up." I spoke as quietly as I could. The situation seemed too delicate to risk waking Ulie.

"I've got you covered, too, Sheriff," said Valentine's voice, equally softly. "I just want to talk."

Her voice came from the direction of the trail. I strained my eyes to see. Nothing on the trail itself, whose pale, packed surface I could see for a good distance. To the left and above it, the next tier of cliff rose almost sheer. No cover there. To the right, the same crumbling slope that lay below the ledge stretched alongside the trail a few meters wide, before it dropped off. Nothing there but loose rocks, weeds and some resin bushes.

"Where are you? Show yourself."

Something moved behind the nearer of the resin bushes, and I saw her shadowy form emerge. Valentine Kelly might be a slender woman, but she was certainly wider than the trunk of a resin bush, and her face showed up clearly now as a pale oval against the rocks. So how in the name of ruination had she gotten so close without me seeing her?

"I just want to talk," she said again. She was keeping her voice as low as I kept mine. Maybe she didn't want to risk alerting Ben that she was talking to the enemy. Or maybe she was just giving him time to move into ambush position.

"Where's your brother?" I asked.

"Asleep. He won't wake up unless we start shooting."

"How do I know that?"

"You ever try to wake up a kid his age when he's sound asleep?"

Yes, I had. But that didn't mean I believed her. While I kept my eyes on her, I was listening all the time for any sound that might suggest Ben was on the move.

"So, talk. I'm listening."

"Two of us, and two of you, and a sandstorm coming," she said. "You'll be in just as much danger chasing us through the sand, as we will being chased."

"Maybe."

"Your brother's even younger than Ben. You don't want him hurt."

"If that's a threat—!"

She shook her head. "No threat. I'm just saying, I want my brother safe. I know you want yours safe, too."

"My brother's not a murderer."

Silence again for a long moment. Then she said, "If you let Ben go, I'll surrender."

"You'll what?" I couldn't believe my ears. After five years of eluding every lawman who had ever come after her, Valentine Kelley was offering to surrender, just like that. What was going on?

"You can do whatever you want to me. I'll answer all the charges. I'm responsible for everything Ben did."

It was not my intention to let Ben Kelley escape. But something was afoot here I didn't understand. I kept talking while I tried to tease it out.

"Are you really? Witnesses in Cotton Flats said you weren't happy when Ben shot the teller. And you weren't even with him last week when he killed those Indians."

"He's my responsibility."

"No good. If you want a deal, give me Ben, and maybe I'll let you go."

"You're not taking Ben!" Her voice rose a little, then she broke off and seemed to struggle with herself. When she spoke again, her voice was low and clear and hard as the rocks around us. "You can take me now, or you can chase us up on the Rim, and Ben will kill you and your brother the first chance he gets."

I didn't answer for a moment. I was trying to put myself in Valentine's shoes, to figure what she might be thinking, but it still didn't make any sense. Finally I said, "You're not thinking this through, Kelley. You want to protect Ben? You're the level head, not him. How long do you think he'll last without you to drag him out of trouble?"

"I have thought it through. He wouldn't last a week in jail. On his own, he's still got a chance. What would you do to keep your little brother safe, Sheriff? Wouldn't you risk anything? Everything?"

She had that figured right, on both counts. Next thing I knew something chunked into the dirt at my feet. Her pistol. I scooped it up and pocketed it as she came slowly towards me, her hands raised. I made her take off her duster and toss it off the ledge so I could see she wasn't carrying any other weapons. Then I made her go past me so I could walk behind her to our camp.

"Why are you doing this?" I said.

"I promised," she said so softly I thought I must have misunderstood.

"You what? You promised? Promised who?"

"You wouldn't—" she half turned toward me, then spun around and screamed, "No, Ben!"

I whirled. Ben stood on the trail not twenty meters from me, rifle at his shoulder. It roared out before I could even think about aiming my own rifle. The bullet passed through my sternum, then I heard a soft thunk and a gasp behind me.

"Val!" Ben yelled.

I didn't waste time looking. I raised my rifle—but he shot it right out of my hands.

"I'm sorry, Ben," said Valentine. I turned then and saw her tottering on her knees, both hands pressed to her breast. "Sorry I left you. They shot the canteen. Not enough water for two." Then she toppled over and tumbled down the slope like a rag doll.

Ben stood staring at me. "I didn't go to shoot her. I shot you, but you ain't hurt. The bullet went right through you and hit Valentine."

"Never mind me. Don't you want to—?" *help your sister*, I was going to say. Then I heard a stealthy step behind me, and Ben snapped up his rifle to fire again. At Ulie, who had stolen out onto the ledge while we talked.

I spun, took a running leap and pushed Ulie back into an angle of the rock face, shielding him with my body so Ben couldn't get a clean shot.

"Don't move!" I hissed.

Ben's footsteps came closer. By turning my head, I could just see him in the corner of my eye, about ten meters from us.

"I get it now," he said. "You tricked me into shooting Val. But it won't do you any good, Wilder." He laughed softly. "'Cause I'm going to shoot you again. And this time it will hit your brother, won't it?"

Only if I let it.

"Jase!" Ulie whispered, trying to push me away. But I was still his big brother, still stronger, and I held on.

What would you do to keep your little brother safe?

I braced myself and *un*-dodged, as Ben's wild laugh and the blast of his rifle sounded together.

The bullet slammed into my shoulder like the hammer of Vulcan, and

159

burned like a red hot wire. I didn't know anything could hurt that much. I felt my knees go wobbly, and tightened my fists in Ulie's shirt front, as much to stay on my feet as to keep shielding him.

"Jase!" Ulie's voice, shrill as a boy's, went through my skull like a second bullet, unbearably.

"So you *can* be shot after all," said Ben.

"Oh, Hades, Jase!" Ulie whispered. "Just hold on, okay? Just tell me what to do."

"Shhh. Don't move."

"But he'll kill—"

I shook my head, glaring fiercely into his face, and he fell silent, his hands now holding me up. I could feel warm blood seeping down my shoulder blade and spreading into my shirt.

Behind me, Ben was still pondering. "Wait now, don't tell me. Is it just luck, or can you choose whether to be shot?" His feet shuffled a couple of steps nearer.

I leaned in closer to Ulie and whispered, "Shoot me."

Ulie stared at me, shaking his head. He still did not understand, and how could I expect him to, when he had just seen me get shot?

"I think you can choose, can't you, Wilder?" Ben said. "And that puts you in a pretty pickle, doesn't it?" He began to giggle like a drunk. "Now you have to choose whether to let me shoot you again, and kill you this time, or let me shoot through you and kill your little brother."

Ulie glared wild-eyed at Ben, his mouth slack with horror. I dug one fist hard into his shirt to get his attention.

"Shoot me. Right here." I tapped my left side, where his right hand could line up his pistol without Ben seeing the movement.

"You should let me kill your brother," Ben was saying. "You made me kill my sister, and fair's fair, isn't it?" He started to giggle again, crazy, hysterical giggling that sounded almost like sobbing.

"Right here, Ulie."

"I can't. Another bullet'll kill you."

"You trust me?"

"Jase...." Ulie was still shaking his head, tears in his eyes.

"Of course, if you want to try to save your brother, Wilder, you can just let me kill you. Then I'll go right ahead and kill your brother, too!" Ben broke into wild shrieks of laughter.

The sound of that insane hilarity reached Ulie in a way that my coaxing couldn't. He met my eyes. His were flinty through the tears, and his mouth closed into a tight line like Ma's when she heard about the saloon gunfight. I felt the barrel of his pistol press against my ribs right on the spot I'd showed him, and he pulled the trigger.

This time, I let the bullet pass.

I looked behind me in time to see Ben fly backwards from the unobstructed, close-range force of Ulie's bullet. It caught him full in the chest. He didn't even have time to be surprised before he was dead on the dirt.

Ulie threw down his pistol and grabbed me. "Sit down, Jase, sit! Gotta stop the bleeding. Hades, Jase, why ain't you bleeding?"

"I am bleeding." I let him lower me to the ground, cradling my left arm to keep the shoulder still. "The bastard shot me in the back. But I'll live. Go see if Valentine is still alive."

"But I just shot you! I—" He ripped my shirt open, exposing my ribcage, and just stared. Then he wiped his fingers slowly across my unblemished skin, and I saw the dawning of understanding in his face.

I said calmly, "No, you shot *through* me to get that backshooter, Ben Kelley. Now go see to Valentine."

He got up to go look for her, moving like a sleepwalker. The minute he stepped away, I let out my breath in a gasp of pain and sagged back against the wall.

He came back only a moment later. "I can't find her. She must have slid over the edge."

Over that edge was a long way down. I sighed. There had been something unexpected about that last conversation, something—promising. But it was too late for second chances now. "We'll tell them where to look for her body in the morning."

"Never mind her, Jase." He bent over me, delicately probing my wounded shoulder. "What in Hades just happened?"

"You just saved the Territory the cost of Ben Kelley's trial," I said, gasping a little at his touch. "That new pistol of yours packs a nice kick, doesn't it? I think I'll have a bruise there for a while." I kept talking, to give Ulie time to get used to the idea. When you're a lawman, you get accustomed to seeing people die. Seeing someone *not* die takes a bit more getting used to.

"Jase, all this time...." Now he was packing the wound in my shoulder like a machine, his mind undoubtedly racing on a different orbit, reckoning back, collecting the pieces. "That hole in your shoulder. Kelley did shoot you today, didn't he? And the shootout this morning—all those holes in your coat—that's why you always go in first, and never get shot. Every damned time!"

"Yeah."

"Why didn't you tell me?"

I let him figure that one out on his own. He didn't spend much time on it. He tied my left arm up in his bandana, then stared square into my face. "Hades, Jase, you let him shoot you! You didn't dodge, you just let him shoot you so he wouldn't get me. You arrogant—! Did you think I wanted you to get shot instead of me?"

"No. But you'd have done the same for me, little brother."

"Yeah, I would." Then his grin flashed in the twilight. "But if you ever ride me again about *me* being reckless, I'll pound you!"

He lifted me to my feet, slid his shoulders under my right arm, and started me on a careful walk back to our camp.

We Wilders always look out for each other.

The Justice Blues

Carla Lee Suson

THE SANCTUM DOORS made a pneumatic swish as Constructor walked in. Per our nightly ritual, I went to greet my husband of over four years in the uniform room. I knew something was wrong when I noticed he was walking stiffly.

"What happened?" I asked as he pulled off his titanium hard hat and peeled off his steel-toed boots.

He lowered his head from its near seven-foot height as I helped remove his armored body cast, hanging it along with the hat on an empty t-square support. The room held five uniforms, all midnight blue with the silver C across the Kevlar-composite breastplate.

"The South Chicago gang got its hands on some high-tech semi-automatics and decided to test them out on me tonight."

"Are you okay?" I exclaimed as the spandex came off next, his body showing an array of large bruises across his chest and back. The sickly green and yellow areas looked like day old injuries rather than hours old. Because of his accelerated healing, Michael only needed the night to mend completely. "Do you need some pain killers?"

He nodded and I grabbed two pills from the medicine cabinet while he talked. "That gang will think twice before taking me on again, though." He washed down the drugs with water. "The damn gun knocked me on my ass and then about twenty punks swarmed out with chains and baseball bats. It didn't last long, though. At least eight of them weren't breathing in the end. I'm telling you, Angelica, we've got to find some way to get the damn breastplates to absorb the punch from the bullets."

"Michael, the engineers have tried to solve the velocity punch. It's simple physics. There's just no way to slow down a bullet before it hits you."

He frowned and headed for the shower. A few minutes later, the steam curls rose above the frosted glass.

I followed him. "Michael?"

"What?"

"I think I should take over the company's books, or we should at least have them audited." Constructor Enterprises, the financial side of Team Constructor, sold the hero-based toys, posters, t-shirts, and anything else that held the trademarked, steel-bolt stylized "C." The profits paid for our large house on five acres of the Wisconsin-Illinois border. They also supported Constructor's many gadgets and cars, as well as an on-call doctor; a crack lawyer; our franchise agent, Larry; and our mechanic, Buck, who also had a Ph.D. in engineering.

"Larry's the money guy. He'll take care of that," he replied.

"But the numbers aren't adding up. Plus, I have an MBA. We don't need Larry."

The glass door opened and a hand shot out, grabbing my wrist and pulling me in. "Michael, no." I shrank back but it was useless. "At least let me get my clothes off!" But by then I was already in the shower. He ripped my wet clothing away like it was paper.

"Women weren't meant for running companies." His voice came out a near growl. "You're my songbird. You'll stay here and make me happy."

"No, Michael!" With my hands flat against his chest, I tried to push him away, but it was trying to move a mountain. He nuzzled my neck, his wet blond hair rubbing along my cheek. "Can we please just talk?"

In the early days of our marriage, Michael had been a gentle and considerate lover. Around two years ago, he began enjoying sex more if I struggled a bit. At first, I had given in to the rape-like play, but after a while, it became less gentle. Now fighting against him resulted in bruises. Sex was to be endured rather than enjoyed.

"I saw your old friend Ramirez today," he said. "He's moved up as one of the leaders of the Southside gang."

I tensed. Michael sometimes had jealous fits over the hint of other men's interest in me. "I always hated him, you know that," I said.

"Yeah, well he sure had a hard-on for you, didn't he, little bird?" His hands began clenching and unclenching in my hair.

"Michael, you're hurting me."

"Yep, Ramirez hated the fact that an Anglo swooped in and stole the neighborhood nightingale away." With his hand balled up my hair, he pulled my head back and planted a bruising kiss on my lips.

"Please let go. Ramirez didn't mean anything to me and I never dated him. You know that. He just showed up to listen to our band, that's all." I tried to move out from under the water, but his grip on the back of my head held me in place. "Why don't we dry off and go into the bedroom? I'll give you a massage and a beer."

Instead, he flattened me against the tile with his bulk. "You know what I want, Angelica," he spoke in my ear. "Women have one function in this world and that is right here." Holding my hips tightly, he picked me up and inserted himself while I stayed pinned against the wall. I whimpered at the force of the violation. "Sing to me."

Thirty minutes later, I still flinched with soreness as I picked up the wet rags that were previously my clothes and mopped up the water with towels. Moving slowly, I got another painkiller out of the medicine cabinet and chased it down with handfuls of water from the faucet. Within a few minutes, the throbbing receded some and I leaned against the wall, silent tears rolling down my cheeks.

What had I become? Five years ago, Angelica Cortez was a rising star. My group, Nightingale, had played at many of the Chicago venues and was poised to begin a multi-city tour. What most people didn't know was that I interwove magic into the music. People thought the Pied Piper was a legend. Truth be told, he was a Spaniard, my direct ancestor. His descendants had the talent at various levels, but the ability soared in me. I could focus the sound and fill it with unimaginable power. I never met a crowd I couldn't bend to my will. When I sang, I could make the audience laugh, dance, weep, or fall to their knees in agony. That level of control frightened me and I kept it locked away.

Nowadays, I stayed isolated in our mansion, a rare toy for a powerful man and Chicago's top crime fighter. I sighed, moving slowly. If I didn't go to the dinner table soon, he would come looking for me.

When I joined my husband for our usual middle-of-the-night meal, Michael was already serving up his second plateful.

"What took so long?"

I waved a hand weakly. "I cleaned up the bathroom." I gathered my food and then sat, pushing the bits around with my fork.

"What's up?" He gestured at my plate. "You're not hungry?"

"I worry about you, that's all."

His chewing slowed before he answered. "I don't want to hear about it. I told you that I was the Constructor on the night before our wedding, so don't go all weepy on me now."

"True, and I told you about my powers too. You could have used extra help tonight."

"What could you do? Serenade them?"

"The sound does damage too." I replied. The painkiller made me feel giddy enough to talk back.

"Yeah? Show me." He smirked as he picked up a glass. "I'm a villain coming to take you down. What are you gonna do?"

I tilted my head up and let off one shrill, clear note, holding it steady. His eyes narrowed as the china plate vibrated and the silverware jittered across the table. The glass in his hand exploded, blowing shards over his dinner. The plate then leaped off of the table, cracking apart. As I ceased, he opened his hand and blood trickled down his palm.

"Great," he snarled, pulling the glass shard out and pressing the linen napkin against the wound. "Thanks for nothing."

"I'm not helpless. I could help you."

"Don't be stupid. Constructor doesn't need a sidekick." He screeched the chair back and stormed out of the room.

Sadly, I picked up the broken dishes and then looked past his chair to the wall. The paint looked splintered into a spider web pattern. I bit my lip, feeling ashamed about the damage I had caused. As I ran a finger along the cracks, the drywall crumbled apart.

By four in the morning, I lay awake, feeling restless. In the darkness, the magic swirled inside me, sharp notes and discordant beats writhing like a living thing. More than two years had passed since I let that much power free. It still frightened me.

I finally got up and walked silently through the house. More tears flowed as I remembered how we met. Michael Dornman saw me on stage in Millennium Park. With high cheek bones, deep blue eyes, and wavy blond hair, he was most women's wet dream. He courted me for months with great romance. The night before our wedding, we shared secrets over champagne and lovemaking. He called me his song bird and told me he loved my voice. The next day, he put me in his gilded cage of a home; his personal nightingale locked away from the world.

A week later, the weather warmed up enough for walking in the park. I took my flute and often played for the children of the neighborhood. The kids came running to me like the Piper of legend as the magic and music weaved in a two-four beat. The mothers often smiled, tapping toes or even sometimes breaking into light steps themselves.

One Monday morning, I sat near the mothers on one of the black iron benches, watching the youngsters romp. A large, brown dog wandered up the walking path, staggering at first and then growling as it approached the children. Its ribs stood out against the dirty hair. Foam dripping from its mouth, the mutt barked and snapped at the children, who began to scream and run from it.

One mother cried out, "It's rabid!"

I ran past the retreating kids, placing myself between them and the canine. The beast lowered its head, growls increasing as it bared its teeth. Pure tones rose up through my throat, fed by intense power. The animal ducked its head, snapping more. I increased the vocalizing as it began to quiver and whine. Soon the dog staggered and fell down. The last breath rattled out of its lungs and it lay still, eyes open and empty.

I cut the sound off abruptly and looked around. Children hid behind their mothers. Everyone stared wide-eyed at me. One woman held a cell phone to her ear and pointed at me. As the sirens cut through the air, I took off down the path back into the trees before the police arrived.

Michael came home that night in a foul mood and covered in patches of drying muck and black soot. "Demolator's back in town," he growled. "The asshole decided to set the landfill on fire. He wanted to ignite the accumulated methane so he could blow a hole in the city. I clogged his flame thrower with the sledge and the damn thing blew me into the pits. Set fire to part of the trash too." He grinned for a moment, a mean leer. "He's dead now, though. Three of the firemen were caught in the blast, too."

"How terrible! Did they survive?"

"No, the damn idiots should learn to stay out of the way." He peeled off the clothing and tossed the body suit over to me. "Clean it up. I hate having that stink in my headquarters."

I followed him into the bathroom and leaned against the marble sink top as he showered. "Something happened today that I want to tell you about. I walked around the park again and this dog wandered onto the playground."

The water shut off and he grabbed a thick blue towel. "Yeah honey. I hear where you're going with this. No dogs."

"What?"

"No pets. Understand?"

"No, I wasn't asking—"

"I work too damn hard to come home and have to deal with dog crap."

"Michael, I wasn't saying I—"

He held up one finger in front of my face, silencing me. "I'm not discussing it. Now where is my food? I'm starving."

I gritted my teeth in frustration. In the kitchen, I pulled the late night dinner out of the oven. He ate the roast chicken heartily. After a few moments, he slowed down and spoke. "What's wrong?"

Shrugging, I said, "I worry a lot, that's all. I think I should go with you some nights."

He frowned and dropped the chicken bone with a hard thunk. "Christ, not this again."

"We could make me a suit out of the same bulletproof material as yours," I said quickly. "I could patrol one section while you did another. We'd get the same work done with half the effort."

"I told you, no woman's going to horn in on the Constructor legend!" He glared at me, face tight with anger. "Besides, how the hell are you going to stop anything? Nag at it?"

I frowned. The music inside began a thrumming that vibrated through my bones. "I have power. I've shown it to you."

"Right!" Mockery filled his voice. "Breaking glasses. That'll work well."

"It's more than that, dammit, and you know it. Do you need more proof?" I stood and took a deep breath, while tightening my abdomen.

As the sound started to come out, Michael bounded across the room, driving a fist into my stomach. The air exploded out of my lungs as he drew his hand back and slapped me, knocking me to the floor. "I don't need my dinner ruined tonight."

Blood flowed from my nose and I coughed and struggled to breathe as he returned to his seat.

"I'm tired of your shit, Angelica. Your attitude has needed adjusting for some time now. You have a good life here. This discussion's closed."

The next morning as the sky brightened, I entered Michael's secret sanctum. The taint of sewage on his costume hung in the air. Rinsing the spandex removed the worst of the debris, but underneath the grime, a red spot on the cleaning rag looked like blood. I stopped and examined the patch of dark material it came from. Too slick for blood, it took a moment to realize the suit contained a long smear of lipstick along the forearm area.

I stared at the stain. I brought my own arm up and wiped my mouth from mid-forearm to wrist, the way I had seen Michael wipe away wetness from his lips. The streak on the cloth followed the same pattern.

After tossing the spandex back into the soapy water, I retreated to the sanctum's computer room. All of Michael's crime-fighting tool belts had GPS locators built in as a safety precaution. I replayed the file from the night before, noting the stops before the fight at the city dump. Around nine o'clock, Constructor had visited a high-rise building for over an hour. I stared at the glowing dots on the map, each with a date and time. Some women threw themselves at Constructor in the heat of rescue. On the newscasts, Michael always gently disengaged their arms and dropped them back to their hero-worshiping toes. I had never seen a lipstick stain on his costume before.

No wiser for all the pondering, I returned to the uniform room's laundry area, stuffed the uniform into a washing machine, then scrubbed the armored chest piece while humming. The magic flowed around my head, easing me into quiet contentment. Afterwards, the place smelled more of lemon cleanser than Chicago trash.

Feeling grimy, I wandered back and slipped into the master bathroom to shower. After I lathered up, the plastic curtain parted. Michael stepped in and pulled me into a tight hug from behind. I stiffened at his touch.

"I didn't mean to wake you," I said cautiously.

He buried his head into the top of my hair. "You were humming."

"I'm sorry."

His hands began roaming across my body. "Don't stop. Sing to me."

I put words to the tune of an old blues song about love and he hugged me tighter, his breath quickening. As his arms encircled my stomach, I hissed in pain as he pulled against my bruised abdomen. He relaxed his grip and I turned to face him, gritting my teeth. He ran a finger across the swollen portion of my jaw. We looked at each other in silence before he muttered, "Whatever," and stepped out of the shower.

I woke up by the early afternoon, finding Michael gone from the bedroom. Thoughts about the lipstick trickled through my mind. Had Michael cheated on me? If so, how much of it was my fault for not living up to the kind of wife a superhero needed? Last night certainly could have gone better. Resolving to be nicer, I got up and dressed in tight jeans, high-heeled boots, and a wraparound top with a plunging neckline. Once done, I wandered through the house, eventually finding Michael working at the computer in the sanctum.

He looked up as I joined him by the console. "Hey, Angel."

"Problems?"

"Nah. I'm logging in last night's attack and reading the police reports."

I ran gentle fingers along his neck and shoulders. "Michael, if things are quiet for the moment, why don't you stay in today? We can grab dinner out; maybe walk down by the lake. We haven't done that in ages."

"Crime doesn't take a day off," he replied while his fingers danced across the keyboard.

"Yes, but crime isn't human. No one will blame you if you didn't patrol every single night. Stay with me."

He spun his chair around to face me, eyes wandering down my cleavage before he spoke. "Tempting offer, Angel. Maybe in a few days." He returned to the computer screen while talking. "The new motorcycle came in. Make sure you take it for a test ride."

Not wanting to be bothered with details, Michael had put me in charge of testing all equipment before passing it on to him. The newest addition to the fleet was a sleek Japanese motorcycle that was reputed to be nearly silent in action.

As I entered the underground garage a few minutes later, Buck, our mechanic, touched his fingers to his dirty ball cap.

"What's up?" he said by way of greeting.

"I'm going to check out the new bike."

He pointed to the left. The midnight blue and silver motorcycle shone with slick aerodynamic lines and painted-on silver flames. I mounted it and started the engine. The machine vibrated though my hips and thighs, but only produced the smallest rumble of sound. The fit and weight were perfect for my body size.

Buck handed me my helmet. "The engine's a beauty and silent as the grave, but the damn thing is too small for the boss."

"It sure is pretty, though."

"Yep, the salesman says it will top 200 miles per hour without even breaking a sweat." He winked. "Not that I would know anyone needing to go that fast. I can strip it down and reverse engineer it. We'll then modify one of the big cruising bikes to do the same."

I patted the blue console. "Not this one, Buck. Order another one to tinker with. I want to keep this one."

He grinned. "Yeah? Whatcha going to call your new ride?"

"My Wings." I put the helmet on and revved the motor, shooting down the tunnel towards the exit.

Within minutes, I blew down the nearly abandoned farming roads that crossed the state line. The speedometer hit 175, but the engine only switched from a low thrum to a slightly higher purr. I laughed and gunned it higher, bending down across the bars.

After a while I slowed down, finally stopping at a small town burger joint for a snack. While I sat inside, an old black sports car turned into the parking lot. No one got out and after a while, I wondered if the driver was a lost tourist. Finishing up the food, I remounted the cycle, and started back toward home at a more sedate speed. The day shone bright, and the trees along the road were bursting forth with new leafy growth.

After a few moments, the black car came up behind me, muffler roaring with noise. The vehicle shifted onto the left, moving to pass me and I slowed down. Instead of continuing forward, it paced the bike for a few moments. I slowed down more and it mirrored my speed.

Suddenly the car surged forward and veered into my lane, cutting me off. I hit the brakes hard and swerved off the road, rolling clear of the bike as I tumbled down the grassy embankment.

I unsnapped and jerked the helmet off, cursing. The car skidded to a stop on the gravel shoulder and three men climbed out. One walked down the embankment, and I recognized the dark skin and acne-scarred face of Roberto Ramirez.

"Hey, *hombres!* Look who we caught!" He shifted a tire iron from hand to hand as he slowly walked toward me. "I knew Constructor would have a *mujer*, but you, Angelica?"

"What are you talking about?"

"A few weeks ago, my gang had a run in with that *bastardo*. While he was down, we planted a bug on his car. We've been watching his home. Then today, a little *chiquita* comes flying out on a rocket."

He got closer, hefting the iron up. "He killed my *hermano*, Angelica. The *bastardo's* got to pay." The other two came forward, flanking Ramirez.

I shifted a couple of steps backwards toward the tree line. "So you're going to kill me instead?"

He grinned, gold tooth gleaming. "No, we're going to take you with us. You're going to be bait for the trap." His eyes roamed down to the deep-cut shirt peeking out of my open jacket. He ran a tongue across his lips. "You look good, Nightingale. Don't worry. Constructor will get his *mujer* back, only a little damaged."

He lunged forward and I reacted with a swinging kick to the face. Although I was no champion fighter, Michael had taught me some self-defense. The boot connected with Ramirez's jaw and his head rocked back. His buddies began to close in from the sides.

Ramirez reared back up quickly. "Bitch," he snarled. He swung the metal bar at my head. I ducked and stumbled back further.

The magic rose in me, fed by my anger and fear. "No, Roberto. *You're* the mad dog and it's time someone put you down."

I opened my mouth, loading the short scream with all the power writhing inside. The sonic punch knocked them all off their feet and sent a crack through a dying tree.

One man stayed down, while the other rolled on the ground clutching his head. Ramirez rose up again, blood pouring from his nose.

"Stay down," I shouted at him. "I don't want to hurt you anymore."

He picked up the metal bar again, holding it like a bat. "You're going to pay for that."

He rushed at me and I screamed again, holding the pure tone. His body began to twitch as he fell to his knees. I gritted my teeth, and pushed the vocalization harder. Blood flowed out of his ears. His eyes rolled up in his head as his whole body convulsed. I cut the sound off and he fell forward in the loamy dirt.

The others were on the ground as well. I looked at the faces one by one. Each lay open-eyed with blood trickling out of ears and noses. None of them were breathing. A panic rose inside of me, and I stumbled back to the bike. Tears ran down my face as I mounted the bike. Hands shaking, I put the helmet back on. Once on the road again, I raced away from the vision of the men that I had killed.

After a four-hour absence from the house, I returned feeling sick and shaky. Buck was gone for the night, and the European speedster spot was empty, proof that Michael had left early.

Once upstairs, I showered, scrubbing my skin raw. Then I crawled into the bed, huddled in a ball and cried until I fell into an exhausted sleep.

I woke a few hours later and stood on the deck, watching the moonlight cover the acres of wild lands around the house. A sad song filled me and I sang a dirge into the night to my loss of innocence. Because I killed those men, nothing would ever be the same again.

That night and several nights afterwards, Michael came home with the smell of Chantilly perfume on his uniform—not my brand. We didn't talk much, and meals often passed in silence. Sleep became harder as nightmares of Ramirez haunted me.

By Saturday morning, life seemed bleaker than ever. In the mirror, I stared into the eyes of a pale mess of a stranger. My face looked thin and pinched, dark rings circled my brown eyes, and the long, black hair fought in wisps to escape the rubber band. My oversized t-shirt and faded jeans also radiated zero attractiveness. Was the stranger in the mirror the reason Michael smelled of Chantilly every night? What happened to the bright-eyed songstress I was years ago?

Michael sauntered in, glancing at me as he went to his dresser. I cringed slightly at his passing, a tear leaking down my cheek.

He towered over me and spoke with a voice edged with irritation, "God, Angelica, you're dragging all over the house. What's wrong now?"

I flicked tears away with a quick jerk of my fingers. "I'm tired and…and lonely. You're gone a lot."

"Is this about getting a damn dog again?"

"No," I bit my lip. "Michael, do you still love me?"

He looked startled. "What an odd question. You're my song bird." He put a finger under my chin, forcing my head up to look him in the eyes. "What's this all about?"

I sniffled. "I've been having a lot of nightmares lately. That's all."

He nodded. "Here." He took a bottle out of his dresser and handed me a pill. "This'll put you out like a light."

I swallowed the white drug down along with some water from his glass, then stretched out across the bed. Tears flowed freely as he walked away and I realized that he had never responded to my question. As sleep tugged at my eyes, my last thought was that perhaps in his silence, I had found my answer after all.

I woke a few hours later feeling better. Ramirez was gone and nothing I could do would bring him back. I needed to save my marriage now.

Picking out clothes became an act of frustration as I realized how badly my wardrobe had declined. Finally, I chose a dark green pullover with a deep scoop neck and the least faded looking pants along with high-heeled sandals. Makeup came next and I pulled my hair off my face with a large metal clip. Silver dangling earrings and matching chain added the touch of extra class.

Overall, the effect looked better than the ghost of a woman I had seen that morning. The transformation also brought a change of attitude from lost to hopeful. Buzzing with a serene melody, I found Michael restocking his tool belt.

He glanced at me and did a double take. "You look better."

"Thank you. I wanted to look nice for you."

Michael hugged me and I responded with a heated kiss.

"Sing to me," he commanded as he pulled me into his lap.

I obliged with something low and bluesy, one of his favorites.

His hands wandered over me, and I began to kiss his throat, moving down his chest.

"Stay with me tonight," I whispered.

He paused. "I can't. I've got some meetings."

I laid my head on his shoulder. "Police chief giving you trouble again?"

"No, it's a...an informant and he doesn't like to meet openly." Michael glanced at his watch and pushed me back to standing. "I've got to go."

Forty-five minutes later, his black sports car rolled up the tunnel and out the secret entrance. Constructor patrolled the night once more.

Silence filled the house. I tried to bury myself in the accounts, but gave up after a few moments. As I shut the bookkeeping program down, an icon blinked in the corner of the screen. It was Michael's tool belt GPS.

I clicked on it and the customized program opened a map with a red dot pinpointing a condominium building near the Navy Pier, the same place he went on the night I had discovered the lipstick. I hit the information icon and a small pop-up window displayed the building's name, address, and the condo number. With a few keystrokes, our specialized database returned the name of the owner, Donna Duquette.

I stared at the screen, feeling numb. Was this Miss Chantilly? Maybe it was high time to find out.

Using the speed of my bike, I arrived at the building within twenty minutes. Michael's car sat in one dark corner on the fourth floor of the parking garage. A hole filled the place where the door lock should have been in the entrance door. In my mind, I pictured Michael thumping it with his finger, shooting the cylinder out the other side. As I walked along the carpeted hallway, wild music pumped inside of me fed by rage.

I knocked at condo number 437. A brown-haired woman swung the door open. As we looked at each other she spoke, half smiling in confusion. "Yes?"

I looked past her and saw Michael. He was half disrobed, his armor thrown over a chair.

His jaw dropped open. "Angelica, what—?"

"*Puta!*" I spat at the woman and shoved her hard.

She fell away from the door, shocked. "Who are you?"

"His wife!" I jabbed a finger at Michael. "Bastard! This is the appointment that couldn't wait? This whore is why you didn't make love to me?"

"Now just wait," he said, hands spread outward in front of him.

"For what? For you to tell me it isn't what it looks like?"

"Settle down!" he snapped back.

But my magic screamed inside. Furious, my words came out in discordant harmony. "This is why you never want me on patrol. You wanted to keep your dirty little secrets. How long have you been sleeping around? Tell me! What crime did you find between that slut's legs?"

His face flushed with redness. Michael rushed at me, wrapping his powerful arms around mine, crushing me against his body.

"Be still or I'll hurt you," he warned.

I kicked at his shins hard, but he lifted me off the ground.

"Want to be the big hero?" he growled. "Well, tell me this, you silly little bitch! Tell me how you're going to get loose from this!"

I opened my mouth to sing, but he tightened his grip, punching my air out in a gasp.

"Oh, no, little song bird. I know you can pacify me with your sounds, but it's not going to happen. So tell me, Angelica, how are you going to fight off bad guys if you can't even break my hold?"

His muscles tensed more. Pain filled my chest as my ribs creaked. Breathing became impossible.

"That's right," he snarled. "You're as breakable as a little sparrow. Some badass crime fighter you'd be."

Spots formed in front of my eyes. As he clenched harder, two pops sounded sharp in the air as I jerked at the agony of my ribs snapping. Writhing, my chest was consumed with pain and the music bled away as darkness filled my brain.

As I started to blacked out, I heard the woman's voice behind me. "Mike, stop! She's turning purple. You're killing her!"

Michael dropped me and I lay in a heap on the floor. My ribs throbbed every time I tried to breathe in.

Moments later, he knelt down in front of me, fully dressed, one hand on my shoulder, shaking it. "Look at me."

I shuddered in agony as the motion caused the broken bones to shift. With tears running down my face, I glared into his eyes.

His words came out low and hard. "I'm going on patrol. This never happened. You'll go home, get cleaned up, and fix my dinner as usual."

I shook my head. One hoarse word came out of my mouth, "Divorce."

He snorted. "I don't think so, Angelica. I own you. You've got no place to go. Plus I can't trust you not to shoot your mouth off about my identity all over town. My reputation won't be dragged through the media mud. No, you're my little song bird and our marriage is until death we part."

He stood and kissed Donna on the cheek. "I'll see you tomorrow."

I flinched when the door slammed shut. After a few moments Donna knelt next to me with bags of ice wrapped in two towels.

"Can you breathe okay or should you sit up?" She placed the cold bundles along my chest. The skin along my arms was turning blue and purple. "We should call an ambulance."

I shook my head slightly. "No ambulance. Call this number and say, 'Man down.' He'll know what to do." Between gasps, I reeled off the number of Team Constructor's emergency doctor.

With a frown, she picked up the phone and relayed the message. After stating the address, she said, "I'm not sure. She's got at least two ribs broken and she's in a lot of pain. Yes, she's breathing okay. Yes, I said 'she'...*Mrs.* Constructor." After hanging up, Donna sat next to me again. "The doctor said he'll be here very soon."

I struggled to rise up and the effort made me moan and shudder. She helped me sit upright. The act of kindness broke through my agony and I began to sob loudly. She held my hand and muttered soft comforting noises while I cried.

When the storm of emotion passed, she spoke quietly. "I'm so sorry," she said. "I didn't know he was married."

I glared at her through teary eyes. "Why are you being so kind to me?"

She let go of my hand and dropped her eyes. "I've had an abusive partner too. In fact, that is how Mike and I met. I'm so sorry."

"I don't care."

She nodded. "I know, but we're not that different. I got smacked around by Joe, my ex, several times. After I landed in the hospital the second time, I left him and moved here. Somehow Joe tracked me down again. He dragged me out of work one night and began whaling on me. Constructor showed up and stopped him. I thought the man was a god. The next night, he turned up and offered to see me home. Then he came again the following night." She swallowed before continuing. "He made me feel safe." She paused and looked me in the eyes. "Before I slept with him, I checked the Internet and couldn't find anything about Constructor having a wife."

"He has a real name." I said softly.

She nodded. "Yes, I checked Mike Cortez and Michael Cortez too."

I snorted. "He lied. Cortez is my name. His is Michael Dornman."

"I'm so sorry."

I drank more water. "Are you going to continue sleeping with him?"

A single tear coursed down her cheek. "I don't have a choice. How could anyone hide from Constructor? Look what he did to you. Can *you* stop him?"

"Yes," I said softly, "I think I can."

"You have superpowers too?" The doubt filled her voice.

"I do. I just never wanted to use them against him."

Donna frowned with disbelief.

I gave her a twisted, hard smile, letting the anger fill my eyes as I spoke. "And I have my fury, which is enough."

When Dr. Heidelson arrived, he gave me painkillers, wrapped my ribs, and drove me home.

The doctor stayed as I faded in and out of sleep. I woke again, finding Michael and Heidelson exchanging quiet, forceful words as Michael watched me with wariness. I closed my eyes again and drifted back off.

A little after five in the predawn hours, the pills wore off and I shifted in an attempt to get comfortable. The bed moved as Michael spooned up close, wrapping his arms around me.

"I'm sorry that I hurt you," he said quietly into my ear. "You surprised me, but I shouldn't have gotten that mad."

"Do you love her?"

He squeezed just slightly before answering. "Does it matter? She's just another trophy."

"It matters to me." The words came out sad as I closed my eyes. My heart filled with hatred, and I gritted my teeth against his touch. Within the year, I vowed to myself, I would rid myself of this man or die trying.

In the many weeks it took for broken bones to heal, I changed my world in secret while Constructor's world continued on as normal. When the bones knitted enough to begin training, I did my chores, but included more weight lifting, pushing myself to the limit on the machines.

I took time to go shopping for better clothes. My evolution into a stronger person also involved changing my hair to a shorter, more modern look. Michael appreciated the more youthful, attractive style, reacting with kinder words and more attention. I sang to him again whenever he asked, all the melodies he loved. I smiled and played his perfect wife, but the core of fury still burned inside.

The nights while he was on patrol were another matter. The profits from Team Constructor had created a multi-million dollar nest egg for the superhero. Over time, I syphoned off most of it. As the final days with him grew closer, a large sum lay hidden in bank accounts in my name.

The uniform manufacturers understood about absolute secrecy. So when I approached them with the design for a different costume, they didn't hesitate. Once ready, the white clothes had the same safety materials as in Constructor's costume, but with an "H" in the center. It was molded

to my curves, and the knee-high, white boots boosted my height. The metal links in the long gloves fit my fingers perfectly, and the mask hid most of my features.

The final day of my plan started with an early morning visit to Donna Duquette's place while Michael slept at home. She answered the door, looking rumpled in pink pajamas.

"What are you doing here?" She glanced into the hallway.

"We need to talk."

She opened the door further, and I took a seat on her couch.

Donna padded over and sat in the matching chair. "You look different, more confident."

My mouth moved in a tight smile. "I could only improve after that night, don't you think?"

She nodded. "Has he hurt you more?"

"No, he's turned into the good husband as long as I remain the dutiful wife. Do you still see him?"

"Not every night, but yes, he comes by."

"Do you love him?"

Her head jerked up. "No. I'm afraid of him." A shadow of pain flickered across her eyes.

"Has he hurt you?" I needed her calm in order for this phase of the plan to work. I began a low, soothing hum, weaving in feelings of relaxation. The tension bled out of her shoulders.

"I told him that I wanted to stop," she said. "He didn't care. He just laughed and lifted me up. He didn't hurt me like he did you, but I could see it in his eyes. We had sex that night, but it was...."

"Rough."

Donna nodded. "He said superheroes deserved multiple trophies and that he owned me now."

I pulled out a cashier's check and handed it to her. Her eyes widened at the million dollar amount. The humming stepped up, moving from relaxation to a hypnotic melody. Then her eyes glazed over as I spoke.

"That's enough to start over anywhere else but Chicago." My words came out in singsong, firm and directed. "But you must leave today, before he patrols tonight. Go get dressed and start packing now. Take only what you can carry with you today."

Without another word, she got up and walked away.

After that, I moved the last of my possessions to my new home. The place sat on the top floor of a high security building. Although it cost a small fortune to buy the rooftop penthouse, the airy view fit me. I had no worries about the future. The millions I had already taken could last me a lifetime if properly invested.

Also I still had my voice.

Michael left by seven that evening, taking the large cruising motorcycle because of the warm summer air. Within the hour, I drove each car out and left them all along the street within blocks of our house. At ten-thirty, the tow trucks arrived to haul off all but Michael's original muscle car. His sanctum stayed safe, I owed Constructor that much, but the cars were donated to the local women's shelter. The only exception was my Wings.

By midnight, everyone associated with Team Constructor had received their final payments and layoff notices. With that chore completed, I allowed my burning fury its freedom. One of Michael's smaller sledgehammers made a satisfying crunch of steel on glass shattering the high tech computer system. Laughing with delight, I smashed and ripped until all the machines lay gutted.

The spandex suits were shredded with a sharp knife and I slashed the boots apart. After piling the armored breastplates into one heap, I added lighter fluid and set them on fire. Once the cover fabric and characteristic "C" burned away, I turned on the extinguisher. The life of Constructor was almost completely destroyed.

Finally, I prepared for the oncoming battle and thought about the evolution of the superhero. Every great fighter started out with good intentions and wondrous acts. Yet somewhere in Michael's career, his power had corrupted him. Constructor had changed over the years. He killed more and took more, like the revolutionary leader, welcomed at first by the crowds only to turn despotic later. Although I had no illusions that I would survive a normal fight with Constructor, it was time to topple the villain he had become. Too many women were victims of abusive men just like him and that needed to change.

I showered and dressed, prepping psychologically the way *he* did before every patrol. The simple actions filled me with a sense of purpose as the black silk covered my calves and thighs, the white body suit stretched over hips and breasts. As I put on the core breastplate, I hummed a tune of confidence in the silent house. The black halo of loose curls framed my white mask. I saw a powerful woman in the mirror, the gold "H" shining in the light.

Tonight Harmony was born.

The magic that filled me had a name both musical and threatening. I became that stronger person, rising from the ashes of my dysfunctional married life. This time, Michael would discover just how much harm my music could do.

At two-thirty in the morning, he came home. The door of the garage slammed shut and the hydraulic lift ground into action. As I sauntered in, white boot heels clicking on the tile, he removed and threw his tool belt against the wall.

"What the hell is going on around here? Did you burn dinner? It smells like smoke." He snarled. "Donna's gone and where in hell are all the cars?" He turned to face me, eyes widening, as he drank in the costume. "Looking like that, maybe I don't need Donna. What are you dressed up as?"

"You're not going to hurt me anymore or bother Donna. People aren't trophies and it's time someone taught you that lesson."

He chuckled. "What? You think you can be a villain?" The humor left his eyes as his hands came to rest on his hips. "What's the 'H' for? Hellcat, or Helpless?"

"Harmony, thanks to you." I stood ready to move, weight forward on the balls of my feet. "Physically you're too strong for me, that's true. But tonight I've destroyed Team Constructor, and now I'm going to stop you. As long as I'm around, you'll never hurt another woman again." I began to vocalize, low alto purring.

The magic started his shoulder and hip muscles twitching although he stiffened against it. He bared his teeth as his hands balled into fists. "I don't mind teaching you another lesson in manners, bitch."

My words came out singsong. "I only plan to hurt you now. Touch me again and I'll kill you."

I increased the pitch, the magic pouring into the sound. His face twisted in pain and he began to sway. He started to move forward, but I stepped up the power.

Teeth grinding, Michael rushed forward, but I swung a roundhouse kick at his head then leaped back out of reach as his head snapped back.

I infused the music with emotion that spoke of pain, sorrow, and remorse. As he began to claw at his ears, Michael dropped to his knees. I kicked him again, a solid blow to the stomach. The big man fell over, convulsing on the floor as blood began to trickle out his nose.

I watched him for a few seconds before backing the magic off. After a moment, the focus returned to his eyes. As his head turned toward me, I squatted down, a safe distance away.

"I'm not going to kill you although I could. I'm going to leave you here in your empty cage. Constructor ends tonight."

He shifted to move upright. Once on his knees, I swung around again, another kick to his face. His head snapped back as I danced away, out of the grasp of those powerful fists.

"I own you," he growled as he struggled to stand again.

"No, Michael, it's over. Don't make me damage you more."

He stumbled upright, and I began the alto notes again. Bits of metal and glass began vibrating across the floor. As he rushed forward, I held my ground and swung a hard fist into his throat. The built-in metal knuckles in the glove crushed his wind pipe. We both fell to the floor. As he struggled to breathe, I kicked and punched with all my might, driving powerful blows into the unprotected parts of his body. Once freed, I shifted quickly away, bruised a little but still singing.

He came up on one knee, wheezing, with one eye swelling shut. "When I get my hands on you, you're dead. Do you hear me? *Dead!*"

I shook my head. "You'll never hurt me again, Michael." As he came at me, the power of my scream drove him back to the ground, hands clenched against his head. As he writhed, I began a new song, filled with my magic-fed rage.

His eyes rolled back in his head, and as the big man's body shook, my words filled the air. "The mighty hero Constructor has turned defective. You see, hero and villain are a matter of perspective. And this one is going down, down...."

Death and Life of The Hero

Ricardo Sanchez

THE MAN WHO opened the door was much older than I expected. His hair was gray and thinning, offering a glimpse of the liver-spotted scalp beneath. Loose skin hung in sagging bags beneath his chin in a rooster's beard. His dark, deep-set eyes were at the center of craggy furrows that radiated out like the edges of an impact crater. His bony arms poked out of the sleeves of a loose, threadbare flannel robe.

Of course he's old, I thought to myself. It was a long, long time ago.

"Can I help you, miss?" he asked politely. His voice was strong, steady and clear. It didn't match the worn-out body standing in front of me. That gave me hope I'd found who I was looking for.

I handed him a business card. "Mr. Weller, I'm Laura Halsey. We spoke on the phone yesterday about a piece I'm writing."

The friendly, open expression he'd greeted me with hardened into a scowl, adding a dozen more grooves to the wrinkles around his mouth.

"I told you yesterday, Ms. Halsey. I'm not going to do any talking about that day, and I don't want to be part of any story! Good-bye."

When Weller shuffled a step back to close the door, I stuck my foot into the gap. He didn't slam my shoe, but he didn't open the door any wider, either.

"Damn reporters," he said, his face reddening in anger. "No! I will not talk about the building collapse. I try never to think about it, in fact. It was a terrible tragedy. So there is no reason for you to keep harassing me."

"Okay," I agreed, not moving my foot. "We don't talk about that day. I'm really much more interested in talking to you about The Hero. It's been twenty years since his death and he's almost been forgotten by The City. I want to change that. You can help me."

Weller's jaw moved silently, as if chewing over my compromise.

"Why do you want to talk to me?"

"Your name was listed as one of the people on the scene when The

183

Hero died. I'd like to hear what happened firsthand."

"Maybe it would be better to just let The Hero fade away."

Lots of people in The City felt the same way. The Hero represented a different time. A golden age we'd lost and couldn't hope to reclaim. It was a response I'd heard before and overcome.

"No," I said. "We need The Hero now more than ever, Mr. Weller. We don't have people to look up to anymore. Our role models all turn out to be adulterers, alcoholics or liars. The Hero represented the best in all of us. Everyone I have interviewed about The Hero has told me that he made us want to be better. To try harder. We need that again."

Weller's resistance faded with each word. His grip on the door relaxed, and I could see his shoulders slumping as the tension eased out of them. His face even regained its faded leather color.

It took him a moment to decide, but he finally pushed the door open.

"Fine," he said. "Twenty minutes. I'll give you twenty minutes for twenty years. And then you're going to leave me alone. Forever."

He turned from me and shuffled into his dark, stuffy apartment on stiff legs, leaving me standing in the hallway.

He stopped after a few steps and said without looking back at me, "Well? Get in and shut the door. And don't expect me to offer you a drink. You won't be staying long."

Twenty Years Ago

The Hero rode the thermals above the manufacturing district. It was his favorite spot. The bustle of activity from below sent warm air pulsing up like a soothing bath. He could just close his eyes, drift on the currents and listen to the city.

Too soon, his extraordinary hearing would pick up a gasp of fright, a call for help or the shattering glass that was the telltale sound of a burglary, and he'd go into action, flying to the rescue. But until then, he would enjoy the quiet moment and the simple joy of flying.

When the call came, it was the wailing drone of a fire truck.

The sirens echoed off of the brick, stone and glass buildings that lined the streets of The City. The Hero closed his eyes and mentally filtered out the reverberating sound waves to identify the original sound. The truck was still moving, but the Doppler effect suggested it was coming to a stop, making it easier to pinpoint. He oriented his body toward the point of origin and willed himself to top flight speed, his cape straining to break free from his neck as he flew. He hated the sound of the siren. It meant he was too late. He'd missed some warning signal. Now lives were at risk and all he could do was react.

The Hero concentrated on the wail of the fire truck. As he got closer, he could tell it was coming from the densely populated Cordoba neighborhood. Decades ago this had been an affluent white enclave in a city of immigrants, isolated from the smells, sights and sounds of millions of people, from dozens of cultures, living amongst each other. But in time, change had come even here. Today, the Cordoba was a thriving, densely populated mix of recent arrivals from foreign shores and long-time denizens of The City.

A blaze here could quickly turn into a staggering loss of life and property. The Hero surveyed the scene from above on his approach, but he could detect no signs of smoke. Vallejo Street had been cordoned off and firefighters were escorting whole families out of a building halfway down the block. There was clearly some threat to their safety, but he couldn't identify it from the air. Whatever the cause, the unit responding to the call was Ladder Truck #2.

Fine men and women, The Hero thought to himself.

He had stood shoulder to shoulder with them too many times, facing down some of the worst blazes in The City's history. With no super powers to protect them, those firefighters had demonstrated a level of bravery in the face of danger that made The Hero proud to call them friends.

Scanning the crowd standing closest to the engine, he spotted their commander directing the evacuation of the building.

The Hero thrust his shoulders back and moved his body into a landing position, aiming for a clear patch of concrete just steps away from Captain Harris. The Hero hurtled out of the sky toward the sidewalk like a comet, but touched down as gently as if he'd just stepped off a curb.

"Captain Harris, how I can I help?"

The Hero's deep, calm voice was quiet, but cut cleanly through the yells from bystanders and the shouted commands of rescue workers.

"It's good to see you, Hero," Captain Harris said. "But I don't think there's much for you to do. Someone called in a tip that the White Right anti-immigrant group planted a bomb in this apartment building. Everyone is out. Now we're just waiting for the bomb squad to sweep the place."

The Hero turned his attention to the apartments. This was the fifth bomb threat in a minority neighborhood in the last month. All of them had turned out to be hoaxes so far, but the possibility that there might be a real bomb kept him on edge.

A curtain on a sixth floor window moved.

"Captain, are you positive you cleared the building?"

"Geffon, you sure you got everyone?" Harris barked into his radio.

"*We knocked on every door, Captain,*" came the static-filled response.

The curtain moved again.

"You missed someone," The Hero pointed to a window. "Up there!"

"Damn. I'll send someone."

"I'll go. Whoever it is may be an illegal and afraid of your uniforms."

Before Harris could say anything, The Hero sprinted away, leaving only a dust devil spinning in his wake. He crossed the threshold into the building, senses on alert to any sign of a bomb. He could detect no immediate danger and started up. The stairs were narrow and steep. The wooden banister that kept climbers from slipping into the well was loose and rubbed smooth by decades of use. A firefighter in full gear would have found it difficult to scale the steps, but The Hero raced upward without even slowing down for the tight corners at each landing.

Stepping into the hallway on the sixth floor, he paused.

Which apartment?

He concentrated his hearing, blocking out any sound that wasn't help-ful. Car horns, the yells of people in the streets, the movement of air through the duct work, all eliminated one by one until his hearing picked out the lub-dub of a heart beat. It was beating quickly, its pace hastened by fear. There was a second heartbeat. Three more.

The firefighters had missed five souls.

The Hero stepped quickly to the door standing between him and the people in the apartment.

"Hello in there," he called out and knocked rapidly. "Don't be afraid. There may be a bomb in the building and I've come to get you all out. Please open the door!"

There was a muffled cry on the other side, some shuffling feet, but whoever was in the apartment continued to pretend not to be home.

"If you don't open the door, I will have to knock it down," he called.

The Hero counted to ten, listening for movement or answer.

Hearing nothing, he pulled his fist back, ready to punch through the center of the door to get a look inside, when it swung open. A small, six or seven-year-old Hispanic girl in pink pajamas stood in the opening. She squinted up at The Hero. Then she threw the door wide open and rushed out to hug his knees.

"I'll get you out," The Hero told the girl, patting her head reassuringly and prying her away enough for him to get a better peek past the door.

On the far side was a large, clean family room decorated in bright reds and blues. Inside were a man and woman, both in their mid thirties, and two more girls, a teenager with long black hair covering her eyes and a two-year-old clinging to her mother's arm. The woman had a cast on her leg from foot to thigh and was sitting in a wheelchair.

"There may be a bomb in the building," The Hero repeated. "We need to get you all downstairs." No one seemed to understand him.

"*La migra?*" the father asked. His voice trembled.

"No. No *la migra*," The Hero said.

The six-year-old squeezed his knees again, eyes closed, smiling. She needed no convincing, but The Hero's reassurance hadn't eased the con-

187

cern on the faces of the mother or father.

"A bomb. *Una bomba*," The Hero said, trying to make the family understand the danger. He put his hands together in the shape of a ball, made a "boom" sound, and quickly pulled his hands apart.

He watched the father's eyes for some sign that he understood.

"*Bomba. Aqui.* Here, in the building," The Hero added, pointing down.

"*Hay una bomba en el edificio?*" the father asked.

He understood. "Yes!" The Hero nodded.

"*Toma a tus hermanas y ve con el Heroe, yo bajaré con tu mama,*" the man said quickly to the oldest girl, who reached to take the toddler from her mother.

Although he'd stayed alert to any indication that an explosive device might really be in the building, The Hero had nearly convinced himself that this was another hoax when his ears picked up a new sound from deep below: crackling, like crunching tissue paper. It was the sound of a fuse burning through.

The Hero grabbed the girl at his knees and rushed into the room, motioning with his hand to get down. "Take cover! Quickly!"

Although they couldn't understand his words, the intent was clear.

The teenager pulled the little one to the floor, huddling with her by the couch, while the father tried to get their mother out of the wheelchair.

The Hero knelt on one knee, pulling the six-year-old tightly next to his body. He was about to tell them all everything would be okay when a blast wave of heat, pressure and shattered wood ripped through the room.

Weller dropped down onto the soiled cushions of his couch, the worn springs twanging and slumping beneath his weight. He didn't offer me a seat, so I found my own. A wooden, hard-backed chair was pushed into an old oak rolltop desk. I dragged it over next to the couch.

"Mind if I record this?" I asked, pulling a digital recorder out of my bag and setting it on the coffee table.

"Yes," he said.

"Oh. Okay. Can I take notes?"

"Fine," he said, waving his hand at me dismissively.

I got out my pen and notepad and flipped to a fresh page.

"So," I said. "Why don't we start by you telling me about the first time you ever saw The Hero of The City?"

"Who said I did?" he answered.

"I've done my research, sir. I know you've seen The Hero," I chided.

That earned me a grumph of a laugh. "Yeah, okay. I saw him the first time when I was eighteen maybe."

"What was he doing?"

"Rescuing a cat from a tree!" he said, and slapped his knee as he cackled in delight at his own joke.

"Mr. Weller...."

"No, really," he said, his laughter subsiding. "First time I saw The Hero he floated up off the ground to pluck some crazy old lady's tabby out of the oak in front of her house."

"I've interviewed, I dunno, maybe a hundred people? Not one of them has ever told me they saw The Hero rescue a stuck cat," I said, making a note in my pad. Cat rescuing wasn't really that interesting, but I hoped if he saw me taking it seriously, he'd be more at ease and willing to open up. "I'm surprised The Hero had time for old ladies and their cats," I said, looking up from my pad.

"The Hero was like that," he said. "Just wanted to help people."

"You know, I believe that, too," I told him. "But a lot of people don't. They think he was out for the glory. Maybe he liked seeing his picture in the paper."

"That's...That's phooey!" he said, jabbing his finger in the air at me.

He made phooey sound like the worst kind of epithet imaginable.

"Excuse my language," he added a bit sheepishly. He seemed almost embarrassed by his outburst.

"Did you ever see The Hero help someone else?" I prompted.

"Sure. Lots of times. Couldn't go anywhere in The City without running into somebody that The Hero had done a good deed for. Most times it wasn't anything that the papers would even report on. There was this old man on Branch Street, Hero helped him get his groceries up the steps to his brownstone every Friday. Is that what a glory hound would do?"

"No, it isn't," I agreed. "But there are people, people who weren't there, that say he showed up at the apartment in the Cordoba that day for the publicity. I've even had people tell me they think he set the bomb."

Weller sprang to his feet, his face turning red again with fury, and made more stabbing motions in the air with his finger. "You! I! Phooey! The Hero never would have...." He waved his hand at me and flopped back down onto his couch. "Aaaaagh. I said I don't want to talk about that day!"

"Heroe! Heroe!"

The Hero blinked open his eyes. Everything around him was a blur. He reached up to his forehead and his fingers came away wet with blood.

"*Despierta, vamos!*"

The Hero shook his head to clear his vision. The movement sent waves of pain rippling through his skull, but the pain helped him focus on his surroundings. The room looked like the aftermath of an earthquake. The floor was fractured and uneven, with jagged sheets of plywood jutting up at odd angles through the carpeting. Fallen ceiling tiles lay in shattered patterns around him where they had hit the floor. Lying next to him was a support beam that had fallen from above. The hardened wood was splintered and bloodied right about even with his head.

Must have been what knocked me out, he thought.

"*Heroe!*"

He propped himself up on an elbow, still dazed. The teenage girl was punching him in the arm, yelling. The six-year-old was sitting in the corner, her knees pulled up to her chest, arms wrapped around them. Tears were running down her cheeks.

Their mother was lying awkwardly on the ground, her cast leg bent into an unnatural position. She was cradling the toddler, who was wailing. A piece of shrapnel from the blast had hit the little girl in the shoulder and blood was running down her arm.

"*Salgamos de aqui,*" the teenager begged.

The Hero climbed to his feet, stumbling. A brief attack of vertigo made the room seem to wobble around him. He closed his eyes until the sensation passed. Opening them again, he saw the father. The man was buried under the same beam that had knocked him out. Blood was pooling beneath his head.

The Hero listened and counted. There was one less heartbeat in the room than when he entered.

The teenager was staring at her father now, too.

"*Saca a mis niñas de aqui por favor,*" the mother called to him from across the room. "*Mi hijas!*"

Her face was a white sheet of pain. The Hero didn't need to speak Spanish to know what the woman was asking him to do.

The Hero scooped the teenager under one arm and reached out to the six-year-old on the floor. She buried her face in her arms and pulled herself into a tighter ball. Still holding onto the teenager, The Hero stepped quickly over to the girl. Crouching down, he tried to grab her up in his free arm, but she resisted, pulling away from his reach.

"*Levántate!*" the oldest sister shrieked.

The yell made the toddler cry harder in her mother's arms.

The Hero couldn't pick up the girl on the floor while he was holding the teenager, so he moved to set her down on her feet.

"*Que estas haciendo? No me bajes!*" she yelled, trying to climb back into The Hero's arms.

Shock. The Hero had seen it before. He ignored the fists beating on his back and reached out with both hands, lifting the balled-up little girl. He held her with one arm, and once their bodies made contact, she opened up, hugged him tightly and sobbed into his side.

He faced the teenager. She had stopped flailing now, and was holding her face in her hands, mumbling. The Hero lifted her up gently and looked at the mother.

"I'm sorry, I can only carry two at a time," he tried to explain. "But I'll be right back."

The mother waved to him to go.

Turning, he ran full speed into the hallway. The corridor and stairwell were in worse shape than the apartment. Entire lengths of stair had been knocked loose by the explosion and collapsed into the center of the well. The Hero could try to float down where the stairs had been, but he'd have to go carefully and slowly.

The smell of rotten eggs drifted up to him from below. The blast must have torn open the gas line. He didn't have much time.

Sunlight streamed through a window at the end of the hallway. That would be the fastest way out.

With a running jump, The Hero leapt forward and into flight. The teenager let out a frightened gasp as they approached the window, grabbing The Hero more tightly around his neck. Rotating around in air, like a high diver twisting into position for entry, he burst through the window back first, protecting the two girls from the breaking glass.

Weller sat sullenly on the couch, his arms crossed across his chest and his head hung low. He was upset, but he hadn't thrown me out.

"You can help me tell The Hero's story," I said. "We can remind people who he really was. I know you were in the crowd when The Hero died. What happened?"

"I said no talking about that day!" he shouted.

"There aren't many survivors who saw it that are still alive," I said, ignoring his protest. "I need you to tell me, in your own words, how The Hero tried to save that family, if we're going to convince people that it wasn't about fame or adoration."

He said nothing.

"Did you see The Hero before he went into the building the first time? Maybe you saw him talking with the fire captain, what was his name?"

"Harris," he said absently, resting his hand in his lap. "I saw The Hero when he arrived. He spoke to the fire captain then just ran in."

"Did he seem apprehensive? Nervous?"

"That was decades ago, how should I know?" he snapped back at me.

"Tell me how you remember it, then."

He mumbled something about nosy reporters before he continued. "He wasn't nervous. He was The Hero. I...*he* saw something inside and just went in. People loved him. He made them feel safe. The Hero, he loved that. And he really loved the way he inspired people to do good. I think that's why he became The Hero." His gaze shifted to the floor and he wiped some moisture from his eyes. "He was a good man."

"He was," I agreed. "You know, when I was doing my research, I discovered an interesting fact."

He looked up at me. All of the anger had been drained out of him. Talking about The Hero had put him in a much better mood.

"Oh yeah? What's that?" he asked.

"The Hero of the City protected us for almost fifteen years."

He smiled at that.

"That long, huh?"

"That long," I said. "But the most amazing thing about his fifteen-year run is that The Hero saved every single man, woman and child he tried to help. Every one."

The smile began to fade from his face.

"Did you see him come out with the last two people he rescued? The two girls from the building?" I asked.

Weller's arthritis-gnarled hand shot out and slapped the coffee table with a thud. "I said no talking about that!" His shout reverberated through the room and rattled the glasses in his cupboards, but silence quickly rushed in to replace the sound.

"How did you happen to be there that day?" I asked.

"Work," he said tersely.

"Really? You claimed to be unemployed on your tax return that year."

"Get out," he said. "Time's up."

The explosion had lifted Captain Harris off his feet and slapped him flat to the ground, winding him. His ears were ringing and the sounds around him were muffled and ghostly. He experienced a moment of panic, but he relaxed and let his training take over. His first priority was to make sure he was okay and could still lead his crew. He'd once seen a man loose an arm and insist there was nothing wrong with him. Shock had blocked the pain. Harris didn't want to be that man.

Starting at his shoulders, he ran his hands down his chest, stomach and legs to make sure he wasn't injured. Reassured he was okay, Harris got to his feet and started a quick mental survey of the damage and casualties.

The civilians had all been moved outside the anticipated blast radius. A quick glance confirmed the barriers had been set back far enough. Although many of them looked scared, they were all still standing.

The firefighters of Ladder Truck #2 hadn't been as lucky. They had been knocked to the ground by the concussive force of the explosion.

"Sound off! Name and status!" Harris barked.

One by one, the firefighters called out their names and let the captain know how they were doing. Fitzhugh was a possible concussion, and a dozen others had shrapnel wounds, but no life-threatening injuries.

Harris said a quick thank-you to Saint Florian, the patron saint of firefighters, that it hadn't been worse, and focused on the building itself.

The bomb had torn away most of the first two floors of the building. A raw, jagged hole was all that was left of the entrance, and the basement had become a blast crater. The loss of support had made the pre-war structure list to the side, but the firewalls put in place between its neighboring apartment buildings were keeping it from collapsing entirely.

There were small fires burning in the shell of the building. What was left would have to be torn down, but it was a small miracle that the explosion hadn't ripped through the surrounding buildings, too.

"They just don't make 'em like they used to," Harris said out loud.

"What's that?" Geffon asked.

The lieutenant was walking over to the captain, finger in his ear, wiggling it in an attempt to improve his hearing.

"Did The Hero get out before the blast?" Harris yelled out.

"I don't think so, sir."

The two men looked around quickly to confirm their fear.

Harris grabbed his hard hat off the ground and strode in front of his crew. "Hey, guys! The Hero was inside that building when the bomb blew. We ain't out of this fight yet," he yelled, goading his men into a rally. "So pick up your axes, get your helmets on. Becker, grab the rookie and get the oxygen and med kit ready. The Hero may be bringing out wounded!"

The prompting triggered routines drilled into his men by endless hours on the hazard course, transforming the disorganized group into the fire-fighting force that was the pride of the department.

At the sight, Harris flashed the scowl that passed for his smile, but the show of teeth hid a concern that was growing by the second. Sure, The Hero could fly, and he was strong as an ox, but Harris didn't think bomb proof was one of his abilities.

Shifting his attention away from the controlled chaos around him, Harris stared up at the building just in time to see The Hero hurtling through a window that had somehow survived the explosion. Shattering glass rained down as The Hero, his blue cape streaming behind him, floated to the ground and touched down lightly with two kids tucked protectively under his arms.

A gash ran from the top of The Hero's head to his hairline. Blood ran down his face and his close-cropped blond hair was red and matted against his skull. The large red star on his chest had been partially ripped away revealing more wounds along his chest. The Hero lowered the two girls to the ground with as much effort and care as he would take setting two delicate teacups on a sideboard.

"Captain, these girls need immediate medical attention," The Hero said, his deep voice resonating with authority.

Harris immediately motioned to Becker. "Get these kids on O_2 and call for a paramedic," he barked.

Becker and the rookie came running up with the tanks.

"Thank you Captain," The Hero said. "I have to go back in for the rest of the family."

Without another word, The Hero rose up into the air and flew back toward the sixth floor window.

"Brave S.O.B.," Harris muttered, then knelt down to inspect the two girls The Hero had brought out.

Becker had placed plastic oxygen masks over both of their faces and was checking the younger girl's pulse. The two were obviously sisters, sharing the same oval faces, dark hair, and bright eyes. The younger girl was huddled inside the folds of the rookie's coat and staring at the ground. The older one's face was impassive behind the oxygen mask, but the quick glances up at the burning building then back down to her little sister revealed the fear and anxiety she was holding back.

"Who else is left up there?" Harris asked.

The teenager shook her head no.

"Uh, *persones, arriba?*" Harris tried again.

She reached up to her mask and pulled it down to speak. *"Mi mamá y mi hermana,"* she answered, her voice quivering.

Harris pushed the mask back in place. "Don't worry, sweetheart."

He was about to say "The Hero will get the rest of your family out," when a second explosion erupted from within the building.

Harris grabbed the oldest girl and pushed her to the ground, covering her with his body. He turned his head in time to see a fireball moving up through the structure, consuming what the first blast had left behind. Whatever support had kept the upper floors from collapsing finally gave out and the building fell in on itself like a house of cards.

The Hero was still inside.

"Get out!" Weller repeated, pointing at the door with his quivering hand.

"You know something, Mr. Weller?" I said, not budging from my chair. "I don't think The Hero died in the fire."

"He did," he insisted, his hand dropping. "The Hero and that family were crushed to death when the building collapsed. We all saw."

"That's not what happened," I told him.

"It is," he said, his voice falling. "The rescue workers found the bodies. The mother and father. That poor baby girl, crushed. The Hero, they found him too, you know! What was left of him."

"I know what they found," I reassured him. "I don't doubt that the building falling in on itself, killing the family, crushed The Hero too. I just don't think the body they found was his. Or that he died there."

"Why are you *really* here?" he asked me.

"Did you ever wonder what happened to the two girls he saved?"

"No."

"Not once?"

"No."

"Well I'll tell you anyway. They went into foster care. Together."

He closed his eyes. "I don't want to hear about this."

"It's okay," I reassured him. "It's a happy ending."

He said nothing so I continued.

"They were taken in by a very nice couple in the North End. Their own kids were already grown, but they were so moved by The Hero's final act that they felt compelled to do something themselves. To help." I couldn't be sure, but it looked like he was holding his breath. "In time, the family adopted the girls. They sent them off to college. The oldest one, Isabel, became a doctor. She works down at Saint Al's."

"I don't want to hear any more," he said.

"The younger one developed, I guess you could call it a hero complex. She wanted to save the world. To be like the man who had saved her. She even put on a costume. The problem was she didn't have super powers, so when she tried to stop a mugging at the tender age of twelve, all she managed to do was get herself stabbed."

"She died?" he asked sharply.

"No," I said. "She was fine. It took me longer than it should have, but I grew out of thinking a cape made me invincible. Or a hero. Now I try to save the world with my pen."

"*You?*" He looked confused.

Nodding, I said, "I changed my name from Noriega to Halsey when my new parents adopted me."

The Hero flew back in through the broken window and alighted in the hallway, just outside the family's apartment.

Something was wrong. The apartment was silent.

He stopped to listen more closely. There was only one heartbeat now and it was weak.

The Hero rushed into the apartment. The mother's body was limp and the pain that had wracked her face was gone. He hadn't come back quickly enough. Remorse welled up inside him. He'd failed these poor girls and their parents. *Face your guilt later*, he told himself. Right now he would save their littlest one, who was still curled up in her mother's lifeless arms, sucking her thumb.

"Come on sweetheart, it's time to say goodbye to mommy," he said gently, and reached down for the toddler.

Far below him, in the guts of the building, The Hero heard the first snapping sounds of fire. Something was igniting the gas he'd smelled earlier. It was too late, and he knew it, but he grabbed at the child anyway. The little girl didn't even whimper as he drew her away from the mother and cradled her against his belly. She just looked up into The Hero's eyes. And she smiled.

"I am so sorry," he whispered to her.

The fireball tore up through the building, eating through the supports that had kept it from collapsing. Carpet melted into puddles of plastic. Drapes caught fire and burned like flash paper. The weight of timber and steel above finally overwhelmed the weakened walls and the building gave in to its destruction. Before the flames could reach the top floors, the roof gave out, and all fourteen floors collapsed to the ground.

"Why are you here? What do you want from me?" Weller was practically begging me now.

"I told you. I wanted to do a retrospective on The Hero and I needed a firsthand account of what happened. I thought it would be a nice way to honor him. I really have interviewed hundreds of people. And I read every story we ever published. He was amazing. One time, he stood in front of a runaway semi truck, trying to slow it down after he got the driver out. The truck plowed him straight through the side of a building at fifty miles an hour. And he survived."

"So what?" he said.

"Your name wasn't in the paper after the building collapse. It was in a private file that Captain Harris kept. He found you staggering down the block after the collapse, dirty and half naked."

"I was down on my luck," he said.

"Captain Harris took you to the Carnby Men's Shelter," I continued. "He tried checking in on you later, but you disappeared one night. You left Carnby's without a word to anyone there. Isn't that right?"

A tear slid down his cheek.

I thought about stopping. Weller was old. If he wanted to hide in the dark, alone, I suppose it was his choice. But I'd already come so far.

"You moved around a lot, but kept coming back here, to this city. Ten years ago you moved into this apartment. And every year, on the anniversary of the building collapse, you put flowers on the grave of Mariela Noriega. My baby sister. The first person The Hero wasn't able to save."

"The Hero died," he protested again. He was crying freely now. Silent sobs shook his body.

"I know," I said gently. "But the man didn't. Captain Harris kept the file secret because he recognized you. He'd seen you up close so many times. Even broken, he knew The Hero when he saw him."

Weller got to his feet and shuffled toward the kitchenette, wiping away his tears with the back of his hand. At the sink, he picked up a glass from the drying rack and filled it with water.

"Why?" he asked me. "The Hero is gone. Why would you care if the man was still alive?"

He raised the glass to his lips and set it down again on the counter without taking a drink.

"Because the city still needs a Hero," I said, standing up. "And because I want to thank him for saving me and Isabel. I also want to tell him I know he did his best to save my mom and my sister."

"The Hero is dead!" Weller yelled and angrily swept his glass and the other dishes on the drying rack to the floor. Glass and ceramic fragments exploded at his feet.

"And so is the man," he said finally.

I picked up my digital recorder. "But the need for The Hero is still alive. In me. In others who would like to know there is someone out there watching over us."

Crossing over to him, I queued up a file on the recorder and set it down on the counter next to him.

"The Hero was never an ordinary man," I said. "In the fifteen years he watched over the city he didn't age a single day. It's true. I had several experts compare photos from his early appearances with some of his last. Not a single new wrinkle or gray hair. And no matter how badly he was injured, he made a full recovery in hours, minutes sometimes."

"Yeah? Well, that's great for him, but I'm just a tired old man."

"From what I've read, I think The Hero's ability to heal would help him recover from just about any injury or illness, if he wanted to. Including old age. I don't think The Hero can die. But he has to want to live."

"You don't know what you're talking about," he said.

"There are over a hundred stories on there," I said, pointing to the recorder. "They're the life stories of the people The Hero helped. People who wouldn't have had life stories without him. I thought you might want to listen to them. And when you get to the end, you'll hear the stories of two sisters he saved from a collapsing building."

"Please," he said. "Just...just go."

I retrieved my purse and moved toward the door. "Mr. Weller...."

"Go!"

I let myself out, but couldn't bring myself to leave.

That didn't go the way I'd hoped, I thought, not entirely sure exactly what I did think was going to happen. But deep down I had expected to see some sign of The Hero. A trace of the man who saved my sister and me.

Maybe I'd been wrong to come here. Weller was a shell of a man who wanted to be left alone. All I'd done was upset him.

I knew I should just leave, but I knocked on the door again anyway.

"Mr. Weller," I called out. "I'm sorry. Mr. Weller?"

He didn't respond, so I tried the doorknob. It was unlocked and I let myself back in.

"Hello?"

The living room and kitchenette were empty. The door to the bedroom was open, so I checked in there. Nothing. Same for the bathroom.

I wandered back into the kitchen. That was when I noticed the drapes covering the living room window had been pushed back. The window beyond was open now, letting in a warm breeze. And the digital recorder was gone, too.

I went to the window and stuck my head out. I scanned the skyline, half expecting I'd see a man flying across the horizon. Like when I was a kid on Christmas Eve, hoping for a glimpse of Santa Claus.

But just like when I was a kid, there was no man in a red suit gliding across the night sky. The absence of proof hadn't stopped me from believing in Santa when I was a girl, and it didn't stop me from believing that The Hero was out there, somewhere, watching over The City.

The Hero closed his eyes and floated on the thermals above The City. Like him, like The City, they were different now. But still familiar.

From down below came the sound of millions of footfalls on concrete. Somewhere a street vendor was hawking fresh strawberries. A conductor was announcing the departure of the 7:15 local.

It was like hearing the voice of a good friend after a long absence.

But The Hero put all those sounds out of his mind and pressed the play button on the digital recorder in his hand.

"Tell me about the first time you saw The Hero?" he heard Laura Halsey ask.

"I was five," a man's voice answered. *"I fell off our fifth floor balcony. The Hero saved me."*

"Little Teddy Harris," The Hero said aloud. "You giggled when I caught you."

The Hero closed his eyes, remembering the little boy. He remembered handing him over to his relieved parents. Remembered the look of happiness on their faces when he waved and flew away.

And he remembered, for the first time in a very long time, what it was like to *feel* like a hero.

About the Authors

The editors wish to give our undying appreciation to each of these very talented and hard-working writers. Without them, this book would not have been possible. Learn more about these literary heroes, including which super power they wish they possessed.

Derek Tyler Attico ("Breaking The Circle") is the author of the critically acclaimed *Star Trek* short story "Alpha and Omega." A native New Yorker, he's exploring the human condition through writing and photography while training to become a billionaire vigilante/strategist (leather optional). Visit him at DerekAttico.com. POWER: Telepathy (it doesn't take a mind reader to figure out why).

Lisa Gail Green ("Identity Crisis") has written numerous short stories and poems. The latest story, "Cursed," is featured in the anthology *Playthings of the Gods*. She lives in Southern California with her husband and two kids. And no matter how much she resembles that one superhero you're thinking of, she vehemently denies any connection. See her online at LisaGailGreen.com. POWER: Unlimited energy, so she can tackle anything—even her laundry.

K. Stoddard Hayes ("The Dodge") spent the first decade of her life reading superhero comics and watching Westerns. She has published hundreds of articles, interviews and essays about science fiction and fantasy on screen, and now does editorial work for two independent publishers. Read her blog at WorldBuildingRules.wordpress.com. POWER: She has always wanted to fly with Superman.

Kevin Hosey ("Blunt Force Trauma") is an author, editor and cartoonist. His short stories have appeared in the *Star Trek Strange New Worlds* anthologies (Simon and Schuster), *Paramourtal* (Cliffhanger Books), *Hint Fiction* (W.W. Norton) and the sci-fi magazine, *Beyond Centauri*. Visit him at KevinHosey.net. POWER: To write compelling stories that change the world. Just kidding. He wants to be invisible so he can sneak into movies.

Ricardo Sanchez ("Death and Life of The Hero") writes comics and fiction. His comic work includes "Resident Evil," "Aion" and the "Telara Chronicles" for DC Comics. He also creates satirical websites and works in the video game industry. You can visit him at ConformAndObey.com. POWER: The ability to teleport so he can see the world but still sleep in his own bed.

Carla Lee Suson ("The Justice Blues") left a career in cellular biology to write and edit. She has written articles and short stories for over twelve years. Her first novel, *Independence Day Plague*, was published in 2010. Carla also creates wood and leather crafts, and often disappears on camping adventure. See her at Blog.NorthOfTheRed.com. POWER: To heal wounds by taking the energy in plants and the earth and focusing it into people.

Jordan Taylor ("Neutral Ground") lives in the Pacific Northwest with several pets. She divides her time between training dogs, collecting canine movie memorabilia, reading classic and modern literature, and writing. Learn more at JordanTaylorBooks.com. POWER: To time travel without physically being there. It would make historical research efficient, enjoyable and incredibly accurate.

Micah Urban ("The Mass Grave of John Johnsons") is a software support technician from Monee, Illinois. He has a background in world history and English literature. He lives as much of his time as possible with his fiancee, their two cats and two ferrets. POWER: To comprehend and speak all languages.

Dayton Ward ("Going My Own Way") is the author of numerous short stories and sci-fi novels (*The Last World War, Counterstrike* and *The Genesis Protocol*). He has also written several *Star Trek* novels, including the recent *Paths of Disharmony*. Dayton has collaborated with Kevin Dilmore on novels, stories, magazine articles, and content for the SyFy Channel website. Visit him at DaytonWard.com. POWER: To stop time. That way, he'd have all the time needed to do everything that needs doing.

Kelly Wisdom ("Daughter of Nyx") spends her summers in Roanoke, Va., as an MFA student in the Children's Literature program at Hollins University. For the remainder of the year, she resides in Mooresville, N.C., and teaches English at Mitchell Community College. She lives in a small house on a big lake with two lazy dogs, two irascible cats and one attentive husband. You'll find her at Kelly-Wisdom.com. POWER: The ability to fly because it is so much fun to do in her dreams.

Thank you for reading

For information on the upcoming volume two
of this series and other exciting books,
please visit us now at

The Edge of Gripping New Fiction

OTHER TITLES FROM CLIFFHANGER BOOKS

Paramourtal™
Tales of Undying Love and Loving The Undead
Edited by
Kevin Hosey and Evelyn Welle

Nominated for Best Romance Anthology of 2010.
A collection of spellbinding paranormal romance stories by some
of the most talented writers today. Suspenseful, dangerous,
humorous, heartwarming and just plain scary as hell, these varied
dark tales will grip your heart and haunt you for days.

PRAISE FOR *PARAMOURTAL:*

"'A delightful book of fairytales for grownups, a touch
of paranormal and hearts that are touched by love."
—*The Paranormal Romance Guild*

"...touching, deeply imaginative and, in a word, spellbinding...
I highly recommend these stories both for their heartwarming
characters and for the intensely imaginative escape they offer.
In a word, this book is enchanting."
—*The Romance Reviews*

"I loved it! There is hot sexual tension....
A recommended read."
—Gina Gordon
Author of Wicked Ride

"...magical yet terrifyingly romantic. It's that wonderful."
—*Ren Thompson*
Writer and Reviewer

www.ingramcontent.com/pod-product-compliance
Lightning Source LLC
Chambersburg PA
CBHW060050260626
47160CB00005B/1643